NO DOORS,

NO WINDOWS

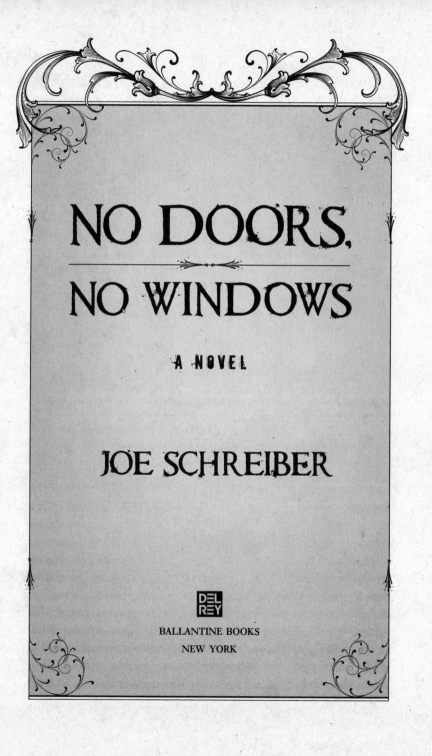

NO DOORS, NO WINDOWS

A NOVEL

JOE SCHREIBER

DEL REY

BALLANTINE BOOKS

NEW YORK

A Del Rey Trade Paperback Original

Copyright © 2009 by Joe Schreiber

Published in the United States by Del Rey Books, an imprint of The Random House Publishing Group, a division of Random House, Inc., New York.

DEL REY is a registered trademark and the Del Rey colophon is a trademark of Random House, Inc.

ISBN 978-0-345-51013-6

Printed in the United States of America

www.delreybooks.com

2 4 6 8 9 7 5 3 1

First Edition

Book design by Christopher M. Zucker

To my father-in-law, Lester E. Arndt, 1933–2008

And I came upon a little house
A little house upon a hill
And I entered through, the curtain hissed
Into the house with its blood-red bowels
Where wet-lipped women with greasy fists
Crawled the ceilings and the walls. . . .
—NICK CAVE

For what other dungeon is so dark as one's
own heart!
—NATHANIEL HAWTHORNE
The House of the Seven Gables

NO DOORS,

NO WINDOWS

CHAPTER ONE

IT WAS A LONG NEW HAMPSHIRE FALL, the kind that stayed mild well into October, and the man and the boy had spent the afternoon in the backyard, throwing a ball back and forth between two worn leather gloves the man had found in the garage. The boy was young, five that summer, but the man spoke to him in the easy, playful way he might've addressed a teenager, with an obvious affection that the boy repaid with rapt delight. They had come outside wearing jackets, but after a half hour of shagging runaway balls past the old toolshed to the cornfield that bordered the property, the man took off his denim jacket and draped it over a low branch of the maple that towered across the yard. Upon seeing this, the boy immediately shed his jacket too and tossed it on the ground. Anyone watching the two of them would've assumed they were father and son.

When he saw the boy winding up to throw the ball underhand, the man turned and began to run back toward the cornfield, where experience had taught him he'd soon be diving to retrieve it. But some eccentricity of wind or gravity interceded, and the ball sailed over his head, momentarily blocking out the midafternoon sun before the man realized its final destination. In a perfect, stretching, never-to-be-repeated arc, the ball closed in on the darkened window of the toolshed, and a moment later, he heard the pop and tinkle of breaking glass.

The boy stood frozen, oval-eyed, the glove dangling from his hand. "Uncle Scott?"

"It's okay." The man, still catching his breath, slowed to a walk, approaching the shed with his shadow stretched out in front of him. Peering between the two or three snaggletoothed rectangles of glass remaining in the frame, he smelled musty canvas and ancient motor oil, dead grass and rotten leaves. Vague piles of equipment and tools loitered in the shadows, crouched low to the concrete floor.

"What happened?" The boy sounded astounded by the enormity of his crime.

"Don't worry about it," the man said, and looked with a rueful smile at the smudges on his sleeves, where he'd been leaning against the sill. "Piece of advice for you, kiddo. Never let a salesgirl talk you into paying eighty bucks for a shirt."

"Okay."

Walking around the wooden double doors, the man stopped again to examine the padlock that dangled from them like a slab of stone. "Ah. The plot thickens."

"What are we gonna do?" the boy asked.

"For every lock, there's a key." He turned from the shed and walked across the yard toward the place where he'd grown up. It was a large, rambling old farmhouse that hadn't changed substantially since his father had built it here fifty years ago. Here was the same enclosed back porch with the same rooty subterranean smell that he remembered disliking as a child and disliked now. More tools. An old railway lantern. A Coca-Cola sign. In one corner, a smiling wooden policeman, cut out with a jigsaw and hand-painted, raised one hand toward the wall. His father had made that, forever ago.

Inside, the house smelled like a dozen different casseroles and hot dishes mingling into one generic aroma pool of gravy and starch. Entering the living room with the boy at his heels, the man, a nondescript New England exile named Scott Mast, walked past the lump on the sofa, mired in front of the television behind a platoon of empty brown bottles. On TV a pretty blonde in a tight T-shirt and tool belt was talking about rehabbing a hundred-year-old Federal house from the ground up. As she dipped her paintbrush and laid down the initial strokes, the creature on the couch made a noise that could've been a belch or a snore and rearranged its extremities among the flattened cushions. Scott and the boy went into the kitchen.

If his mother had been alive, he knew she would've been mortified by the influx of perishables that had arrived after his father's funeral. But Eleanor Mast was fifteen years in her grave, killed in the same fire that had taken Great-Uncle Butch and a dozen others. And now they had buried their father. At the memorial yesterday, Owen had already started making noises about moving out of the rented mobile home where he and Henry lived and coming back to live in the old house. Scott visualized the two of them here in the kitchen, feasting for months off defrosted meat loaf, venison sausage, and turkey and cranberry wreath.

He reached over and retrieved the Mason jar from the shelf above the sink. The jar rattled with spare coins, loose nails and screws, paper clips, bits of scrap wire, and empty wooden spools, a trove of ageless, useless junk. When he and Owen were kids, their mother had always kept a few dollars rolled up inside it for school lunches or ice cream in the summer. The paper money had long since vanished, leaving only the most clamorous and least valuable contents gleaming dully in the rays of afternoon light. Scott dumped it upside down on top of the stove, sorting through sticky pennies and two-cent stamps.

"What the hell's going on in there?" the voice from the living room called.

"Nothing." Scott raised his voice but didn't look up. "Just looking for a key."

Within seconds, Owen had lumbered into the kitchen doorway, head cocked and eyes squinting at Scott beneath a hood of thatched black hair. At thirty-one, he was three years younger than Scott but seemed both older and slower. He wore a black Jack Daniel's T-shirt that wasn't quite long enough to cover the droop of his belly above the low-hanging waist of his Levi's. With him came the aroma of beer and stale synthetic fabric mingled with chewing tobacco—old, familiar smells that came together in Scott's nostrils in a weird combination of nostalgia and almost unbearable sadness. Owen took another step, brushing the boy aside, his flushed and faintly perspiring face still turned up to maintain eye contact with Scott. "What key?"

"To the shed."

"Yeah?" Owen's eyes narrowed. "What's out there?"

"Nothing," Scott said. "We just lost our ball. Went through the shed window and—"

"You kidding me?" Owen finally seemed to notice the boy standing between them. "Henry, what did you do? Did you break that window out there?" He grabbed the boy's arm hard enough that Scott saw his head jerk forward, upper and lower teeth clicking together, a reaction that only seemed to disgust his father. "Don't pull that act on me. That didn't hurt."

"Owen," Scott said, "it was my fault. I threw the ball."

"Yeah?" Owen's head twisted slightly sideways toward him, sly fascination spreading over his face. "How come?"

"I lost control of it."

"Typical." Owen reached around and scratched the back of his thigh. "I guess you figure you can just break Pop's shit all you want now that he's gone, just fly on home and not worry about it, huh?"

"Come on, man," Scott said. "I'll replace the window before I go." Throughout the course of this conversation, he'd found three possible keys in the morass of items from the jar and slipped them into his pocket, then scraped up everything else from the range, wanting to be away from his brother as quickly as possible.

"Damn right you will. Just 'cause Pop's gone don't mean you can bust the place up and leave." Owen was following Scott back down the hall, still talking, and noticed the boy was trailing along behind. "Where you think you're going? This is man talk."

Letting the screen door bang shut behind him, Owen followed Scott off the porch and fell into step a stride or two behind him, a lurching, trudging shadow in Scott's peripheral vision. "I don't really mind about the window," he said. "Probably nothing out in the shed except a bunch of junk anyway. Pop hardly ever went out there anymore."

Scott realized his brother was afraid he might find something valuable out there and keep it for himself. "I just want the ball back."

"Bunch of crap," Owen said. "You never know when you might get lucky, though. Stuart Garvey was telling me about this guy down in Nashua, his grandfather dropped dead of a stroke, and when he went out to the barn, he found about eighty thousand dollars in cash stuffed into coffee cans, packed into a hole in the floor." He whistled softly. "Eighty *grand*, you believe that?"

Scott tried the first key in the lock, but it wasn't even close. The second one was noticeably larger, not even a possibility. That left only a small brass key. He slipped it in the padlock and felt the internal mechanism of the thing yield with spring-loaded eagerness into his palm. No sooner had he lifted it off than Owen reached past him and swung the doors wide open, throwing a widening trapezoid of daylight across the floor and stepping into the shed. After an interval of breathless silence, a layer of disappointment spread rapidly over Owen's face, reverberating through his entire body, as the prospect of sudden riches deteriorated before his eyes. Yet again, fate had cheated him out of his fortune.

"Bunch of shit," he muttered, glaring at the old tools, the rusty wheelbarrow leaned up against the wall, the lawn mower and rakes, the piles of cinder blocks, old bags of mulch, and boxes of seed. "What'd I tell you?"

"Uh-huh." Squatting down, Scott saw the softball resting on the bottom shelf of the bare-bones workbench their father had built along the back wall of the shed. When he reached down to retrieve it, something else caught his eye, and he stopped thinking about the softball completely.

"What's that?" Owen asked over his shoulder, instantly attuned to his brother's heightened interest. "You find something?"

Still squatting down, Scott leaned forward, resting one shoulder against the corner of the workbench for leverage as he dragged the heavy, square object into view. It was an old office manual typewriter, battleship gray, with round black keys. He ran his fingers over them to reveal the gleaming Bakelite laminate beneath a silky layer of dust.

"Great," Owen said, not bothering to hide the disappointment in his voice. "Anything else down there?"

Scott reached deeper. Wedged against the wall, behind the bare spot where the typewriter had been, he saw a bundle of pages tied together with twine. Like the typewriter, they were heavier than he'd expected; only when he pulled the stack out did he realize how thick it was, two inches at least and weighed down with untold seasons of

absorbed moisture. It had been rammed back there with such force
that the top page had folded crookedly onto itself. Smoothing the page,
he read the words:

THE BLACK WING

By
Frank Mast

Scott stood up. Owen was standing in the corner, completing a
desultory investigation of a stack of wooden apple crates.

"Pop ever say anything to you about this?" Scott asked.

Owen didn't look up. "What is it?"

"Some kind of manuscript. It's got his name on it." He flipped
through the pages. They were numbered in the upper right-hand corner, and the last page was marked 138. Each one crammed to the margins with single-spaced type. There were occasional words x-ed out
and corrections handwritten between the lines. "I didn't know he ever
tried writing."

"Who knows?" Owen straightened, wiping his hands on his jeans.
"After Mom died, Pop did a lot of crazy shit. Wandering around, not
making any sense. Frank Whipple told me he saw him just a couple
months ago, parked outside the old Exxon on 743, trying to pump gas
from a phone booth."

There was more to this remembrance, but Scott wasn't listening.
Grasping the stack of pages in his hand, letting it dangle off his index
finger by the neatly squared and knotted twine that held it together, he
stepped out of the shed and into the afternoon. It felt cooler outside
now, the light slanted a bit lower between the mostly empty branches,
another slice of autumn irretrievably lost in the shadow of the waning
year. Scott was halfway across the yard when he saw Henry standing
on the porch, still wearing the leather glove, and realized that he'd forgotten the ball in the shed. When he looked again, the boy was gone.

"Where'd Henry go?"

"Who the hell knows. Kid's like his mother. You never know what
he's doing, half the time *he* doesn't even know." They went back into

the house, and Owen shot a glance at the clock above the fireplace. "Quarter to four. Too early for a cold one?"

"Why not?"

Owen snatched two clinking bottles of lager from the refrigerator and banged them on the table. Of the case Scott had brought home the day of their father's funeral, only three bottles now remained. The rest had flowed through his younger brother in a steady river of barley and hops that seemed to propel him through the days, and wherever he sat, the clear empties gathered around him like friends who had nothing more to say.

"We still on for dinner tonight?" Owen asked. "One last family meal before you sail on out of here?"

"Sure." Since coming home for the funeral, Scott had taken them out to dinner every night. The town didn't offer many more options than the ones he remembered from childhood: the Pantry on Main Street, Fusco's, and Captain Charlie's, a steak and seafood place just outside of town that still sold "freedom fries."

"Hot damn." Owen grinned. "Happy hour starts in fifteen minutes at Fusco's." Already invigorated at the prospect of a night of free drinking, he grabbed the stack of pages from the table, riffling through them like a dirty magazine. "So the old man thought he was Stephen King, huh?" He dropped the manuscript on the table, where it landed hard enough to rattle Scott's beer bottle. "I'll have to check it out."

"He must have kept it private." Scott picked up the bundle and tucked it under his arm, heading out of the kitchen and up the stairs. Reaching the room at the top of the steps where he was staying— Owen had immediately staked his claim on the bedroom they'd shared as boys—he took his wallet from the dresser and stopped to look around one last time.

The air hummed with familiarity. When they were young, this had been his mother's sewing room; for years it had been the wheelhouse from which she had steered the goodwill of the town. In perfect counterbalance to their father's stoicism, Eleanor Mast had been chatty and extroverted, an organizer, a volunteer, facilitating countless bake sales and fund-raising events for the Milburn Fire Department, somehow finding the spare time to take in sewing for extra money. In town people still spoke of her as a kind of female folk hero. At his father's funeral yesterday, Conrad Faulkner from the *Chronicle* had come up to Scott with the remembrance that it was almost the fifteen-year anniversary of her death—the night of the Bijou fire. When he'd noticed Scott's anguished expression, Conrad had attempted to change the subject. *Hey, speaking of the Bijou, it looks like somebody finally bought that old eyesore. Maybe they'll make something out of it. Stranger things have happened, right?*

Scott looked around the sewing room, aware that his breathing had become shallower, more deliberate. The past was here, had never left. Yellowed envelopes of Singer patterns still occupied the built-in shelves beside the window, next to a worn mannequin, above the old-fashioned sewing machine that folded down into a flat table in the corner. Tiny bits and scraps of fabric lay in the gap between the rug and the wall.

"Yo, Bro, you ready?" Owen bellowed from the bottom of the stairs, voice lubricated by fresh drink. "You've got hungry men down here."

"I'm coming," Scott said. Descending the stairs, he felt his chest beginning to unclench, expanding with a sensation he didn't immediately recognize. They were halfway to town before he identified it as relief. It was an old habit—whenever he put the past in his rearview mirror, he inevitably felt as if he had saved his own life.

CHAPTER TWO

TWO HOURS LATER, SCOTT DROVE THEM HOME in Owen's truck, a putty-colored Ford F-150 of uncertain age whose alignment scraped and dragged as if it had been slammed into a tree and repaired just enough to keep it running. Owen had passed out in the passenger seat, cheek flattened against the glass, while Henry sat buckled in between them with his small hands folded on his lap, staring out the bug-flecked window. The boy had hardly touched his cheeseburger during dinner and spoke only when Scott asked him direct questions about school or movies he'd seen lately.

"You're leaving tomorrow," Henry said finally.

Scott nodded. "In the morning."

"Why can't you stay here?"

"I have to go back to Seattle."

"Why?"

"It's home."

The boy fell silent, powerless before the logic of the statement. "I could go with you," he said in a small voice, as if he were afraid Owen might hear him. "I could live with you."

"Think you'd like it out there?"

Henry considered, then nodded.

"Not too rainy?"

"I like the rain."

"I don't think your dad would like it so much." The truth was, upon first meeting his nephew, Scott had thought of little except how it would be if Henry were his son and not his brother's. Henry's mother wasn't part of the picture. She had been a local girl, the daughter of someone's housekeeper, with no interest in raising children. From everything Scott had seen, his brother had taken the anger and humiliation of her desertion out on Henry, pretending the boy didn't exist or criticizing him for being clumsy, lazy, or disrespectful.

Once or twice in the last four days, usually after several drinks, Owen would embrace his son with gruff affection, a crooked hug or beery kiss that would bring a cautious smile to the boy's face before Owen lost interest and drifted back to whatever he was watching on TV. Then the boy would sit with him on the couch or on the floor, watching Owen with a child's clear-eyed lack of sentimentality, loving his father but never fully trusting him.

Scott pulled into the driveway and parked, rousing Owen with the silence where the sound of the engine had been. "Thanks for dinner, bro," he muttered, climbing out and ambling up the walkway to their parents' house. Scott and Henry followed, the boy looking as if he wanted to say something else but wasn't sure what. In the living room, Scott heard the TV switch on, followed by the scrunch of compressed couch springs and, seconds later, the rumble of deeply sedated snoring.

"You want to come upstairs and help me pack?" Scott asked, and Henry responded by following him up to the sewing room, installing himself on the single bed with his legs dangling off the end. Something was on his mind: something that took a moment to find its way out.

"Was Grandpa crazy?" Henry asked. "When he died?"

"He had a disease that made him forget a lot of things."

"Alzheimer's?"

"Right." At first, Scott had been floored by his nephew's capacity to seize on a name or concept upon hearing it only once; now he simply accepted it as part of some inexplicable cosmic whim. "People with Alzheimer's can't really take care of themselves. They'll walk away and forget where they live or forget to take their medication."

"My dad says Grandpa used to cry a lot."

Scott paused to weigh his answer. "I think it's been hard for him since your grandma died. He probably spent a lot of time feeling frustrated and confused. It's hard to understand, even for grown-ups, but there are times when it's better to let go of life and find some kind of peace—even if it makes the people around you sad."

"Yeah, I guess." Henry was looking past him, at the laptop on the sewing table. "Do you have any games on your computer?"

"I might." In fact, the same day he'd booked his flight to New Hampshire for the funeral, Scott had gone to Best Buy and purchased a dozen games designed for elementary-age kids, patiently installing them on the computer's C drive, one after another. Henry found one that he liked, something about hunting robot sharks from a speedboat, and sat down to play.

At ten o'clock, yawning, he slipped down from the chair and lay down on the air mattress where Scott had spent the last few restless nights. Within moments, he'd rolled onto his stomach and was breathing deeply into the pillow, one arm flung up above his head. Scott slipped Henry's sneakers from his feet and drew the blanket up over his shoulders, paused, and after a moment, bent down and kissed the boy's cheek just above a dried ketchup streak.

At length, he found himself picking up the manuscript with his father's name on it, scowling more at the existence of the pages than at what they might actually convey. He opened the drawer of the sewing table, brought out a pair of his mother's old pinking shears, and snipped the twine. The sheets of paper, long bound together, were released with an almost audible sigh.

Peeling back the title page, Scott glanced at the first typewritten lines:

Chapter 1

From the outside, the house appeared completely normal.

My father wrote those words, he thought, a low-wattage tremor running down to his fingertips. Without realizing it, he'd already continued reading:

> They had followed the dirt road at least a mile through the woods to get here, and Faircloth hadn't gotten a good look at it until the real estate agent stopped to open the iron gates. It was a tired old relic from some other time, smooth where it should have been angular, angular where it should've been smooth, at least a hundred years old, with sprawling wings and dormers and porticoes that seemed to have been added on as afterthoughts. There was nothing beautiful about it. But it was in his price range, which by itself made it exceptional.
>
> The interior, however, was where it all changed.
>
> The real estate man stood back, letting Faircloth wander into the foyer, where something caught his eye.
>
> "These corners," Faircloth said, pointing.
>
> The agent smiled in anticipation of the question. "Yes?"
>
> "They're all rounded." Faircloth squinted up where the walls and ceiling came together, not in sharp angles but in edgeless curves. He looked down at the floor. It, too, blended into the walls without any definitive line of demarcation.
>
> "Most people don't notice that right away," the agent said. "You're a very observant man, Mr. Faircloth."
>
> Faircloth, who didn't consider himself particularly observant but recognized a salesman's flattery when he heard it, continued to inspect the rooms.
>
> "Look all you want," the agent said. "You won't

find a single true angle or straight line in the place--an eccentricity of the original designer. The effect is quite singular. If you get out a carpenter's level, you'll discover that the walls and ceilings, even the windowsills and doorways, all have a slight inward curve. Hence the name of the property."

"What's that?"

"Round House."

Faircloth snorted. Entering the dining room, he found himself standing in front of a doorway that seemed to have no place in that particular spot. He paused in front of it, resting his hand on the brass handle, and that was where he stopped. Despite the August heat wave, which this afternoon had brought the temperature throughout this part of New Hampshire well above ninety degrees, the handle felt ice-cold.

"What's this?" Faircloth asked.

The real estate man didn't answer immediately. Perhaps he'd been woolgathering and needed a moment to catch up. "That? Another closet, I suppose. I haven't looked in it myself."

Turning the handle, Faircloth opened the door and looked inside. At first, he had been sure that what he would find would be a closet, with an empty metal bar and a few forgotten wire hangers, some old newspaper laid across an upper shelf, or maybe just another small, rounded-off room.

But it wasn't a closet.

And it wasn't a room.

Opening up in front of him on the other side of the door was a long, narrow hallway with black walls and a black ceiling. It appeared to go straight back, perhaps twenty feet or farther, before ending resolutely with a plain black wall. There were no wall sconces or fix-

tures in the hall, but with the natural sunlight
streaming through the dining room to his back,
he could see quite well that the hallway in front
of him had no doors or windows either, that it
just ran its course and stopped.

"That's strange," the real estate man said,
from immediately behind him, and Faircloth
jumped and looked back, feeling silly at his
startled reaction.

"What?"

"You don't even notice it from the outside."

Without bothering to reply, Faircloth stepped
into the hallway, sure that he'd overlooked a
closed window or doorway in there upon first
glance. A hallway without windows or lights was
poor planning; a hallway without doors simply
didn't make sense, even in a place as decidedly
eccentric as Round House.

But there were no doors. He walked the length
of the wing, running his fingers along the
smooth walls, wondering if the previous owners
had sealed the doors shut and plastered over
them, but he felt nothing. It was almost as if the
entire addition had been built for the sole purpose of being shut off, walled away from the
rest of the sad old house.

I'll read just a little further, Scott thought, in the silence of the
sewing room, *and I'll go to bed.* He flipped the page, his eyes already
moving over the words he found there.

CHAPTER THREE

IT WAS FOUR THIRTY IN THE MORNING when Scott turned the last page of his father's manuscript. He laid it aside and stood up to stretch, squeezing the pins and needles from his legs, bent down to pick up Henry, and carried the boy back to his own bed without really thinking about what he was doing. In every significant way, he was still engulfed in the world of his father's story.

Set in 1944, *The Black Wing* told the story of Karl Faircloth, a shell-shocked soldier sent home early from Europe, put to work in his ailing father's machine shop, and engaged to Maureen, a teller at the local mercantile bank. Scraping together what little money he's saved, Faircloth decides to buy a home for himself and his new bride, the old house in the woods outside of town. Round House—with its queasy lack of angularity and its peculiar hidden wing, the long, black vestibule containing no doors and no windows—seems the only affordable option.

Faircloth and his wife haven't been living long in Round House when they begin hearing strange noises coming from the shuttered wing off the dining room. Sometimes it sounds like a scratching noise, like an animal trying to get out. Other times it sounds like whimpering. Upon investigation, the couple discovers that the corridor has grown both longer than before and rounder. After a night of quarreling and heavy drinking, they find themselves lost in it like two children in a fairy tale, simultaneously giggling and frightened. Uncertainty has begun to pluck at the strings of their marriage in other ways as well. Faircloth is convinced that Maureen is having an affair with a loan officer from the bank, and his drinking gets worse, compounding his jealousy and catalyzing into a speechless, suffocating rage. With their domestic life disintegrating around them, he finds himself increasingly drawn to the windowless corridor and the soft, irregular scratching noises that emanate from it while he lies awake in their marriage bed, the room spinning, waiting for his wife to come home.

One night, waiting for Maureen to come home, Faircloth drinks himself to the brink of oblivion, staggers to his old footlocker, and unwraps the Luger he smuggled home from Germany, stolen off the body of a dead German soldier. He is sitting at the dining room table loading bullets into the clip when the hallway door clicks and swings open, releasing a gasp of violently cold air. Faircloth shivers and looks up.

That was where the story ended.

At first, Scott was sure there must have been some mistake. For a moment, despite the lateness of the hour, he actually considered going back out to the shed with a flashlight and nosing around for the rest of it. What stopped him wasn't the inconvenience of putting his shoes back on and getting cobwebs on his face but the awareness, the implacable certainty, that there *were* no more pages. For whatever reason, he knew that this was where his father had stopped.

That was when he lost his mind.

The thought threw a jolt through him. It implied that the manuscript was recent, something generated in the final years, as the old man's dementia had taken root in the floorboards of his psyche. It seemed impossible. Almost as unsettling was the fact that he'd written this at all—after all, he was Frank Mast, the town electrician, a stoic man with a purely utilitarian view of language.

And then there was the other thing.

His father's book—what there was of it—was good. Damn good. The pain inside it felt urgent, white-hot, and inevitable, as if sprung from a wound in the old man's side. The situation it described felt real, an honest attempt to exorcise demons from a mind driven mad by guilt.

Scott had gone to college to be a writer. Back then, he had sat through countless writing workshops, had endured whole reams of terrible prose, his own and others'; he had hung out in coffee shops with his computer, tapping and tinkering away without ever completing anything of substance. His sketches evoked unhappiness in detail without any particular point of reference, the malaise of characters smoking and drinking too much while waiting around for something to happen. Rarely, if ever, had they become actual stories—like his would-be fiction career, they were never completed, only abandoned.

He lay down on the mattress, shut his eyes, and slept hard, without dreams. Daylight woke him, and he glanced at the clock and saw it was almost nine. He had a noon flight out of Manchester, ninety minutes from here. Scott brushed his teeth and showered, bundled up his clothes, and, at the last moment, grabbed the stack of manuscript pages and stuffed it into his suitcase, zipping it up like a thief, and then took it out again and looked at it, feeling ridiculous. The manuscript wasn't his. But he wanted to take it.

Gathering the pile of pages in his arms, he started downstairs, rounded the corner, and saw the woman standing in the kitchen.

"Hello?" she said. "Anybody home?"

She wore a black sweater and form-fitting jeans and was holding a large cake pan. Scott was immediately struck with the feeling of having seen her somewhere before. She had significant brown eyes—city eyes, was his first thought—that appeared to be simultaneously guileless and guarded against any potential fiber of ill will.

Only then did he realize who she was.

"Sonia?"

"Hi, Scott."

"Hi. Wow." He stood there blinking, waiting for words to come, and realized he was going to have to go searching for them. "It's great to see you."

"You too."

"I didn't hear you down here." His lips were tingling weirdly and felt disconnected from his face, as if he'd just taken a bite of some extravagantly hot pepper.

"I let myself in. I hope you don't mind. The door was unlocked."

Now they felt numb, as if the pepper had been poisoned. "No," he said, "that's fine." When, he wondered, was this going to stop feeling unreal? "How have you been?"

"Good."

"You look great."

It might not have been the right thing to say, perhaps too superficial given the circumstances. She stood there for a moment watching him carefully, as if the compliment had been some kind of clumsy negotiating tactic.

"I'm sorry about your father," Sonia said. "I heard—"

"Thanks."

"We weren't able to make it to the service, unfortunately. Dad's doctors have him on permanent bed rest these days. You remember my dad."

"Sure," Scott said, still feeling vaguely like a subpar actor who had wandered out onstage without first reading the scene. He was beginning to realize that the disconnected feeling wasn't going away anytime soon.

"He's got end-stage lung cancer, and there's not much time left. You must know how hard that is." She drew in a breath and held it, most likely auditioning possible things to say and approving none of them. "Anyhow, look, I don't mean to bring you down, especially not now; you've got a lot on your mind already. I don't know how you feel about it, but I just think it is so unnerving, watching your parents become . . . childlike again."

"I didn't really know my father all that well." He'd never said anything like that out loud—never even consciously *thought* it—yet here it was anyway, this unspeakable confession, unable to be retracted. "After my mom died, everything else . . . It all sort of happened while I was away doing other things." His hands were restless, moving up to cover his arms. "I could've checked in with him, picked up the phone, got on a plane, but I never seemed to find the time."

"I know what you mean."

"Would you—" He realized he ought to at least look at her cake, but he literally couldn't drag his eyes away from her face. "I was just about to make coffee. Do you want some?"

"Sure."

From the living room, a floorboard squeaked like a nail being pried from a rusty pipe. Another creak followed—a whole chorus of them, in fact—as if some giant of unreasonable bulk were challenging the tensile strength of the floor itself, and Owen came around the corner in his T-shirt and jeans, scratching under one arm and wincing at the light. His face was pouched and swollen and seemed to hang in irregular bags of flesh from the oversized box of his skull. "Better make an extra pot."

"Owen, you remember Sonia Graham."

Owen chuckled; Scott looked at her for an explanation. He wasn't aware of how effortlessly this came back to him, silently glancing at her with the expectation that the message would arrive intact. And, of course, it did.

"I tend bar at Fusco's," Sonia said. "Three nights a week. That's how I found out you were back in town."

"Fusco's?" Scott frowned. "We were just there last night."

"That was my night off. Lisa told me you came in." Sonia fired a sidelong glance at Owen. "Your brother must've neglected to mention you were back in town."

"Hey, I figured *everybody* knew that Hallmark boy was back," Owen said with an overtly florid gesture. "He's the talk of the town."

Sonia cocked an eyebrow. "Hallmark boy?"

"It's a long story," Scott said.

"Scott's a grown-up," Owen muttered. "He can take care of himself. Just like you." And then, with real interest: "What you got there?"

"Chocolate cake," Sonia said, holding out the pan.

"Fuckin' A." Owen nodded, the hungover smile on his whiskered face looking real, and Scott remembered, as if realizing it for the first time, how Sonia Graham could have that effect on people, tricking them into exposing their finer qualities, whether they intended to or not. "Save me a piece, I'll be right back."

Sonia smiled. "You better hurry."

Owen trudged up the stairs, and a moment later, Scott heard him chatting with Henry, who must have been up in their old bedroom, reading the tattered comic books that he'd found in a box under the bed. In the meantime, he was aware that he had been left alone with Sonia, neither one of them knowing quite what to say until her eyes settled on the stack of pages lying on the table.

"What's that?"

"It's a manuscript."

"Yours?"

Scott shook his head. "I wish. It's actually my dad's. I found it in the shed."

"*The Black Wing*," she read. "Your dad was a writer?"

"I never thought so, but . . ."

"Any good?"

"It is," he said, "but it needs an ending."

"He never finished it?"

Scott shook his head, got up, and began to make coffee. A moment later, Owen and Henry came downstairs, and Sonia cut them each a wedge of chocolate cake. Henry drank orange juice and continued to stare intently at the panels of the Daredevil comic that he'd brought down with him, while Owen and Sonia had an animated conversation about the proper method of making a margarita. Scott tried not to stare at her, but it was almost impossible, particularly when she looked directly at him and smiled, reached up to tuck her hair back behind one ear, or shifted sideways so her knee brushed his beneath the table.

"Hey, bro," Owen said, "don't you have a plane to catch?"

"I can always fly standby."

"You'll end up paying more," Sonia said. "When does your flight leave? Where are you headed?"

"Seattle."

"The big city."

"Yeah, he's leaving all us real people behind," Owen said, brushing crumbs from his stubble. "Ask him how much he paid for those shoes. Go on, ask him. Cheap bastard still won't spring for a rental car, expects me to drive him halfway across the state like a chauffeur."

"I'll drive you," Sonia said.

"That's silly." Scott felt a surge of embarrassment baking his face like the blast of a sunlamp. "You don't have to do that."

"Are you crazy, man? Let her." Owen was already lumbering away to find his tool belt, leaving the three of them in the kitchen. "Some people have to earn a living around here. Henry, get your stuff, let's roll." The boy was observing Scott carefully over his comic book, as if he feared his uncle might try to slip away without saying goodbye. In that instant, Scott was given a brief but utterly compelling glimpse of what life would be like if he could take Henry with him. There was plenty of room in his house and he'd let his nephew decorate his room any way he wanted, taking trips to Pike Place Market and Mount Rainier. On weekends, they would go to the mountains or make the ferry trip out to the islands in Puget Sound, scouting for whales.

"Come here." He lifted the boy from the chair and hugged him. "You and your dad are going to come out and visit me for Christmas, right?"

The boy hugged back, hard, and nodded against his shoulder.

"Take care of yourself," Scott said.

Take him. You could do that. Just take him and run.

But Henry had already kissed and hugged and obediently released him, sensing with a child's clarity that the deal was done. Scott looked up the hall. "Owen," he called, "I'm leaving."

"See ya," his brother's voice hollered down. "Say hi to the beautiful people for us."

Sonia blinked, clearly puzzled by the briskness of his goodbye, but Scott expected nothing less. His family had always been bad at farewells. Even their mother, who had never forgotten to kiss their cheeks on the way to school, had ultimately found no better way of saying goodbye than dying.

CHAPTER FOUR

THEY DROVE TOWARD TOWN in her immaculately maintained Corolla, Sonia changing radio stations while she fingertipped the steering
wheel with small and subtle movements, hardly seeming to consult the
street. "So," she said, "how long has it been since you were back?"

"Fifteen years."

"That was for your mother's funeral, wasn't it?"

Scott nodded, wondering at the implication that death was the only
compelling reason that one might revisit the past. But Sonia seemed
distracted, lost in her own thoughts. A fat squirrel shot out in front of
the car and across the street, chasing a loose tangle of leaves. He
caught a whiff of wood smoke drifting in the bright distance balanced
with the scent of apples, smells and sights crisper than normal, and
realized that he hadn't taken his pills yet today, or yesterday for that
matter.

"What about you?" he asked. "How long have you been back?"

"Almost two years now."

"Weren't you going to law school?"

"I dropped out of Loyola after my second term. . . ." She reached for a Styrofoam cup of coffee in the cup holder, took a sip, and put it back. "It's only temporary. Circumstances with my father . . ."

"Right," he said, and they both went quiet again.

"But, hey, look at you." She flicked her eyes up and down, from haircut to shoes, seeming to take his measure in a single glance. "You've done all right for yourself."

Scott felt the first pinpricks of sweat tickling his hairline. The car abruptly felt too small. He ought not to have accepted this ride from her; he had allowed himself to get caught up in the immediate and visceral thrill of seeing her again without considering the implications of being stuck in conversation for a ninety-minute drive. But there was no getting out of it now.

"You always said you were going to be a writer," she said. "Is that what you're doing?"

"I write greeting cards."

"Hallmark boy." She nodded. "Now I get it."

"I still manage a little fiction on the side." This was a flat-out lie, but he made it sound slightly better by adding, "Not that I've had much time to do it lately. Random House isn't exactly knocking down my door."

"Hey," Sonia said, "relax. It's great that you're getting paid to write anything. Who gets to do that?"

"It's not exactly the great American novel."

"Yeah, well"—she gave him a wry half smile—"pouring beers isn't really practicing law either. But I guess nothing ever turns out quite the way you expect it, does it?"

"Yeah, I guess not."

Another silence, this one heavier somehow, measured in miles, and Scott felt it now, the past riding between them like a hitchhiker they'd picked up along the way. It might have been that notion in the abstract—the almost palpable presence of the past—that triggered the next idea in his mind. Once acknowledged, it wouldn't go away.

"Do you mind if we take a detour before the airport?"

She frowned. "What about your flight?"

"We've still got time."

"You're sure?"

Scott nodded. "Turn here. Take a left on Broad, follow it down."

They drove half a mile, and he gave more directions, wondering now if Sonia realized where they were headed. If she did, she said nothing. Their route became a country road, climbing, dithering, and unmarked except for an occasional mailbox, up to an unassuming intersection marked only by a black smear of tire marks and the bright yellow sap of the broken tree.

"Is this where your father . . . ?" She let the question fade, unfinished.

"Yeah." He climbed out, trembling only a little, wishing now he'd remembered to take his pills but not wanting to pull them out in front of her. Under his boots, tiny fragments of grit spangled the roadside. This was all that was left of his father, a pair of black tire marks, crumbs of broken windshield glass, a demolished young pine—and then he remembered the manuscript, more marks left across a blank surface, more dead pulp. Looking at the angle of the swerve, Scott felt his eyes drawn back to the unmarked dirt road that joined the main highway here, and found himself wondering what a man like Frank Mast might have been doing up there.

Whether he saw it then—a glint of old iron, buried a hundred yards back in the woods—or only thought he did when he later remembered that moment, he didn't know. He walked back to the car.

"Let's go up that way," he said, pointing up the dirt road.

"Why?"

"I just want to check it out." He got in, still watching her. The moment felt odd, a segment of the past spliced into the present. "You mind?"

Shrugging, Sonia put the car in gear. The bare dirt surface bumped and scraped underneath them. It was a bad road and she drove slowly, mindful of the car's suspension. The trees grew thick and low above the road, and pine boughs hissed off the roof like stiff brooms brushing metal. After a few minutes, Scott could see that the old gates really were there after all, still partially disguised by the piney overgrowth that surrounded them. They stood ajar, as if the last person to come along hadn't had time to get out and close them behind him, and he stared at them as they passed through, turning his head to watch them go by.

That was when he first saw the house.

CHAPTER FIVE

IT STOOD BY ITSELF, STARING BACK at them from a clearing in the trees. Parts of it looked three stories high, others four, and there was the feeling that if you walked its circumference, you'd find that the whole thing went much farther back than expected. Wings and cupolas sprouted not quite randomly from its sides, outbuildings, additions that might have been tacked on as afterthoughts. The result was shapeless and unfocused, a house that looked big enough to get lost in.

Smooth where it should have been angular, his father had written, *angular where it should've been smooth.*

"It's real," Scott said, more to himself than Sonia, stepping out of the car.

"What?"

"Round House. It's exactly like he described it." Taking a few steps toward the house, he glanced up, feeling a single fleck of rain strike his nose. Through the treetops, the sky had gone low and mottled, and he could smell the threat of a downpour rising up from the woods around them.

He walked across the neglected lawn to the porch, just ahead of the rain. The old wood was silent under his feet. In front of him, the brittle scroll of an ancient advertising circular poked out of the mailbox, looking as if it would turn to dust if he touched it. He saw a faded business card wedged inside, a local real estate office. Plucking it out, he dropped it in his pocket, turned, and looked back at Sonia's car. It was reassuring to see her there, only fifty yards from where he stood. Maybe it was just the clearing, or the sudden arrival of the autumn storm, but the distances out here felt magnified, even warped, as if the sheer size of the house itself created its own gravitational field. He couldn't see her expression through the falling rain.

He jogged back to the car and got in.

"You're soaking wet," she said. "What were you looking at?"

"This house. It's the one my dad described in this manuscript I found. I thought he'd made it up, but it's actually real." He looked at her and saw color rising in her neck that hadn't been there a moment earlier, flushed against the darkness of her hair. "What?"

"Nothing," she said. "I just hope you've got dry clothes for your flight home." She watched him dialing the number from the business card. "Who are you calling?"

"The Realtor."

"Are you serious?"

"I'm interested in seeing what it looks like inside, that's all."

"Don't you still have a plane to catch?"

He did. But at the moment he had forgotten all about it.

MARQUETTE LUTHER, THE REAL ESTATE AGENT who came to open up the house for him, was an unflappable African American woman in her midforties with a black umbrella and sensible black shoes. She was not the kind of individual whom Scott typically associated with this part of New Hampshire, and if the house itself hadn't been such a distraction, the inquisitive part of him would have labored to keep from asking how she'd ended up here.

The rain had hammered the clearing and tapered off prior to her arrival, but the air remained absurdly frigid, trapped inside his clothes, right up next to his wet skin. The muscles in his jaw ached from trembling. Up on the porch, he and Sonia waited while Marquette bent her right leg at the knee and flicked a leaf from her heel.

"We actually had to check our own listings for this one," she said. "I didn't even know it was out here. And I've been with the office for sixteen years." She took a key out of her purse with a round paper tag attached to it and tried to fit it in the door, but it didn't work. "That's strange. This should be the right key." She ducked back out of the shadow of the porch to check the label on the tag.

Scott reached out and tried the door. It clicked and turned easily, without resistance. "Looks like it's open."

"You're kidding."

Behind them, Sonia made a sound of amused incredulity and gave him an "after you" gesture. With a half-comic sense of a man going to meet his destiny, Scott stepped through the entryway.

Part of him, maybe the majority of him, had expected to find it dirty and damp—cluttered, probably, with old newspapers and water damage, sheet-draped furniture, cobwebs, and whole layers of dust, maybe even a broken window or two. But the air was dry, and the vacant hardwood floors of the foyer and adjacent sitting room looked freshly swept. Past an open walk-in closet, an enormous metal radiator sat beneath one of the windows, coiled like a python.

"My goodness, look at these floors," Sonia said. "How old do you think they are?"

Marquette checked her paperwork. "Built in the 1870s."

"Do you have any idea who the owner is?" Scott asked. He had started the other way and, realizing he didn't know where he was heading, turned to look back at the Realtor.

"It's been empty for quite some time. I could certainly look into it."

"What did you call it when we were outside?" Sonia asked Scott. "Round House?"

"That's what my father called it, in his manuscript." He nodded and pointed up. "See?"

Marquette Luther studied the ceiling for a long moment and followed it down to the floor, then forward to the doorway, squatting down and running her fingers along the frame. "That's very unusual," she said. "The whole place kind of . . . curves around you, doesn't it?"

"Yeah," Sonia said.

"What?" Scott looked back at her. "You don't like it?"

"It reminds me of something I read somewhere about dreams. They say if you're not sure whether or not you're dreaming, you should look for a place where the walls come together. Apparently in dreams they never form a sharp angle."

"How interesting," Marquette said, but her voice sounded hollow and strange, and Scott realized that Sonia's comment had struck him the same way, the huge emptiness of the house sucking the familiarity out of it. For the first time, he felt as if maybe he shouldn't have come here, shouldn't have opened the door and allowed himself to go inside.

"I guess that makes this a dream house, then," he said, but Sonia didn't say anything, and the real estate agent's obligatory laugh was so dry that he wished he'd kept his mouth shut.

Scott walked across the sitting area and opened the French doors to the formal dining room, the space largely empty except for a few haphazardly placed pieces of furniture. Although he had never set foot in the room, he felt as if he'd stood there before, right in that spot. In his father's manuscript, this had been where Karl Faircloth first encountered the door to the long black hall that went nowhere. Scott paused and let his gaze settle on the oak door in the far right corner of the room, unremarkable except for its odd placement and the long brass knob, exactly as his father had described. He touched the handle—it was cold, as if all the coming blackness of winter were waiting to be released from the other side.

He let out his breath, only then realizing how much air he'd been holding in, looking at the place where his father's book and reality finally parted company, and his first conscious thought was *Thank God*, followed immediately by a sense of how silly he'd been. *What did you expect?*

The space on the other side was just another closet. It was shallow and plain, not much bigger than the one they'd passed in the entryway, and it was certainly not a hidden wing. Two unpainted shelves, each slightly curved, lay bare in front of him, and Scott found himself reaching in to tap the back wall. Two knocks and the whole thing would swing around, wasn't that it? Or would there be a hidden lever, à la Scooby-Doo? He stood back with a peculiar combination of relief and disappointment, and that was when he noticed the scratch marks inside the door.

They were narrow and deep, like the work of a chisel or file. The markings came in sets of three and four, sometimes five, as if some animal had been trapped inside or, he supposed, a person—they were about chest-level to him—or perhaps a child, though, of course, no child could've mustered such force.

"Scott?" Sonia's voice was distant, buzzing through the ductwork like the two-cans-and-a-string telephone game he'd played as a kid. "You have to come up and see this!"

"Coming," Scott said, and pushed the door firmly shut.

"WHAT DO YOU THINK?" SONIA ASKED, gesturing into the open room at the end of the second-floor hallway. The hall was long and straight and would have been utterly unremarkable if not for the almost cavelike effect of the rounded ceiling and floor. The room at the end was somehow both bigger and smaller than it should have been. Scott stepped inside. After the rain, little drizzles of gold-orange and yellow afternoon light trickled down through the surrounding trees outside. The light ought to have revealed desiccated insect corpses and dust bunnies, but there was only freshly dusted spotless cedar, which he could feel bowing just slightly under his shoes. Built-in empty bookshelves lined the walls, floor to ceiling, separated by wide windows. A single glassed-in dormer projected from the sloping wall, surrounded by treetops and overlooking the lawn, big enough for a desk and chair. "It's the perfect office. Think of the writing you could do here."

"You're a writer?" Marquette asked.

"Scott's a novelist," Sonia said. "They're calling him the next Nicholas Sparks."

"Really?"

"No." Scott felt his face getting hot. "She's joking."

"He's going to finish his father's novel," Sonia said, seemingly oblivious to his stare. "His father passed away recently, and Scott found this unfinished manuscript. Now he's going to complete it for him—right here in Round House. It will be published under both their names, a father-and-son collaboration, like a tribute to his father. Right, Scott?"

"No," he said, horrified. "I—"

"What a *wonderful* idea." Marquette held up her arm, pulling back her sleeve for him to see skin. "I've got goose bumps," she said. "I think that's a marvelous thing to do. You can certainly put me down for a copy." She looked at Sonia, beaming. "And you're so right, this house would be the perfect place for a writer . . . secluded, quiet, with plenty of space to spread out. I believe it's available for rent, but let me call and confirm that."

THEY FOLLOWED HER OUT TO THE PORCH, neither one of them speaking until Marquette climbed back into her car and shut the door. Then Scott turned and looked at her. "The next Nicholas Sparks?" he asked. "What the hell was that about?"

Sonia shrugged. "You're a writer, right? Why not give it a shot?"

"I told you, I write greeting cards."

"And fiction, you said."

"Some." The lie, already coming back to haunt him, and he thought of something he'd once heard his father say: *The more you lie, the more you have to remember.* "Not novels, though."

"Well, maybe it's time to branch out and try something a little different. Don't you think you're up to it?"

"That's not the point."

"What happened to being so intrigued with this house?" She was driving them up the bumpy road, keeping her eyes straight ahead, but Scott felt as if she were staring at him, waiting for an answer. "All of a sudden you can't wait to run away again?"

"I'm not running away from anything. My life is in Seattle, my job—I can't just drop all that and move back to town."

"How long would it take you to finish it, a month or two? You're telling me that your employer wouldn't give you a leave of absence so you could help get your father's affairs in order? I thought you were the big swinging dick back at the greeting card factory."

Scott looked at her. "What are you doing?"

"I'm helping you gain closure."

"What, you're a shrink now?"

"You could use one."

"I've got that covered." It was silent in the car as they reached the intersection where the dirt road merged onto the two-lane highway that would take them back toward town. Sonia stopped the car and looked at him thoughtfully across a distance that seemed to encompass all the years they had spent apart.

"Let me ask you this," she said. "Do you think you *could* finish the book? Do you have any idea how you would end it?"

Scott opened his mouth to tell her no, it wasn't his story to tell. But what he said instead was, "I don't know. Maybe I might have a few ideas."

"So give it a week. See what happens. If nothing comes of it, hey, it's an extra week you got to spend with your nephew."

He wanted to look at her and tell her to take him to the airport. Instead, he found himself looking back over his seat and through the trees, to the house.

CHAPTER SIX

THE NEXT DAY, SCOTT WROTE A CHECK for six hundred dollars plus a security deposit and signed a one-month rental agreement for Round House. Owen picked him up at Marquette Luther's office and drove him down to a Hertz in Manchester to rent a car for the time he'd be staying here in town. When Scott had called Seattle to ask for extra time off, the reaction from the home office had been what he'd expected: *Of course, Scott, take all the time you need. Please don't hesitate to let us know if there's anything we can do for you.* His boss had gone on to share a story about losing his own father to a massive coronary, and Scott had felt obliged to listen until the man, realizing what he was doing, had signed off with a beefy "Be well."

If Owen was surprised by Scott's decision to stay in town—or indeed felt anything particular at all about it—he kept his feelings to himself. The drive down to the car rental place was quiet except for the electronic chirps and blips from Henry's handheld video game. It looked expensive, and Scott wondered where it had come from. Owen, who wore a flannel shirt with a T-shirt underneath reading *I'm not a gynecologist but I'll take a look*, smoked cigarettes and blew the smoke out the window. His ashtray was already a carcinogenic pincushion bristling with yellow-stained filters.

"You ought to come out to the house yourself," Scott said.

Owen grunted.

"Dad never said anything to you about it, did he?"

"About what? Some house in the woods?"

"Yeah."

"Dad and I didn't really talk."

"So, then, he never mentioned anything about a house?"

"What?"

"Dad never told you about—"

"Jesus, man, *no,* okay? Fuck." Owen shook his head, inexplicably furious. Scott had told him all about the house and how it matched the one that their father described in *The Black Wing,* and Owen seemed to have nothing to say about that either. The miles spun out indefinitely. The radio was broken; it only got static and talk radio. At last they came to the Hertz near the airport, and when Owen pulled up in front of the office, Henry put down the video game in alarm, as if he'd forgotten that Scott would be following them back to Milburn. Owen was scowling at him as well in what looked like expectation and discomfort, shielding his eyes from the midafternoon sun.

"You got money for gas?"

"Sure." Scott took out his wallet and withdrew four twenties, handing them to Owen. "That okay?"

His brother took the bills and folded them between dirty fingers. For the first time, Scott noticed how badly the yellowing nails were gnawed down. "I was wondering if you could maybe float me. You know, since you'll be around for a while. Until work picks up."

"How much do you need?"

"A few hundred, just for groceries and shit."

"I'll hit the ATM on the way home."

Owen nodded as if he'd expected nothing less. He looked back at Henry, still gripping his video game. "Put that goddamn thing away already. Giving me a freakin' headache." Then he swung the pickup around, tires squealing, and drove out of the lot, leaving an exhaust cloud in his wake.

Scott was watching him go, thinking it wasn't safe for Owen to be driving like that with his son in the truck, when he felt a sudden electric shock go through his head. It was so surprising that, for an instant, he thought he'd somehow bumped his head into a live wire, even though there was nothing behind him. He looked around anyway, rubbing the back of his skull, too stunned to think. Within seconds the spasm was gone. He stood outside the car rental office for another moment before going inside.

CHAPTER SEVEN

ROUND HOUSE WAS COLD.

On his first night, Scott put two sweaters on and wandered the first floor, stomping his feet and hugging himself while he explored the various doorways and slanting side halls, searching for the source of cold air. He almost expected to find a window wide open or a hole in the wall. Some of the doors were locked, but the only key he had was for the front door. Walking from the kitchen through an oval antechamber into the extremely old sitting room with a hearth and mantel, he found a window. It didn't open to the outside but onto another room, perhaps ten by twelve, with two rocking chairs, shelves, and a wooden cradle in the rounded corner. The air here felt particularly still, as if it hadn't moved in decades, and was as glacial as a deep freeze. Scott looked at the cradle, too small for anything but a child's doll. Who had lived here, and when?

Did Dad come out here and write? he wondered, and then: *Did Mom know?*

He followed the flight of stairs to the second floor. Here was the sinuous hallway that ran the entire length of the house, with closed doors that had stared blankly at one another like frozen corpses for the last hundred and forty years.

Frozen corpses? Where did that come from? The writing room that Sonia had shown him stood at one end of the corridor, the door open just as he'd left it. They hadn't needed a key to get inside the house, but many of the upstairs doors were locked.

SCOTT WENT BACK DOWN TO THE KITCHEN. He had picked up a few supplies—deli meat, peanut butter, multigrain bread, instant coffee, and a bottle of Bombay Sapphire gin. He busied himself with putting away the rest of the food, found a dusty glass in the cupboard and rinsed it out, added ice and some gin and an olive. He'd never been much of a drinker—he'd bought the gin only because he thought Sonia might come by for a nightcap—and it felt particularly strange to be sitting here under the cold kitchen lights, shivering like an arctic explorer, drinking alone. Regardless, he took a sip, gasped, shuddered, and took a bigger gulp, letting it warm him slowly from the inside.

At length, he returned to the dining room.

For some reason, he'd set up camp here rather than in one of the upstairs rooms. Moving his belongings upstairs felt too permanent, and he liked the feeling that he was here only temporarily, until he came to his senses and realized the absurdity of this whole enterprise. So this was where he had put his suitcase and his laptop bag, along with an inflatable air mattress borrowed from Owen, a sleeping bag, and a pillow. He opened the suitcase and took out the stack of pages that comprised his father's manuscript. Lacking a table or desk, he took the pages and his laptop to the settee and sat down, immediately uncomfortable. He was going to have to get some real furniture in here, even if he had to rent it. Temporary or not, four weeks was more than enough time to earn yourself a sore ass.

He turned to the last page of the manuscript. The text went all the way to the bottom of the page, but it ended with a paragraph break. The last thing that his father had typed was:

```
    Faircloth heard the door swing open and
  stopped his ministrations with the pistol to
```

```
look up. What he saw standing in the entryway
made him suck in his breath and then fall
absolutely still.
     The thing in the doorway grinned back at him.
At once, with the clarity of absolute terror, he
understood everything that had happened up till
now--and he grasped what had occurred here, in
this place, and what it meant for him, forever
after.
```

Okay, Scott thought, *but what?*

Knowing he was only going to make himself miserable, he turned on the laptop, already feeling awkward about the writing process. Greeting card copy was so short, usually fifty words or fewer, that he always wrote it by hand, often on Post-it notes stuck on corkboards he kept hanging around the office. One of the things he always liked about it was that with the right background music and atmosphere, he could usually bang out the whole thing in one night—from inspiration to execution. Sometimes there was even an element of self-hypnosis to it. If he had to write a Christmas card in July, he'd turn the air-conditioning down to sixty, put on a sweater, and mull some cider. No need for that now. He slugged gin and shivered.

Reading the last paragraph of his father's story over again, he opened a new document and looked at the blank screen, the blinking cursor.

He closed his eyes and tried to imagine what the book cover might look like. *The Black Wing*, by Frank Mast and Scott Mast. And a picture of a dark, spooky, slightly curved hallway leading into darkness. Or maybe the oak door in the corner of the dining room, halfway open.

He got up and walked over to the door. Was his story somewhere behind it, waiting inside? He touched the cold doorknob, so cold it could've been hot, turned it, and opened the door, looking at the empty closet. Why, of all the doors and hallways in the house, had his father chosen this particular one to imagine the hidden wing behind? Scott looked at the scratch marks inside the door and touched them, running his fingers into the random, reckless grooves.

It was late. He blew into the air mattress until he was light-headed, but it still wasn't firm. There was a leak somewhere. He unrolled his sleeping bag and lay down on it anyway, suddenly too tired even to brush his teeth, and switched off the flashlight. His first breath in the dark tasted of metal shavings, a slightly toxic flavor. In the silence there was the faint hiss of the mattress softening beneath him. The sea was lapping up, rising to engulf him, and he sank down beneath the waves.

SCOTT AWOKE IN THE MIDDLE OF THE NIGHT with a start, his heart pounding. It was as if there had been a loud noise somewhere in the house, a thump or a crash that had startled him from his slumber, that had ended just as he'd come awake. It was completely dark. Why hadn't he left a light on?

I did. I know I did.

He sat up in the sleeping bag on top of the completely deflated mattress and waited, counting the seconds, but it was resolutely silent. The house was freezing, and he had to pee. The feeling of urgency versus the cold air reminded him of going camping as a child.

Groping for the flashlight, he climbed out of the bag, still fully dressed, mouth thick and gummy from the gin, and walked out of the dining room and down the hall that led to the entryway. The house had several bathrooms on the first floor, but he still wasn't sure where all of them were; the closest was under the stairway ahead of him. He went in, emptied his bladder, splashed water on his face, and drank from his cupped hands. Now the water tasted slightly rusty. Wasn't it supposed to get better, the longer you used it? The pipes shook and rattled deep in the walls. He glanced at his watch: It was three in the morning. No more sleep for him.

The insomnia had been a parting gift from his mother. When he was a child, his nights had been filled with the reassuring sounds that emanated from her sewing room, the steady whir of the Singer machine and the occasional creak of her footsteps as she got up to get something, a piece of fabric or a cup of tea. In the master bedroom, his father snored thunderously, gnashing his teeth and fighting the Vietcong in his sleep, while his mother sat sewing, tapping the Singer's foot pedal, a woman driving nowhere. In the mornings, she had looked harried and run-down, burning toast, spilling juice, touching the corner of her lip as if trying to remember something from the drawn-out hours of the night. When Scott and Owen came home from school, she would be normal again, smiling, but Scott had found himself wondering what that thing was that she'd wanted to tell him after a sleepless night. After her death, he was struck by the fact that his relationship with her had been an unfinished conversation. In death, she had become much more articulate. At the funeral, he remembered Owen looking at him out of the corner of his eye, and Scott had gone back to the house afterward, up to the sewing room, and slammed his head into the wall hard enough to crack the plaster. Right away it had made him feel better. Ten years later: therapy. White pills. The crack in the wall was still there.

A sharp electric jolt ran up the right side of his neck. He winced, not moving, waiting to see if it would happen again. It didn't.

He walked out of the cold bathroom, wiping his hands on his jeans, and went back to the dining room, searching his suitcase for his medication. He had the vague memory of leaving the pills at his father's house—Owen's house now, he reminded himself, home of the cracked wall. He could visualize it so clearly. Was that part of not taking the meds? He conjured up a memory of his mother's pale face, standing in the kitchen with burned toast in her hands, crying about something. It made him wonder what other memories might be lying dormant in the corners of his mind, waiting for the lights to come on.

In the hallway, something rattled, and Scott felt his blood jump. He stopped in his tracks and held his breath. The radiator clattered a second time, the noise fading into a sustained gastrointestinal gargle. All around him, the subtle irregularity of the house made its minor incidental noises. Scott thought about the locked rooms upstairs. It would be good to explore them by daylight with Sonia, if he could ever get the right set of keys.

He crawled back into his sleeping bag on the flattened mattress and lay staring blankly at the ceiling, waiting for morning to come. Time passed in the funny way it did in the middle of the night, somehow quicker and more slowly, in fits and starts; every time he looked at the clock on his cell phone another twenty minutes had passed while he'd lain there listening to the house, thinking of nothing.

When day came, it was raining.

CHAPTER EIGHT

OWEN DIDN'T TALK TO HIS SON on the ride to school. His head was throbbing from last night's bender, and the world felt far away but still too close, muffled by a thick layer of insulation with an occasional spike of noise or sunlight piercing through. Going back to bed felt like the best way to handle it, a few more hours of sleep followed by some strong coffee, but he had things to do today, chores that wouldn't wait.

He pulled up in front of Henry's school, pressed both hands against his eyes, and pushed until it hurt. "You got your stuff?"

Henry nodded and climbed out, putting on his backpack.

"Okay, then."

"Bye, Daddy." Leaning over to kiss his father's stubbled cheek, Henry slipped out and ran through the puddles, jumping over some and into others. Owen sat watching him melt together with all the other kids until he couldn't see him anymore. He drove his truck back through town in the pouring rain, wipers slashing at the downpour. Dead leaves caked the road, plastered to his tires in a soggy brown mush. November had arrived, the fall already shot to hell; at the ripe old age of thirty-one, he could feel it, not just in his pounding skull but in his busted knuckles and arthritic knees, blizzard weather here before deer season even got started.

For a native New Englander, he'd been caught embarrassingly off guard by the sudden drop in temperature. Tonight he had promised Red they'd go out to Lawson's Woods and jack a deer. Owen didn't savor the idea of bundling up and trudging through the rain-soaked trees with a gun in his hand any more than he cherished the certainty that he would be the one dressing out the animal, hacking its hide off while Red stood by, slugging coffee brandy and reliving his glory days in the NFL.

Nobody knew exactly what a guy like Red Fontana was doing up here in Milburn anyway. At thirty, he'd played professional football, a big-shot New York playboy with a smoking-hot supermodel for a wife and a multimillion-dollar career. A year later, he was washed up, finished, a late-night talk show punch line. The supermodel wife was dead—a dance club overdose—and rumor had it that Red had gone broke defending himself against speculation about his involvement in her death. Bye-bye, contract; so long, endorsements. He was done with football, done with New York, done with the tabloid columnists who had been his best friends. He had retreated north with his new wife, Colette McGuire, who—rumor also had it—had married him mainly to piss off her parents. Attaching himself like a tick to the McGuire bloodline, he'd moved into the house and made all sorts of new friends and local suck-ups here in town. Chief among those friends and suck-ups—for reasons Owen had yet to fathom—was he himself.

He drove down Main Street, toward what was left of the Bijou Theatre, pulling up in front of the blackened, sloping shell of the building where workers were hauling wheelbarrows of black debris out into the rain. They all looked as miserable as he felt; without realizing it, Owen drew some measly measure of comfort from watching them shuffle about their work anyway, heads down, backs stooped. He'd gone to school with some of those guys, played ball and run around with them, making plans for the future. After a certain point, who had a choice how their lives went? Owen tried to remember where the point had been for him.

Instead, he got a flash of his mother running up the aisle with her arms raised and her hair on fire, screaming, a burning angel.

Owen parked and got out, lit a cigarette, and walked over to the temporary chain-link fence that surrounded the demolition site. For fifteen years since the fire, the Bijou had sat here with nobody doing anything to it, rotting like a corpse at a viewing. Now the Milburn Historical Society, headed up by none other than the McGuire family, had finally decided to fix it up.

Flicking the cigarette into a puddle, he looked through the fence at one of the hard hats, a Latino guy with an earring, leaning on his shovel. "Hey."

The wetback turned around, water dripping off his helmet.

"You speak English?" Owen asked.

"Yeah."

"Lemme talk to your foreman."

"Who the hell are you?"

"Just get him, okay?" Owen heard his own voice rising slightly. "Before I sic INS on your ass."

The guy tossed his shovel and walked over, and Owen felt the adrenaline swelling in his temples, temporarily overtaking his headache. Eight thirty in the morning and he was already in a fight. That moment of critical decision—he'd missed it again.

"I'm a fucking U.S. citizen, asshole."

"Oh yeah?" Owen showed teeth. "Let's see your green card, shitbag. Or did you leave it in your car with your seventeen kids?"

"The fuck did you just say?"

"You heard me."

The guy was starting to come over the fence when a man in rolled-up shirtsleeves and a tie stuck his head out of the trailer. "Hey!"

Owen and the wetback both stopped and looked over.

"What's going on here?"

"You the foreman?" Owen called back.

The man came down off the steps, scratching his head with a pencil. Off to the left, the Latino employee had already faded away. Owen imagined him muttering to himself in Spanish.

"We ain't hiring," the foreman said.

"Red sent me."

"Is that a fact?" The foreman looked him up and down, visibly underwhelmed by what he saw. "What's your name, gruesome?"

"Owen Mast."

"Is he gonna know you if I call to check it out?"

"Be my guest."

"Great." Now the man just looked tired. "Come on around the side, go on up to the trailer, and talk to Mike, he'll get your paperwork. We pull a twelve-hour shift here, half hour for lunch, no benefits. This ain't no union shop. You call in sick, you show up hungover, you're fired, no second chances, I don't care who your friends are. Got it?"

"Yeah, yeah." Owen was already walking toward the trailer. He felt a hand on his shoulder, stopping him.

"You ever done work like this before?" the foreman asked.

"What," Owen said, "demolition?" He gave the guy a grin that cut deep into the corners of his cracked lips. "My whole life."

CHAPTER NINE

DURING HIS FIRST TWO WEEKS in the house, Scott fell into a routine, a means of breaking up the day, not that it amounted to much in the end. He spent the morning drinking coffee in his makeshift office in the dining room, staring at the blank computer screen like a passenger staring out the window on a transatlantic flight. Usually he'd type a dozen words and delete them, go to the kitchen for more coffee, come back, sit down, and repeat the process. On-screen, the view remained unchanged with no land in sight.

Ladies and gentlemen, the captain has turned off the FASTEN SEAT BELTS sign; you may now feel free to roam about the house.

At midday, he would give up and wander upstairs, turning on lights as he went, exploring the rooms whose doors were unlocked, catching an array of peculiar smells—mothballs, wet wool, and rotting cedar. He checked out closets and cupboards and doorways that led nowhere, telling himself that if there was inspiration here, he'd find it. But all he found was emptiness, that same sulky, sullen vacancy that seemed to radiate from the hub of the house in vast invisible spokes.

Then, late one Saturday afternoon, just before dark, while walking through the hallway outside the sitting room, he found something new.

It was an old theatrical poster, probably from the sixties. It was hanging on a narrow patch of wall behind a door that he hadn't opened before. The poster art was so simple as to be almost meaningless, a line drawing of a room with three walls that didn't quite come together in the corners. Below it, the text read:

One Room, Unfinished
Debuting in September at the McKinley, 23rd Street

And below that, in small, almost reluctant letters:

A play by Thomas Mast

Scott looked at the poster. He saw no year on it anywhere, no indication of its age except for its overall poor condition. There *was* something familiar about it, though, not just the name of the play but the odd artwork as well. Thomas Mast had been Frank Mast's father, Grandpa Tommy, Scott and Owen's grandfather, a man Scott had never known, a name that didn't come up often in conversation. "Not a New Englander," Frank had said. "A city man. Too slick for his own good." Coming from his father's lips, it was nothing less than a condemnation. But what was the poster doing here?

Scott unpinned it from the wall, peeled one corner back as if there might be some further indication of its meaning on the other side, saw nothing but blank space, and wondered what he'd been hoping to find. Some hidden message? A note written just for him from some half-forgotten relation? It was the sort of detail you could use only in the world of make-believe, where clues added up to full and satisfying explanations. Even the title of this play—*One Room, Unfinished*—suggested nothing of the sort, though Scott thought it was absolutely appropriate. No one in his family had ever finished anything. Rather, it seemed that things—fires, ambition, alcohol, madness—were always finishing *them*.

He stared out the window. It wasn't raining anymore, but the sun was already draining from the western windows, creeping away in embarrassment of another wasted day. His spine ached and his

stomach was sour from the coffee, the computer screen still blaz-
ingly blank. He held his trembling hand in front of his face, but he
couldn't tell if it was his hand shaking or his eyeballs. His blood
sugar was crashing; he had to be hungry, but the thought of his
provisions—dry cereal, canned tuna, lunch meat—only made him
more nauseated. Returning to the kitchen, he went against all con-
ventional wisdom, poured himself a gin to settle his nerves, and
called Sonia.

"It's me," he said. "You want to get some lunch?"

"At four thirty in the afternoon?"

"Dinner, then." The gin was already working. He thought about
swinging by his father's old house and picking up Henry, seeing if the
boy wanted to come along with them for a meal, even if it meant bringing Owen too. "Are you at the bar tonight?"

"Lisa and I split the weekend," Sonia said. "How's the writing
going?"

"Good."

"You've been at it for what, almost two weeks now? Making any
headway?"

"Yeah, it's actually going really well." Another lie—one more to
remember. Why did he feel compelled to hide the truth from her?

"You sure you want to knock off for the day?" Sonia asked.

"You should always quit when you've still got some momentum."
Over the years, his brain had become a tip jar full of writing nostrums,
often contradictory. Quit while you're ahead. Don't stop if you're
rolling. Keep regular hours. Don't hold yourself to routine. Make an
outline. Go where the story takes you.

"Okay," Sonia said. "Why don't you come by the house in an hour
or so. Does that sound all right?"

"Sounds good."

"Scott?"

"Yes?"

"Nothing." She paused. "See you in a while."

Hanging up, he allowed himself to breathe. They had history
between them, a lot of it, maybe more than he had with anybody else
on this earth that he wasn't related to by blood, and he still didn't
know where to begin. He didn't know exactly when he'd first met
her—growing up here, it seemed as if they'd known each other forever—

but he remembered exactly when and where he'd first become completely, agonizingly aware of her.

They had been in English class, in the spring of their senior year, laying out an issue of the school newspaper, the Milburn High *Graduate*. All the other students had left for the day, and Mr. French was back at his desk, correcting papers, while Scott and Sonia tried to find enough space for the Ski Club photo. They'd reached for the picture at the same time, their hands brushing against each other long enough for them both to realize they'd touched, and she'd looked up at him. Later that afternoon, they walked home together and talked on the phone that night for two hours—about school, and their families, growing up in Milburn, which Sonia called "the ghastliest little hamlet in New Hampshire." Like him, she had dreamed of running away; but she had actually done it at age twelve and gotten as far as the city limits before the sheriff caught up with her and brought her home. Scott, who'd always dreamed of leaving but had never mustered the nerve, could only stand in awe.

A week later, she'd invited him over to her house for pizza, and they planned their escape together, just the two of them, for real this time. At the end of the night, Sonia had kissed him, and Scott levitated home feeling like he'd just discovered an antidote for gravity, the omnipresent loneliness that he'd lived with for so long that he was scarcely aware of its existence. In all the years they'd known each other, he felt as if she'd been hiding this side of herself, or he'd just been too blind to see it. Now, with graduation less than a month away, he couldn't believe he'd waited this long. He felt like a man on a long train ride looking at a pretty girl, waiting to talk to her, only to exchange a brief word before she stepped out of his life forever.

So he took a chance and wrote her a long letter. In essence, it said he really did want to run away with her, wherever, to do whatever—college, Europe, the Peace Corps—as long as they were together. He finished it by saying that he'd fallen completely, totally in love with her, and if she didn't feel the same way, he'd understand, but he couldn't just let her walk out of his life without knowing how he felt. He passed it to her one morning before class and spent the next three hours squirming in his seat. At lunch, she'd found him outside the cafeteria and led him outdoors, under the shadow of the old gymnasium, and kissed him. "You jerk. What took you so long?"

What followed was a week of pure bliss like nothing he'd experienced before or since, sneaking out at night, crawling in each other's bedroom windows, staying up late and never sleeping. Then, the day before the senior prom, he'd tried to call and she wasn't home. When he'd driven by the house, her father had come out and told him to go away. "She doesn't want to talk to you."

After that, it didn't matter how often he called or came by, the results were the same. They didn't see each other that summer, and when fall came, they both ran away, but in different directions. When he thought back on it, he wondered if he'd scared her off or whether—in his darkest imaginings—it had been something worse.

She doesn't know about that, he thought. *She couldn't.*

But in the back of his mind, he wondered.

HE SHOWERED IN THE DOWNSTAIRS BATHROOM, pulling back the mildewed vinyl curtain to peer through the steam into the opaque mirror as if he expected to see someone looking back at him. As children, he and Owen had scared themselves with the story of Bloody Mary, whose face would appear in the mirror if you stood in front of it and chanted her name thirteen times.

By the time he'd shaved and gotten dressed, it was almost totally dark outside. Gusts of wind tumbled dead leaves the size of giants' hands across the huge, empty yard that divided the house from the surrounding woods, and he recognized the smell of snow in the air. It was the first time he'd been out that day, and the change in weather shocked the Pacific Northwesterner in him, which was far more used to rain and fog. *Winter's here,* he thought, with an irrational sense of panic, and then immediately: *I'm not ready. I shouldn't even be here.*

Pills, he thought absently, and reminded himself to get his prescription refilled at the pharmacy. He thought of the random brain zaps he'd been experiencing, something to tell his doctor about back in Seattle.

Driving into town, he marveled at the illusion of distance between his house and civilization. Surely an illusion was all it was, a minor miracle of subjective perception. It seemed to take longer than ever just getting to town, and he passed no other cars, the damp, empty road telescoping in front of him, stretching out like a child's idea of time. Two miles east of downtown, he followed another country road to a four-way intersection where a ramshackle junk shop stood under a bright lamp with a hand-painted wooden sign that read EARL'S EMPORIUM. He parked and went up the steps, knocked on the front door, and saw Sonia on the other side, smiling a little awkwardly, making him think of how she'd looked eighteen years ago, almost half a lifetime.

"Hey," she said.

"Hi." And then, because of the fine lines above her eyebrows: "Is everything all right?"

"Sure. Good to see you. Come on in."

As always, they had to navigate the coves and shoals of Earl Graham's junk shop to get to the actual house. Sonia led him between long tables piled with tagged items, old parking meters and drive-in speakers, racks of incomplete military uniforms, ear trumpets, and glass cases of campaign buttons for losing senatorial candidates whom Scott had never heard of. Earl had been an old Communist from New York back in the post-Eisenhower era, cranking out a mimeographed newsletter from his one-room flat on Mulberry Street, but sometime in the 1960s, he'd gotten tired of politics and headed up here to get married and sell junk to tourists. Some of this stuff had no doubt been here the last time Scott had set foot in this place; the nearness of the past both warmed and chilled him.

"Dad?" Sonia stuck her head around the corner of the living room. "I'm going out now, okay?"

Behind her, looking into the room, Scott glimpsed a skeletal, trembling, almost unrecognizable wreck of a man he barely remembered, his nearly translucent skin colored only by the glow of the plasma TV screen. Oxygen tubes ran into the plastic mask covering his nose and mouth. A machine beeped. Scott looked away, abashed by his own reaction. It was as if some smaller, weaker organism had donned the skin of Earl Graham and was rapidly suffocating within it, and there was really nothing to say. He told himself Earl hadn't seen him standing there; he could still slip away unnoticed.

He walked into the living room.

"Mr. Graham?"

Sonia's dad glanced up at him, almost alarmed.

"It's good to see you again," Scott said. "It's been a long time."

Earl nodded guardedly, not moving. "Uh-huh."

"I remember Sonia and I used to come out here and play board games on Friday nights, right there in the junk shop. We got pizza and stayed up late. You always kicked our butts at Trivial Pursuit."

"I don't know about that."

"No, you did," Scott said. "I still don't know how many golf balls there are on the moon." And he did a peculiar thing, something he'd never imagined himself doing, certainly not spontaneously. He touched Earl Graham's shoulder, not patting it exactly, just allowing his hand to rest there on the fragile bone for a moment, an acknowledgment of the memory connecting them. "It's good to see you again."

The old man cleared his throat and looked away.

SONIA WATCHED HER FATHER turn away from Scott, wincing at the rawness of the moment, like discovering a bruise where you didn't know you had one. It seemed like forever since they'd sat together here playing board games and talking about the articles they were writing for the school paper. Every so often, Earl would interject some comment about how they ought to publish one purely Communist issue, just to see how big of an uproar they could create. He even came up with headlines for them: *Students! Throw off the shackles of capitalism! Embrace the Workers' Alliance! You have nothing to lose but your pencils!*

Thinking back on it now made her lonely for those days, when her dad was strong enough to carry an armoire into his shop all by himself and his laugh could fill the entire house. They'd all been so much younger then—the world itself had felt like a lighter place, spacious and more promising.

"Go ahead," Sonia told Scott. "I'll be right out." After he left, she went back into the living room and bent down next to Earl. "You're sure you don't want anything while I'm out?"

The old man moved his eyes back and forth instead of shaking his head. He was pretending to watch TV, the way he sometimes did when he was upset, so he wouldn't have to look at her. Sonia guessed he was embarrassed that Scott had seen him like this—he didn't like unexpected visitors seeing him on the couch, hooked to his oxygen. Most days he didn't even open the shop. The tourist trade was dried up, and few of the regulars came by anymore. It was too awkward.

"I won't be gone long," she said. "I left spaghetti and meatballs on the stove if you get hungry."

"I'm fine."

"And there's some French bread in the oven."

Earl picked up the remote and changed the channel with a murmur of appreciation. "Look at that, will you? Ava Gardner in *The Killers*. Look at that and tell me Frank Sinatra wasn't one lucky son of a bitch."

"I've got my cell phone."

He gave her a sidelong glance. "You still here?"

She kissed his cheek and walked toward the back of the house.

"Kiddo?"

Sonia looked back. "What?"

"Your friend out there—tell 'im three."

"Three?"

"Golf balls on the moon."

EVERYTHING OKAY? Scott asked, out in the car.

Sonia just nodded. There was silence in the car as they drove away from Earl's junk shop. It was beginning to snow, individual white flurries swirling down, sticking to the windshield and blowing off. Finally Scott said, "Do they know how long he has?"

"Months," she said. "Probably no more than a year."

"I'm so sorry."

"You know that line from Frost," Sonia said, "'the slow smokeless burning of decay'? That's how it feels. Hurts like hell, but I'm glad I can be here for him." She took in a deep breath and released it, wanting to change the subject. After eighteen years apart, she didn't feel as though she knew him well enough anymore to go into it any further. "So the book's going well?"

"Huh? Oh yeah."

"You know where it's headed?"

"I've got a pretty good idea," he said. "I know that it's got to center around the house and how it fits into the history of what happened there."

"What did happen there?" Sonia asked. "In the story, I mean?"

"I haven't figured it out yet."

"You think your father knew?"

"I guess," Scott said. "I mean, he must have, right?"

"And you're on the same track that he was?"

"I hope so. I keep telling myself it's helpful to be in the house. If nothing else, the atmospherics can't hurt."

"Right. Well, I guess places can be funny like that."

He looked at her.

"Funny how?"

Sonia glanced over, uncertain whether he was curious or just making conversation. He actually seemed interested, so she thought back, trying to remember the theory that her father had described to her, what, four or five years ago? It had appeared on one of those ghost-hunter shows on the Discovery Channel. "This scientist was explaining how certain old places, for whatever reason, can generate a kind of field around them, the way high-tension wires create electromagnetic fields. Anyway, he said that sometimes if these places are around long enough, certain intense emotional states—anger, grief, loneliness—can get imprinted there, like a scratch in a record, playing over and over again."

Scott nodded. "A scratch on a record, huh? That's not bad."

Sonia saw him turning it over in his mind as a possibility, not for application in his life but maybe as something he could include in his novel to make it work.

"Have you . . . experienced anything like that?" she asked.

"In that house?" He shook his head. "No. Although . . ."

"What?"

"Nothing."

She felt him going quiet, inhaling whatever he'd been about to confide, and wondered if she was supposed to chase after it. Scott had never been coy that way, though; if he wanted her to know something, he just said it, and she sensed whatever reluctance he felt was probably justified.

They arrived at his father's old house and got out. Henry stood waiting in the driveway with a flashlight. Sonia watched Scott's mood lift at the sight of his nephew. It still freaked her out a little how easily she could read his moods after all these years, without even trying.

Scott hugged the kid, picked him up. "Hi, Henry. What's up?"

"Catching snowflakes on my tongue."

"How are they?" Sonia asked.

"Not big enough to fill me up," Henry said. "Are we going out for pizza?"

"Whatever you want." Scott glanced at the front door. "Where's your dad?"

In the glow of the flashlight, Henry's smile faded a little and then withered away completely. From across the lawn came the faint but distinct sound of glass breaking inside the old toolshed, a pop, a smash, a tinkle. Sonia heard a voice that she immediately identified as Owen's. It was followed by a louder crash, and the boy shuddered. In the fading daylight, it sounded like the noise of a wounded dog.

"Wait here," Scott said. "I'll be right back."

CHAPTER TEN

HE FOLLOWED THE FLASHLIGHT BEAM across the yard through snow-veiled heaps of dead leaves, over to the shed where the baseball had landed. In the darkness, the landscape felt lifeless, as barren as tundra.

In front of him, the noises inside the shed grew louder, rusty objects clanging together like old tools in a bucket. As he approached the entrance, he could hear Owen muttering under his breath, a succession of muffled curses and threats punctuated by a resonating explosion of loose metal. It was strange hearing his brother talking like this, talking to no one; the broken, start-and-stop cadence of Owen's speech made it sound as if he were actually carrying on a conversation with some voice that he alone could hear.

"Hey, man." The door had been torn off its hinges, and Scott stepped over it, into the shadows. "What's—"

The words broke off in his throat. All around him, illuminated by the flashlight, the shed stood in ruins, crates overturned, farm tools scattered, bags of fertilizer and grass seed spilled across the floor. In the middle of it, Owen stood squinting at him blearily, shoulders rising and falling with the force of every breath. A galaxy of empty beer bottles, many broken, lay at his feet, and there was a wild slash of dried vomit cutting almost diagonally across his shirt, as if he'd thrown up while running or spinning around. In the confined air of the shed, the stink of stale beer came rolling off him in waves, no longer the smell of a brewery but more of rancid, rotting yeast.

"Don't you knock?"

"What, on that?" Scott looked at the torn-off door lying on the bare concrete. He made his way forward, stepping over a shattered jar that looked as if it had contained about a thousand nails, some of them old enough to have crucified Christ. "What are you doing in here?"

"Mind your own goddamn business."

Scott saw blood leaking from the back of Owen's hand, dark red and encrusted with dirt. "Did you cut yourself?"

Owen snorted, picked up a box, and shook it, scattering empty oil-cans across the floor, kicking one as hard as he could against the wall.

"What are you looking for?"

"Nothing." Owen stumbled and tried to catch himself; Scott caught him, surprised at his brother's weight in his arms. Yanking himself free, Owen lurched forward with a snarl and almost immediately lost control of his legs in a tangle of old extension cords. Dropping the flashlight, Scott caught him again and Owen exhaled in his face. It was like grabbing hold of a great, stinking pile of soiled hospital linen.

"Come on inside. Let's get something on that hand." Before Owen could argue, Scott directed him out the door and across the yard, making his way by moonlight. He was all too aware of Sonia's and Henry's eyes watching from the end of the driveway as he walked his brother up the steps. It didn't bother him so much that Sonia was watching—she must have seen Owen like this before—but no child needed to see his father being half dragged, half carried, raving and shuddering, across the lawn into his own house. They went through the front door and inside, Owen bumping into the furniture as he proceeded. His words came out in spurts, convulsively, along with his stumbling gait.

"Lemme go. I'm fine." One arm swung, knocking a tower of dirty bowls and plates from the arm of the couch. "Fucking *fine*," I said. The crash seemed to remind him that Scott had brought him inside, and he jerked his arm back, pivoting on one heel.

"Owen—"

"You think I need *your* help?" But Owen was fading fast, tears and fatigue and bitterness brewing up in his eyes, strangling out his voice. It was like watching a man drown from the inside.

Scott somehow managed to lever him into a kitchen chair, pushing it over to the sink to run cold water across the gash on his brother's hand. It was bloody but superficial, nothing that would require stitches. The vomit on his clothes stank worse in here, and Scott reached down and peeled the shirt off, Owen's arms going up to allow the sleeves to slide over, then flopping limp at his sides. On his brother's back, between his shoulder blades, Scott saw a small tattoo he'd never noticed before, one word: *Henry,* with a heart around it.

He finished rinsing his brother's cut and wrapped it with a towel. Owen had stopped talking and sprawled back in the wooden chair, as if he'd passed out with his eyes still open. After a moment, Scott picked him up under the arms and dragged him out of the kitchen, across the cluttered living room. He lay Owen on the couch and covered him with a fairly clean-looking fleece Patriots blanket, brought over a glass of water, a bottle of aspirin, and a bucket from underneath the sink. He doubted his brother would wake up before they got back or, if he did, whether he'd be in any condition to read a note of explanation.

Walking back outside, he saw the faint, reluctant eye of the flashlight inside the shed and went back in to retrieve it. The beam was pointing across the floor at a partially demolished shelf. Amid a pile of broken glass was a single sheet of paper, plastered to the wall with mildew. Scott bent down and peeled it free. It was a typewritten page numbered 139:

    The girl in the doorway wore a blue dress. She
    couldn't have been more than twelve, maybe
    younger. Her hair hung in flat tangles around
    her face, eyes sunken deep in their sockets, her
    skin bluish with mold.
        "Who are you?" he asked.
        She raised one hand, one hooked finger to the
    inside of the door leading to the house's hidden

wing. Her ragged nail dragged across the wood,
scratching it, making the letter Y. Then, just to
the left of it, she wrote an R. And then an A, followed by an M, an E, an S, and an O. To the very
left, in front of all these letters, she etched a
crooked, spidery letter R.

He read the letters backward.

"Rosemary." Faircloth felt faint. "Rosemary
Carver?"

He had heard of her, an outsider who had run
away from home in another part of the state,
come to town, and disappeared back in the late
1800s without a trace. Her father, Robert, had
come around looking for her, and the local
police had launched an investigation, but no one
had ever found her body.

Looking at her now, Faircloth realized why he

End of page.

Scott stepped out of the shed with the lost page in his hand, fold-
ing it and sliding it into his hip pocket as he walked back toward the
driveway. The voice that came to him out of the darkness was first a
surprise, then a reassurance.

"Is he all right?" Sonia asked.

"He will be."

She gave him a dubious glance but said nothing. It was Henry's
expression that worried him. The boy looked pale and dazed, as if
shaken from a feverish state and dragged out of bed. His normally
bright eyes had a ghastly, glassy sheen.

They drove out to a pizza and burger joint on Ware Lake, a summer place that stayed open late in the season for the deer hunters who
would soon be buying supplies—jerky, sandwiches, and six-packs to
take into the woods. Sitting in the diner, waiting for their pie, Scott
had to forcibly resist the urge to get out the sheet of paper he'd found
and read through it again.

"Was your dad out in the shed all day?" he asked Henry.

His nephew just nodded and looked back down at his pizza.

"You want to spend the night at my house tonight?"

Another nod, delivered with a slight upward glance, as if Henry feared he might turn around and revoke the offer at any moment. Scott got up and walked around to the other side of the table, put his arms around the boy, and squeezed. "It's going to be all right," he said. He felt Henry clutching on to him, not wanting to let go. "I promise." Henry's nod was just a slight, almost imperceptible twitch against his chest, something that happened between heartbeats, barely there at all.

AFTER DINNER SCOTT DROVE back over to Earl's Emporium. There were lights on in the living room and he thought he saw the shape of a face between the curtains, a bent shadow stooping toward the glass. Sonia said good night and started to get out. Scott leaned over the seat. "Hey, Sonia?"

She stopped, looked back at him.

"Have you ever heard of a girl named Rosemary Carver?"

She thought for a second and shook her head. "Name doesn't ring a bell. Who was she?"

"I'm not sure," he said. "Maybe just a character in my dad's manuscript, but he makes her seem like a real person."

"Am I ever going to get a chance to read this legendary manuscript?"

"If I ever finish it."

"Patience isn't my strong suit." She was still looking at him. "Can I ask you a question?"

"Yeah?"

"Is any of this weird for you?"

"What?" he said. "Being back?"

"All of it."

"Yeah," he said. "You?"

"A little."

He watched her walk into her father's house and drove away. Taking Henry home, he found Owen sitting up on the sofa staring blankly at the Home Shopping Network, clutching a bag of frozen peas over his hand.

"You okay?"

Owen didn't look at him.

"I thought maybe Henry could sleep over at my place tonight."

Silence. Water from the bag dripped down between Owen's knees into a wet spot on the rug.

Scott went upstairs and gathered the boy's pajamas and toothbrush in his Finding Nemo backpack, along with a fresh change of clothes and some toys and comic books, and his sleeping bag. When he came down, Owen hadn't moved, and the puddle between his feet had grown slightly larger.

"We're leaving," Scott said. "I'll have him back in the morning."

"Yeah, great."

Scott took Henry's hand and they went outside.

THEY DROVE OUT OF TOWN, along the empty highway to where the woods got thick, and down the dirt road leading through the open gates. Scott stopped, and Henry looked blankly at the enormous house without comment. He clutched Scott's hand tighter as Scott led him across the yard and up the stairs to the front door. It was late, but the boy didn't seem particularly tired. As they went into the entryway, Henry stopped and gazed at the different hallways and doors that went off into separate parts of the first floor. Something about his calm, introspective expression made Scott feel sleepy.

"I'm camped out in the dining room," Scott said. "It's this way." He unrolled Henry's sleeping bag next to his. "I've got a bunch of movies if you want to watch one on the laptop."

"Sure."

He had patched the air mattress with duct tape; it finally stayed inflated. Scott dozed off a little while later with the sounds of a Disney movie droning in the background. Sometime later that night, he woke up to find Henry playing on the other side of the dining room, pushing a small toy car along the rounded embankment where the wall met the floor, making small growling noises as he crashed it over and over into the radiator.

"What are you doing?" Scott mumbled.

"They're crashing," Henry said, not looking up. "They're all crashing and dying."

"What time is it?"

The boy didn't seem to hear.

"You don't want to lie down?"

No answer.

"Henry?"

"I can't sleep."

"What's wrong? Is it the house?"

A shrug. "Just can't."

Scott lay back down, allowing his eyes to sink slowly shut. A moment later, just as he was falling back asleep, he heard light footsteps and the boy crawled onto the air mattress next to him. The warmth of his small body felt gaunt and rail-thin. As he huddled closer, Scott caught a whiff of something sour coming off his skin, the odor of dried sweat and oily hair. Was there a washer and dryer in the house? He couldn't remember. In the morning he would bathe the boy and take him shopping for new clothes, something he should've done a long time ago.

Next to him, the boy stirred and settled. Scott was just beginning to doze off again when he heard noises from across the dining room.

He opened his eyes, lifting himself up on his elbows, and saw that Henry was still by the radiator playing with cars. He'd never come over. Jerking upright, Scott looked down at the empty spot on the air mattress where he'd felt the small body curled next to his.

It was still warm.

CHAPTER ELEVEN

THE NEXT MORNING, HENRY woke him up and asked what day it was.

"Sunday."

"Are we going to church?"

"I don't know," Scott said. "Do you go with your dad?"

"If he's not too sick, sometimes."

"Which one do you go to?"

"The stone one."

When Scott was growing up, his mother had taken them to First United Methodist at the corner of Hawthorne and Grove, four blocks from the Bijou Theatre. It was one of several local churches that had supported Great-Uncle Butch's mission trips. Scott vaguely remembered hearing that his father had stopped going after the fire. His wife's funeral had been the last time he'd set foot inside a church.

Outside, the world lay buried under six inches of snow. The parking lot of First Methodist had been freshly plowed and was nearly empty. They crept into the sanctuary and sat in the back row amid old people in black suits and archaic clothing from unfamiliar epochs, dresses and jackets that seemed to have emerged from steamer trunks and mothballed closets. None of them recognized Scott, or if they did, they didn't say anything. The boy sang the familiar hymns from memory and doodled through the sermon, airplanes and bubble creatures. Scott kept his phone on vibrate. When he didn't hear from Owen by noon, he put the boy in the backseat of his rental car and drove into town to the library, figuring that his nephew could occupy himself in the children's section for an hour. Henry followed along with a reluctance that wasn't like him.

"Don't you like the library?" Scott asked.

"We never come here."

"When I was a kid, I'd go here just to walk around and pick out books. They've got everything here."

They walked in, and Scott stopped in the entryway, startled enough to wonder if he'd somehow gone into the wrong building. It was even emptier than the church, and cold enough that he could see his breath. Most of the shelves were vacant, stripped to the walls, and the remaining books sloped against one another like rows of sloppy drunks. Even the drinking fountain had been removed, leaving a dripping yellow pipe sticking out of the wall with a bucket underneath. Boxes and crates of books stood in unsteady piles with no discernible sense of organization.

"Hello." He looked up and saw a pretty librarian, close to his own age, holding a stack of newspapers. She had gray eyes and a small, sweet smile with a brown birthmark immediately off to one side. "Can I help you?"

"I'm looking for some historical records."

"Oh." The librarian nibbled the cushion of her lip. "Well, there's not much left here, I'm afraid. We're closing down."

"Permanently?"

She smiled sadly. "Budget cuts."

"You're kidding." Scott looked around, seeing the place with new eyes. He'd actually downplayed his affection for the place as a kid. For years, he'd fantasized about having a key to the library so he could come in at any hour of night and peruse the holdings by flashlight.

The librarian was still nibbling her lip. "You needed some historical records?"

"I'm wondering if there was ever a girl in this town named Rosemary Carver." Saying the name out loud didn't lend his cause the legitimacy that Scott had hoped. If anything, he felt more foolish than ever, hoping to find historical evidence of a character that his father had probably just made up for his novel. "How far back do your local newspapers go?"

"Our holdings don't go much further back than the 1940s, and most of that has already been packed up. Of course, you're welcome to browse. I can't vouch for our inventory." She hesitated, glancing over at Henry, and added in a lower voice, "Be careful, though. There are rats."

He looked at her, sure that he'd either misheard her or that she was kidding.

"They've been breeding in the basement. I think the move must have riled them up."

Scott held the boy's hand while they walked through what was left of the stacks, Henry whispering *rats, rats, rats* to himself as they walked, trailing his fingers along the dusty metal shelves. In the corners, beneath the fixtures, Scott began to notice the traps, lethal-looking spring-loaded contraptions complete with big chunks of stale cheese or rancid salami on their triggers. He could tell that Henry saw them too, but the boy said nothing.

After twenty minutes of searching, he found what was left of the local history section, just a few dusty tomes of names dating back to the 1850s. The last book on the shelf looked as if it had been left behind purely because of its size—it was as big as a tea tray and oddly grimy; no doubt its cloth covers had absorbed decades of dust and the gaze of a thousand disinterested local scholars. Hoisting it from its place, Scott opened the book and found more names, pages and columns of birth and death dates, organized by decade, by township, alphabetically by name. There were plenty of Masts, distant cousins and relatives, and when he flipped forward to the *C*'s, sliding his index finger down the page, he found only one Carver, dating from 1883— first name Rosemary.

"Any more like these?" he walked over and asked the librarian, pointing to the name. "This is the girl I'm trying to find out about."

The woman shook her head. "We had more volumes on this shelf," she said. "It used to be full. They just packed them up a few days ago."

"Where are the books going?"

"Anywhere and everywhere. The rats will have the whole place to themselves soon." She seemed more comfortable talking about rodents than books. "You didn't see any, did you?"

"Any what?"

"Rats."

Scott shook his head. "No."

"Oh," she said, sounding only slightly disappointed. And then, almost as an afterthought: "Don't I know you from somewhere? Scott Mast, right?"

"Yeah."

"I knew it. You were best friends with Sonia Graham. I'm Dawn Wheeler. I was friends with Marcia O'Donohue?" She looked almost pleading. "We did yearbook together senior year."

"Dawn," he said. "Sure."

"It's okay if you don't remember. That whole yearbook experience was so embarrassing. I had the biggest crush on Adam White, and I remember all I wanted to do was a full-page layout about him jumping off the diving board. Remember that break-dancing exhibition he did at the talent show?"

"Sure."

"Well, if you want to find those books, you might want to head over to the McGuire farm. Some workmen took about sixty boxes of them over there last week."

"Colette McGuire?"

"Mm." Dawn hesitated and lowered her voice, seeming to taste something bad that had come up from her throat. "Now *there's* someone who hasn't changed very much. Of course, why would she, when she was already Miss Smell So Sweet the first time around, right? Things aren't so perfect for her these days, though, from what I hear, ever since she married that football player."

Scott looked up. "What?"

"Red Fontana." She looked at him. "You didn't know? Colette married Red in New York and brought him back here. She did it to shame her parents, and it worked. They were dead a year after the wedding—matching heart attacks. Of course, from what I hear, Red's already lost interest in her. They say he's been spending his time down at Fusco's with . . ."

Dawn realized what she was saying, and her voice trailed off, a red rash spreading across her face. Suddenly Scott remembered her from the yearbook office, a blushing, venomous, unhappy girl whose mouth had run away from her even then.

Behind him, from somewhere deep in the empty library stacks, came a sharp metallic crack.

CHAPTER TWELVE

WITH CHARACTERISTIC BLUNTNESS, Scott's father had always said that the only thing that ever actually grew on the McGuires' so-called farm was "dirty money," a phrase that boyhood Scott had imagined as a particularly noxious strain of weed, its leaves and stems stamped with the faces of scowling presidents. Rumor had it that Conrad McGuire had been an old-school war profiteer, a bootlegger who had run Canadian whiskey during Prohibition, not above shooting a man in the kneecaps to solidify his market share. Some of the old-timers still held that his wife had been a failed actress and nymphomaniac with a weakness for farmhands, strapping young northerners whom her husband recruited for her while he stood inside the closet and watched with a bottle of whiskey and a belt around his neck. They were all long since dead, granted legitimacy in death that they'd never had in life. Their home was a fabulously appointed Georgian mansion in the foothills to the west of town, removed but not so much that it couldn't be seen by those below; an inspiration and a warning to anyone who might similarly aspire to such heights, it simply stated, *This space taken.*

Scott hadn't been out here in eighteen years, not since the day before his senior prom, when his mother had sent him up here with Colette McGuire's prom dress, which she'd spent a week altering at the behest of Colette's mother, Vonda. He remembered unzipping the garment bag on the way over and peeking in at it, stroking the satiny fabric with his fingertip and imagining her flesh beneath it until he was queasy with arousal and self-loathing.

Now Henry sat quietly in the backseat, gazing out at the snow-covered scenery. The boy had been talking about the rats in the library but had fallen quiet when the white hills had soared up around them.

"If you kidnapped me," Henry said, "I wouldn't turn you in."

"I'll think about it."

"We could go to Mexico."

"What's in Mexico?"

"Chalupas." Henry pointed to the McGuire farm as it emerged from the trees in front of them. "Why are we going to this house?"

"I'm looking for something."

"More books?"

"Yeah."

"About what?"

"Somebody who lived a long time ago."

He pulled into the circular drive in front of the main house and saw a red convertible parked crookedly in the driveway. A groundskeeper in a grubby orange sweatshirt was shoveling the walkway, a pair of earphones jammed up under his black knit cap. He didn't glance up as Scott and Henry got out of the car and walked past him to the front door to ring the bell. They waited for a moment, and Scott rang it again; when no one answered, he walked back over to the man with the shovel and tapped on his shoulder.

"Is Colette home?"

The man turned to reveal a face the color of a boiled potato. Up close, Scott could hear the tinny squawk of whatever music he was listening to, heavy metal cranked up loud enough that there was no way he could have heard the question. Scott started to repeat it, and the man squinted at him and shook his head before falling back to work. Scott was about to walk up and try the doorbell again when Colette came around the side of the house. She was wearing jeans and a black leather motorcycle jacket and stopped and took off her sunglasses, looking at him for a long time as if he might have been a hallucination, the end product of an inadvisable pharmacological dalliance.

"Scott Mast," she said. "Now I've seen it all."

"Hi, Colette." Up close, everything about her looked slightly more magnified than he remembered—breasts, lips, cheekbones—the result of subtle but comprehensive plastic surgery done to enlarge every salient feature while the rest slid back into obscurity. She looked like an overinflated sex toy. "How have you been?"

"Well, what can I say?" She spread her arms, and the jacket's buckles jangled in the cold air. "I'm here. The one place on earth I swore I'd never end up, and here I am." She flicked something off one sleeve, and Scott caught a glimpse of a puckered scar on the inside of her wrist, like a sloppy soldering job, as her wedding ring caught the light.

"You're married."

"I'm a lot of things. You?"

Scott held up his left hand, his ring finger bare.

"Crazy," Colette said. "I always pictured you and Sonia together." He couldn't tell how serious she was. "But you didn't even make it to the prom that night, did you? Word is she stood you up."

"That was a long time ago."

A crow landed in the thin crust of snow, blinking at them, flustered its wings, and flew away.

"So," Colette said, "what brings you sniffing around my little empire of shit?"

"I'm doing some research on my family. With the library closing, I heard you've got a lot of the old town records and articles here."

"Yeah," Colette said, "it's really sad about the library. Breaks your heart."

He couldn't tell if she was kidding or not. It was beginning to make him uneasy. Despite the temperature and the wind, a shimmer of sweat had formed over his skin, and he was sure she'd noticed it.

"Can I have a look at what you've got?" he asked.

"You want to check my stacks?" Now the smile looked as though it were held in place by deep surgical staples, an extension of cosmetic surgery by other means. "Sure, come on back."

She led Scott and Henry across the landscaped yard—"over hill and dale" was the children's book phrase that popped into Scott's mind—as they followed the mansion's outer wall past a marble fountain and a vast, dying plot of snow-buried wildflowers. He felt better now that they were walking. At the outer edge of the lawn, he saw a long building rising up against the thickets of trees that encompassed the property.

"What's that?"

"The granary. My great-grandfather used to stash his booze here. Word is he castrated one of his competitors here too, sent his balls home in a beer bottle. Cold-blooded old times, right?" The granary's door stood on rusty metal hinges that looked as if they were dripping with tetanus, and Colette gripped the handle with both hands, yanking it open with exaggerated difficulty. "Help yourself."

It took a moment for Scott's eyes to adjust; at first, he registered only the smell of decayed paper and cardboard, damp mildew, and, faintly, the smell of old liquor and stale urine. He thought abstractly of pulp and the Frenchman who had invented it, inspired by wasps and the way they mixed spit and wood to create cheap paper. Split-open boxes, spilled books, and old documents flourished everywhere in four- and five-foot drifts. Some of the boxes were crawling with weevils. Others buzzed with lazy, half-dead flies that didn't realize their season had long since passed.

"What is all this?"

"The town history," she said. "Sometimes I wander out and think about burning it all to the ground. Of course, I couldn't, without losing my inheritance—Daddy's lawyers made sure of that, just like they made sure I have to live here the worst six months of the year. But I do come down and kick it around from time to time when I'm piss-ass drunk enough. Speaking of which . . ." She gestured back at the house. "Too early for you?"

"Just a little."

"Oh, come on. The sun's over the yardarm somewhere in the Western world, as my father used to say."

He shook his head. "We may stay out here and poke around if you don't mind."

"Poke all you want. I'm up in the house if you get thirsty." She bent down and smiled into Henry's face. "Got some cookies for the little guy too—yummy chocolate chip."

Henry stood watching her go. "She's scary," he whispered.

"Tell me about it." After holding back a moment until he was sure she had returned to the house, Scott waded into the depths, venturing between the stacks of paper, books, and split-open binders, fat accordion file folders spewing yellow clippings and handwritten records. Something scurried over the back of his neck, and he flicked it off without looking at it.

"What do you want me to do?" Henry asked behind him.

"Nothing. Don't touch anything."

"What are you looking for?"

"A name."

"Rosemary Carver?"

Scott glanced up, startled.

"I heard you talking to that library lady," Henry said, "the one with the spot on her face. She lived a long time ago, right?"

"Back in the 1800s," Scott said, and his foot crunched on something, glass breaking and grating against the floor. "Oh shit." Bending down, he saw it was a broken picture frame leaning against a damp box with the handwritten label, one word, block letters: OBITS. Scott opened the soggy flaps and peered in, reluctant to stick his hands into the mess. It was a warren of newspaper obituaries. Some of them went back to the Depression and even further, though the oldest were so faded that he could make out only the headlines. Scott dug his hands into the paper, felt it crumbling between his fingers. Every so often, he'd grab a swatch of paper and look at a name or a photo. He'd never heard of any of these people, though he assumed they were all townies. Then, after ten minutes, toward the bottom of the stack, he found one for Hubert Gosnold Mast, from the local paper, dated 1952.

Scott picked it up and studied it in the thin early-winter light.

According to the article, H. G. Mast had been a painter, educated at Boston College and abroad, and had spent years traveling in Europe before landing at a small prep school in Vermont. His teaching years were described in loving detail, focusing on the dedication he brought to the job; it was here that he'd met his future wife, Laura, and had their only son, Butch. That would have been Scott's great-uncle, the missionary whose movie would eventually become synonymous with the Bijou fire, meaning Hubert Mast had been Scott's great-grandfather. The obituary went on to mention that after the war, Mast had divorced his wife and left her and young Butch to return to Paris, where he had rented a loft on the Left Bank. He tried to resume painting and struggled through a string of unpaid debts, failing health, and "moral degradation," a phrase the obituary writer seemed to use as an implication of wanton homosexuality, venereal disease, or both. Toward the end, he'd made some halfhearted plans to return to the States and the wife and son whom he'd left behind, but it was too late. One afternoon in May of 1952, his French landlady had come upstairs for the rent and discovered that he'd hanged himself.

"Scott?"

He flinched around and saw Colette back in the doorway of the granary, her blouse zipped up in her leather jacket.

"It's getting dark," she said, a little unsteadily. "Are you sure you don't want to come inside, stay for dinner?"

"We should be going."

"Find what you came for?"

"Not really."

"What a shame," she said. "Maybe you're not looking in the right places." Her lips, tongue, and teeth were stained pink as if she'd been drinking cherry Kool-Aid mixed with cough syrup. "We can't have that now, can we?"

Scott stuck H. G. Mast's newspaper obituary in his back pocket. "There's so much material here, it's hard to know where to begin."

"My Aunt Pauline might be able to help," Colette said. "She's the local authority on scandals and town legends. She knows where all the bodies are buried."

"Where is she?"

Colette nodded back at the main house. "She lives upstairs. Come on inside."

He and Henry followed her up a winding path of slick flagstones, through a pair of glass doors that led directly into the formal living room. The furniture was perfectly arranged, the oyster gray carpet swept in seamless unerring waves. It was as humid as a greenhouse inside, so sweltering and queasy-sweet with conflicting smells of imported southern flowers that Scott almost expected to see bumblebees wafting through the air from petal to petal. Beneath that smell hung an even more artificial sweetness, more syrup than sugar. Colette stopped at the bar and picked up a nearly empty pitcher of something red and sticky-looking, pouring a glass tumbler full. "Drink?" A lime fell into the glass, splashing droplets across the backs of her hands. "I'm having rum punch," she said, slurring her words now.

"No thanks."

"Something else, then?" She whisked a tall bottle of vodka from one of the shelves, poured two fingers, and clinked in ice, thrusting it at him. Scott took the glass to keep it from spilling. "Follow me."

They twisted around the corner to a spiral staircase that he remembered from his one visit here, the way it looped in showy circles as it ascended through volumes of open, pollen-thickened air. Colette clung to the railing like a brown recluse spider, leading them to the landing, down another corridor to a closed door. She tapped on it briskly, waited, tapped again. "Aunt Pauline? It's Lettie. I brought visitors."

No sound came from inside. Scott watched as Colette turned the knob and opened the door. The bedroom was huge, dominated by an elaborate four-poster canopy bed where a tiny old woman in a diaphanous white gown lay propped on a mound of pillows, her eyes sparkling with a kind of brightness that might have been dementia. An old-fashioned wheelchair sat next to the bed. Heavy curtains blocked the remaining daylight, and from somewhere, big band music played—Benny Goodman, Gene Krupa, Glenn Miller, or Count Basie's orchestra playing "One O'Clock Jump." The walls were decorated with framed theatrical memorabilia—playbills, publicity photos, programs and newspaper clippings, reviews and advertisements. Setting down his drink to take a closer look at one of the old photographs, Scott decided that at least some of the pictures had to be of Pauline when she was much younger, when she had resembled a slightly less angular Barbara Stanwyck.

"Aunt Pauline, I want you to meet a friend of mine, Scott Mast, and his nephew."

The doll-sized woman sat up to light a cigarette with a gold lighter that looked as big as a grenade. Coughing, waving away smoke with a miniature hand, she favored Scott with a crooked but genuine-looking smile that faded only slightly when she got a good look at his face. "I know you, don't I?"

"My family's been here in town for a long time."

"No," she said, "you personally. *You* were here in this house before . . . I remember, you brought Colette's prom dress." She tapped a bent finger against her temple and gave him a sly, narrow, not entirely pleasant look. "I don't forget things like that."

Snorting, Colette tipped back her glass so that a thin runnel of pink liquid trickled up one cheek. "Scott's doing some research on local history."

"Oh?"

"Someone named Rosemary Carver."

Inside the cloud of smoke, a light flickered in Aunt Pauline's eyes. "Oh," she said. "That poor little dead girl."

"YOU'VE HEARD OF HER?" Scott asked.

"Every town has its ghosts," Pauline said, not bothering to look around at her great-niece. "Rosemary . . . well, I like to think she was just an angel, a little one called up to heaven before her time."

"What happened?"

Pauline didn't answer right away; she puffed luxuriously on the remains of her cigarette, allowing the cloud to thicken around her head. "She disappeared."

"Was she from around here?"

"From one of the outlying areas, I believe, yes."

"How old was she when it happened?"

"Twelve or so, I believe. Thirteen at the oldest—still an innocent. Little lambs so often go astray. Don't you find that's true, Colette?"

Colette sniggered. "Yes, Auntie."

"What about her parents?" Scott asked.

"Her mother died in childbirth. And her father—Robert, his name was—he was a schoolmaster. Not a pleasant man, by all accounts."

"How so?"

From inside the cloud of smoke, a sigh. "His temper was legendary. His students were all terrified of him. There was one boy in his class named Myron Tonkin, a soldier's son, a real hell-raiser, they say. Myron's favorite trick was sneaking out to the outhouse to watch the girls when they went to pee. And then one day Mr. Carver caught him staring in at his own daughter. But the boy wasn't just staring, if you get my meaning."

"What happened?" Scott felt himself preparing for the worst. "Did Carver beat the boy?"

"Oh no." Aunt Pauline shook her head. "He just *spoke* to him."

"What?"

"For about five minutes. To this day, no one is quite sure what the schoolteacher said. But they say when the boy came back into the classroom, he was completely pale. He stood there staring at nothing, trembling, his hands stretched out in front of him. At first, people thought he was just pretending, staring at nothing, bumping into walls and furniture, then they realized it was real—the boy had gone blind."

"Did anyone ever question Mr. Carver about it?"

"Of course not," Pauline said, tongue probing the corner of her cheek. "The only thing he said about it was that the boy had finally cured a bad habit. In certain circles, there were rumors and allegations about how Mr. Carver had . . . done something to him, but no formal accusations were ever made. Over the next few years, there were other, less dramatic occurrences—one little girl, an incurable gossip, developed a sudden, debilitating stutter. Another boy, a bully who liked to torture animals, was trampled to death by his father's horse. They were all troublemakers of some sort, all repaid in kind."

She paused, looking around the bedroom, and Scott realized that the music had stopped playing long ago.

"In any event, Carver stopped teaching when his own daughter disappeared. A few people whispered that he had it coming, after what he did to the Tonkin boy."

"You mean, was *supposed* to have done," Scott said.

"Mr. Mast, I trust you've been schooled on the etiquette of correcting your elders." Her voice betrayed no change in tone. "Whatever the case, Robert Carver threatened to do much worse to the person who had abducted his daughter."

"Why would anyone want to hurt his little girl?" Scott asked.

"Why does anyone hurt anyone?" the old woman shrugged. "The blood cries out for it."

Scott found this statement chilling, like a biblical proclamation gone profoundly wrong.

"Did he ever find her?"

"On the contrary," she said. "He disappeared immediately afterward. No one saw either of them ever again."

———

"ISN'T AUNTIE A HOOT?" Colette asked.

She walked Scott and Henry downstairs, clinging to the railing so tenuously now that Scott braced himself to catch her if she fell. On the first floor, the ripe sweetness of flowers hit him again, overwhelming and sickly. He knew he would smell it in his clothes when he got home, and it bothered him more than Aunt Pauline's cigarette smoke.

"I don't see how she could know all of that," he said, "since it happened so long ago."

"Are you kidding? Auntie knows everything. The ancestors of these people still live around town and they all spin their yarns. That one little boy, Myron Tonkin? His great-great-granddaughter Anne works over at the hospital. When Auntie broke her hip last year, those two spent hours hobnobbing together, swapping spook stories—they were inseparable."

At the bottom of the stairs, Colette made a hard left to the bar, where the bottle of vodka was waiting for her. She poured a glass without so much as looking at it. "What happened to your drink?"

"I must have left it upstairs," Scott said.

"You sure you don't want to stay for dinner?"

He glanced out the window. It was already dark enough to count the first stars. Down below, where the circle drive curved around, he heard an engine growl, and a pickup truck came barging into the driveway with a squeak of brakes. Scott heard country music cranked to speaker-distorting levels, the thudding and squealing of guitars and drums and bass. It stopped and a man climbed out. He had a flat, blandly handsome face and wore an expensive topcoat perfectly tailored to fit his broad shoulders, striding forward with the exaggerated swagger of one who imagines whole universes trembling in his wake. Scott realized he'd just gotten his first glance at Red Fontana.

"We should get going," he said.

Colette smiled. "Don't worry about Red," she said. "He's just going to go upstairs and change and then go out to the bar to drape himself over Sonia Graham all night. Then he'll come home at two A.M. and try to screw me—that's always good for a laugh." She lowered her voice to a stage whisper of mock confidentiality. "There's a special thing he likes. He likes it when I just lay there and let him do whatever he wants."

"Stop it." Scott covered Henry's ears with his hands. "That's enough."

Colette wobbled down in front of Henry, lifted his chin, and inspected his eyes as if searching their depths for some hint of comprehension. The boy gazed back at her, expressionless as ever. Scott tried to imagine what her breath must have smelled like in his face at that distance. Finally she touched his nose with the tip of her finger. "If you could have any wish," she asked, "what would it be?"

"I wish I was a ghost," Henry said.

Colette laughed, bent down, and whispered something in his ear. She stood up and looked at Scott. "You know, it's a shame things never worked out between you and Sonia."

"Thanks for your help."

Once they got into the car, he asked Henry, "What did she say to you?"

"She said I already was a ghost."

Through the darkness, Scott looked up at the wide bedroom window and saw a face peering down from between the curtains. It was the old aunt. She had worked herself into the wheelchair and sat, watching them from inside the scented house. The smoke around her head had cleared. She wasn't smiling anymore. He felt the now familiar tingling in the back of his skull, a moth floating dangerously close to the bug zapper, and braced for the shock.

CHAPTER THIRTEEN

ON THE WAY HOME, they stopped for a fried fish dinner at Captain Charlie's. The counterman had a tattoo of a lizard on the side of his neck. He sat behind the register reading his newspaper, and Scott and Henry carried their cardboard baskets of fried perch and hush puppies over to a booth on the far side of the restaurant. It was decorated in fishing nets and plastic crabs, and they sat underneath a framed picture of one of the owners standing next to John Travolta for a movie that Travolta had filmed here some years ago. The movie showed up occasionally on cable, and Scott realized now how strenuously he had endeavored to avoid it, streets and storefronts of his hometown shown from strange Hollywood angles.

Afterward, Scott drove to his father's house and walked Henry to the door. The boy seemed reluctant to go inside.

"I'll see you later," Scott said.

The boy looked hopeful. "Later tonight?"

"Probably not. It's getting late."

"What's your hurry?" Owen's voice demanded, from somewhere inside. A football game was playing on TV.

"I've got work to do back at the house."

Owen gave a mocking laugh. "*Work,* huh?"

Scott walked into the living room. His brother was stationed in front of the television rummaging through a bag of potato chips the size of a pillowcase. Bottles and trash surrounded him like the swath of a tropical storm. A battered old guitar leaned against the fireplace, a reminder of the years Owen had spent locked in his room, brooding over the same three chords.

"What were you looking for in the shed last night?" Scott asked.

Owen's shoulders went rigid and he withdrew his hand from the bag. A bloody piece of paper towel hung from his palm like a tattered flag, held in place by strips of Scotch tape with salted yellow crumbs stuck to them. Without looking at Henry, he said, "Go up to your bedroom."

When the boy went upstairs, Owen turned and faced Scott squarely.

"How much longer are you planning on sticking around?"

"I haven't thought about it," Scott said.

"Yeah, well." Owen peeled back the paper towel, sucked some of the salt from his wounded hand, never looking away from Scott. "Maybe it's time you start."

"You still haven't told me why you were out in the shed."

Owen looked down, found his beer on the floor, and drained it. "If Dad left anything else around here, I'm entitled to my share."

"So you were looking for money?"

"I'm not going to spend my life dragging wheelbarrows and hauling scrap." Owen's face was reddening as he spoke, spitting the words as much as speaking them, and Scott glanced at the empty bottle in his fist, wondered if it might shatter. As genuine as his brother's anger appeared, he somehow felt as if he wasn't getting the whole story from Owen—as if perhaps Owen himself didn't know what he'd been doing out there. *He's scared,* Scott realized. *I've asked him to explain something about himself that even he doesn't understand, and it's making him feel like a cornered animal.*

Owen took a deep breath and put the bottle down on the end table to his right. "You remember that time in fifth grade, that kid Brad Schomer who kept messing with you? One time he pushed you from one side of the cafeteria to the other, waiting for you to fight back."

Scott felt the tips of his ears growing hot. "Yeah."

"You finally broke down and started bawling."

"Until you stepped up and hit him for me," Scott said. "I've never forgotten that."

"I always wondered why you never stood up for yourself. But now I get it. In this life, you either fight or run away. You've always been a runner."

Scott glanced at the scrap of paper towel flapping from Owen's hand. "Take care of that cut," he said. "And let Henry know I said good night."

He could feel Owen's eyes on him until he got back into his car.

SCOTT DROVE OUT OF TOWN with a sense of renewed urgency, a stopwatch twitching in the pit of his stomach, a sense of time running out. Seeing Colette and her ancient aunt had reminded him that everything had a deadline, the present bulldozing forward into the future, carrying all the weight of the world with it. Colette had once been so fetching, the sort of girl whose face and body were enough to make you believe in God's almighty grace, impervious to the ravages of time. All that was gone now, spoiled and sodden.

And Owen—had Owen ever really had a chance? A permanent storm cloud of doom hung over his brother, portending endless disappointment, from as far back as Scott could remember.

What about you? What have you got?

As if in answer, he reached for the front door and turned the knob, stepping inside. The cold within the house slipped around him, insinuating its way through the protective layer of his clothes, finding his core. Scott turned on the lights and stared slowly down the hall, half expecting to see someone—or something—waiting for him here. Time was moving here too, but the stopwatch feeling was gone, replaced by the steady and somehow more apt image of sand through an hourglass. Scott could almost feel it trickling away. He thought of something a writing professor had once said: *We write as a means of stopping time; paradoxically this allows us to see how things change.* Arrows on a chalkboard, diagrams, equations—action and reaction, cause and effect.

He mounted the stairs, unconsciously counting them, and stopped at the landing, then turned and went back down again, up the hallway and around the corner.

TWENTY MINUTES LATER, he was sitting back in the dining room with the laptop on his knees. It was 8:02. He had returned expecting nothing more than another marathon of head-pounding frustration and even now stared at the blank screen and the blinking cursor.

8:07.

8:13.

8:22.

Creative visualization: He'd used it to write greeting cards—why not fiction? Shutting his eyes, he imagined the room around him, the way Faircloth had it arranged on page 138 of the manuscript. The Luger sat on the table next to the open bottle of I. W. Harper bourbon, half full, although a man like Faircloth would see it as half empty. A pack of Lucky Strikes and a red and white box of kitchen matches. And Round House itself, the huge old manse and all its endless subconscious curves and eased edges warping around him in the night.

I'm Faircloth. I'm Faircloth. And I'm waiting . . .

But the last page kept intruding on the rest of the story. Next to the pistol and the whiskey and the cigarettes, Scott began to imagine a stack of old papers, research material, notes, all of it pertaining to a young girl named Rosemary Carver. Old articles. Transcribed court documents. Eyewitness reports of the girl who had disappeared, Milburn's little lost lamb. What had Aunt Pauline called her?

An angel, a little one called up to heaven before her time.

Scott's eyes opened. He glanced down at the computer screen and knew what he needed to write next. There was no sense of realization—the words were just there, almost as if his father were standing beside him, whispering in his ear. Without hesitation, he started typing.

```
    Faircloth looked across the table at the
articles he had assembled there. Maureen would
be home soon, drunk and stinking of another
```

man's cologne, and she would start yelling at
him for making a mess in the dining room, but
suddenly he didn't care about any of it. He didn't
care about his pig of a wife and the way she
cheated on him right under his nose, and the
pathetic, impotent weakness that he felt when he
pretended it wasn't happening. The only thing
that mattered was Round House and the girl, an
angel called up to heaven before her time, sad
and lost and alone, who had died somewhere
under circumstances so horrible that he could
only guess what might have happened to her.

Faircloth looked back at the old pages and
felt something stirring somewhere in the room.

Then, unexpectedly, in the front of the house,
he heard a sound. It was the unmistakable
scrape and click and rattle of a key turning in
a lock. Maureen was

Click!

The noise was faint but perfectly clear. It had come from the direction of the front door. Scott stopped typing, fingers still hovering over the laptop's keys, and cocked his head, listening for the sound to come again, metal on metal, a key in a lock.

When he didn't hear anything more, he took the computer off his lap and stood up from the settee, heart thudding sickly in his chest as he walked out of the dining room and into the long, empty corridor that led to the front door.

He could hear his own footsteps creaking along the boards, faster now, as he approached the entryway. There was the ridiculous urge to shout "Hello, who's there?" and he managed to quell it, barely, but only by *running* the last few steps, determined to bring the ridiculous moment to a close, gripping the handle with both hands and flinging the door open.

The porch was empty.

Of course it was empty. His mind was playing tricks on him due to his not having taken the medication prescribed for him—

He stared at the outside of the door.

There was a key stuck in the lock, attached to a ring with a dozen other keys dangling from it. Scott touched the key ring, weighing it in his palm, the metal keys tinkling against his fingers, their ridges making them feel more real. They were startlingly cold, as if they'd just been removed from a deep freeze. He pulled them free, expecting resistance, but the key in the doorknob slid loose from the lock with oily ease. They must have been here for a while, he thought; maybe the Realtor had dropped them off after he had arrived home earlier.

But where had the recent noise come from?

It had come from the house.

He carried the keys back inside and shut the door.

And locked it.

BACK AT THE LAPTOP, he wrote:

> Maureen was coming around the corner, trying to move quietly but far too drunk to succeed. Her cheap high heels clattered like stones along the hardwood floor; she would have woken him from even the deepest sleep.
>
> When she saw Faircloth at the dining room table, her doughy face flushed bright red and spread into an idiotic smile.
>
> "Karl? What are you still doing up?"
>
> "Just working on my scrapbook."
>
> "Scrapbook?" Her watery eyes took in the piles of paper, the old articles and historical documents. "You don't have a scrapbook."
>
> "I'm just starting one," he said with a smile.
>
> "It's after midnight, honey. Aren't you tired?"
>
> He shook his head and stood up slowly, seeing the nervousness drifting over her face like a cloud scudding across the moon. It didn't bring the rush of pleasure he'd hoped--he felt it only

faintly, as if his own nerve endings had been worn down. Through a glass darkly was the Scripture that ran through his mind.

"Well," she said, "I'm going to bed. I'm bushed."

"Maureen . . . ?"

She turned and saw the Luger in his hand, pointed at her. Her eyes widened, and she emitted a single shrill giggle that died almost before it left her lips.

"Karl." It wasn't quite a whisper. Her hands opened, showing pudgy, glistening palms. "Don't you love me anymore?"

"Of course I do."

"Then why--"

The sound of the gunshot was much louder than he'd been prepared for. It boomed through the house, deafening him. Maureen's entire body flew backward, jerked by invisible cables, and she hit the wall in silence, dropping to the floor. A pool of dark blood was spreading steadily from beneath her, seeping into the rug, darkening it.

Faircloth put the gun aside and went over to her. There was no feeling of panic or disbelief, no rise in heart rate or shortness of breath, none of the physiological symptoms that he'd wondered if he would experience. He felt absolutely calm and sane.

Kneeling down, he rolled her body in the rug where she had fallen. When she was bundled the way he wanted her, he hauled the whole package across the dining room floor to the oak door in the corner. He laid it aside, opened the door, and gazed into the deep and windowless black space, which seemed to go on and on forever.

Turning around, he began dragging her body inside.

Scott stopped typing and sat back to reread what he'd written, allowing himself a little thrill of satisfaction. Finally, it was going well. Not *great*, not yet, but at least it was on track with what his father had been writing. For the first time, the sight of words on the page didn't bring a dull drumbeat of incipient dissatisfaction.

He stood up and stretched his back, then glanced at the clock and saw that it was almost midnight. His spine ached but it was a good ache, a manifestation of hard work.

Quit while you're ahead. Go back in the morning when you're fresh.

Don't quit when you're on a roll.

Tonight he was on a roll and he knew it. He put his hands back on the keyboard and kept going.

CHAPTER FOURTEEN

OWEN WAS DOZING on the couch when the car pulled into his driveway, its headlights strafing the room with slatted yellow bands that slid across the walls and disappeared. He sat up with a grunt. The TV was on, showing infomercials for machines that promised to tone and shape your abdominal muscles in thirty days. At the other end of the sofa, Henry lay curled up like a cat, half covered by his coat, dreaming his secret little boy dreams. Owen shivered and looked around. The living room felt deep and cold, piled to the ceiling with unfamiliar shadows.

From outside, a car door opened and shut. The night was so quiet that he could hear footsteps coming up the driveway, a steady and unhesitant *crunch-crunch*. Owen stood up, stepped over his last empty beer bottle, and looked across the kitchen at the shape rising up onto the porch, gaining both height and bulk as it approached. He could see it through the glass, moving toward the door. The pulse in his throat was beating hard enough that he knew he'd be able to see it in a mirror. Before he could decide what to do, there was a sharp knock.

He opened a drawer, rummaged through it, and pulled out a steak knife. "Who's there?"

The shape just knocked again, more forcefully this time. Owen's mind flashed to a recurrent childhood nightmare—a faceless man in a black slicker standing outside the house shouting his name in the middle of the night, while he cowered under his covers and waited for the thing to go away. *Go away. Go away.* But the thing in the slicker never did. It just bellowed for him furiously, endlessly. *Owen Mast! I know you're in there! Come out!* It never said what it wanted, but that didn't matter. Owen knew that if he ever did go down there and the creature in the black slicker got its hands on him—hands he somehow knew would be wearing black leather driving gloves that ended at the wrist—he would die of fright.

He swallowed, the walls of his throat lined with sandpaper. Now his head had cleared, and the throb of his pulse in the side of his neck had become almost painful. He wished he hadn't thought about that old nightmare. He hadn't remembered it in years.

Still holding on to the knife, he took another step across the kitchen and squared his shoulders, feigning confidence in almost perfect counterbalance to what he felt.

"Who's there? Scott? Is that you?"

When there was still no answer, he touched the knob, realizing too late that he'd never locked it. It swiveled in his grasp, the door swinging open to reveal a woman in a leather jacket standing on the other side, clutching two brown paper grocery sacks in her hands. It took Owen a moment to recognize her and a longer moment to process the reality of her appearance here at this hour.

"Well, can I come in?" Colette McGuire said. "Or are you just going to stand there getting a hard-on?" She looked at the knife in his hand and started laughing. "Oh God. You already got one."

Owen lowered the knife, opened his mouth, and closed it again. The winter night had drawn all the color from her skin, and the effect was striking. She looked as though she had just stepped out of a Kabuki theater where her entire face had been painted white except for the two almost perfectly round rosy patches on her cheeks. When he still didn't respond, she pushed past him and into the kitchen, hoisting the brown bags up and then dropping them on the table with a thump.

"It's cold as hell out there," she said, turning back to him and rubbing her hands together. The vapor of booze hung around her like perfume, a cloud so ripe and familiar that he felt as if he could reach up and pluck memories out of it. "Windchill is thirty below. And you want to hear the kicker? I've got a place in Key Biscayne, right down on the water. When I close my eyes, I can practically smell the tanning butter."

Owen shrugged and shook his head, hoping for a clue or at least something to say. Inside the brown paper bags, he could see two six-packs of Schlitz beer, cold cuts, bread, milk, a box of Cap'n Crunch, and some peanut butter and jelly piled up.

"What is this?" he asked thickly.

"What?"

"This." He gestured at the food and beer. "What, did you get an early dose of the Christmas spirit over at the McKennedy Compound?"

Colette shrugged and did a precise little pivot in the middle of the floor, pointing her chin at him. "You've got a little boy to take care of, don't you? And he's got to eat?" Her eyes sharpened the slightest bit. "And last I heard, you like the occasional beer."

"I'm not looking for charity."

"The only Charity I know is a whore down in Memphis. This is just me trying to help you out."

"At one in the morning?" A thought occurred to him, not a pleasant one. "Did my brother put you up to this?"

"Whatever." Colette waved a hand in his face as if the topic no longer interested her. "The food's here. You can either take it from me or throw it in the trash. At this point, I'm totally indifferent."

"You drove all the way out here to tell me that?"

She had already turned away from him, rounding the corner into the living room, where Henry lay on the far end of the couch. Owen went to follow her. The idea of Colette alone in the room with the boy made him uneasy in some ill-defined way, the way he might feel if an unfamiliar animal had entered the room with his sleeping son. When he came in, he found her standing over him, watching him.

"Don't worry," she said, not looking up. "I don't bite."

Owen didn't say anything.

"They came by my house today."

"Who did?"

"Scott and Henry."

Owen frowned, feeling the ground slope downward under his feet, as if he were sinking into the deeper end of the pool. "So he did put you up to this."

"Hardly." Colette reached into her jacket pocket, swaying a little, and snapped the cap off a small airline bottle of Jack Daniel's, opening it and pouring it down her throat without seeming to swallow, then followed it with an equally small bottle of vodka. "Single servings," she said. "They're never quite enough, are they?"

"You're trashed."

"Another country heard from." Colette smiled, her lips wet and sticky-shiny with whiskey; he knew if he kissed her, he'd taste it. "You know what I am, really, O-wen? I submit to you that I am queen of the dead." She spread her hands, gesturing outward to an invisible empire. "Here's to me, the newly appointed matriarch of all that is cold and calculating."

"Jesus." In spite of everything, he found himself nodding in appreciation. "How shit-faced are you, right now?"

"How the hell would you even know?" She was still looking down at Henry. "At this point, everything in a twelve-mile radius of you reeks of whatever was on sale at the liquor store this week." She reached down toward the boy's hair, almost running her fingers though it, and Owen's hand slapped it away.

"Don't touch him."

"Paranoid much? Maybe you're right to be."

"What are you talking about?"

"Think about it." She gazed up at him, a different kind of smile making its way over her face now, slow and leisurely, like a serpent stretching to sun itself across a rock. "Little Henry here likes Unkie Scott a lot, you know. In fact, I bet little Henry would give anything to just leave here for good and fly back out west with Unkie Scott forever. He wishes Unkie Scott were his daddy. It's written all over his face. I was blind drunk today on three kinds of medication, and even *I* could see it."

Owen felt a bright bolt of pain shooting across his chest, but he got a grip on himself, took in a deep breath, and an instant later it was gone. "You think you're telling me anything I don't already know?" he asked, surprised at how steady his voice sounded. "You think I even *care* what you think?"

"I think I'm looking at a guy who has reached the end of his rope and realized it's tied around his neck," she said. "I mean, come on. Look at this place. You can't even take care of yourself."

"Yeah, well, I didn't inherit a fortune, like some people."

"No, and you didn't work for it either. Your brother, Scott, on the other hand, he's a goddamn American success story. I bet he could afford some good lawyers. If he decides to get serious about helping your little boy get free of this half-assed kennel you've got him in now—"

"You listen to me." Owen grabbed her by the collar of her leather jacket. "Me and my little boy are no business of yours." The surprised expression on her face, however short-lived, eased the tension clamping down on his chest, and for an instant, he felt back in control of the situation again. Then Colette blew the hair out of her face and shrugged, her swollen lips parting to release a soft, smoky chuckle so quiet that he felt it rather than hearing it.

"You want something from me, Owen? You just give it a name."

"Does Red know you're here?"

"Red?" Colette snorted. "Please. He's got his own little extracurricular activities to think about." Her voice became a mocking lilt. "Don't you even want to know why Scott came over to see me today? Or are you too stupid to even ask the right questions?"

He realized that he was on the verge of hitting her, punching her in the stomach, and how satisfying it would be to watch the self-satisfied smirk fall away from her face once and for all. Once, he'd gone through court-mandated psychological counseling, and the therapist had stressed the importance of visualizing his reactions. But his problem was, the only reactions he could truly visualize were the wrong ones. So, instead, he put his hands under his arms and clamped them so tightly that his biceps ached.

"Scott wanted to know about Rosemary Carver," Colette's voice drifted in. "My aunt Pauline gave him an earful. Good old Aunt Pauline, always happy to receive a visitor."

Owen shook his head. "I don't know these people."

"Oh, that's right," she said, "you don't need anybody, right? The last man on earth out here with his son. Good thing you can always rely on the kindness of strangers, isn't that—"

A pulley cracked somewhere inside him, and his arm flew out like a mast breaking loose from its moorings, knocking one of the bags of groceries off the table. A jar of peanut butter hit the floor and rolled away in a lazy semicircle until it bumped into the cupboard. "Get your ass out of my house."

"Tsk." She clucked her tongue. "Sounds like someone woke up on the grumpy side of the bottle."

"Blow me."

"I'll take a rain check." She sauntered out, slammed the door behind her, and Owen went back into the living room and sat down next to his son. His heart was choking on an undigested bolus of rage and humiliation. He put one hand on the boy's shoulder, felt his chest rising and falling, and closed his eyes, hoping to find reassurance in this simple moment. Despite everything—his inexplicable anger at Colette, and whatever it had turned into in the final moments before he'd thrown her out—he could feel the rest of the beer in the kitchen calling out to him. There was something comforting in its siren song, and eventually he went to answer it.

As he cracked open the first can, he thought he heard her laugh.

CHAPTER FIFTEEN

IT WAS TEN A.M. when Sonia woke up in the motel room with Red still snoring beside her. She climbed out of bed, heading for the bathroom and hearing him sit up behind her.

"Hey," he said.

She shut the bathroom door and turned on the water so she couldn't hear him. Splashing cold water on her face, she did a quick scan of the amenities. You didn't get much in the motels where she and Red ended up. No complimentary shampoo, no fancy body wash, nothing but a tiny bar of soap the size of a credit card to get the smell of last night's smoke, sex, and whiskey out of her pores. Sometimes it seemed as if the more you had to wash out, the less they gave you.

No matter; she'd catch a shower at home. Back at the house, Earl was going to be wondering where his breakfast was. Or *not* wondering. Her father often knew more than he let on.

She turned the water off and heard Red moving around outside the bathroom door, not hurrying, enjoying the leisurely morning after. For him, she knew, these small moments were all part of the disproportionate pleasure he took from their nights together, few and far between as they were. Whatever else his day might hold in store, lying in a motel bed listening to her get dressed and hurry through her morning bathroom rituals was the high point.

"You all right?" he asked when she came back out of the bathroom. He was still naked, sprawled out on the sheets, idly playing with himself as he watched her get dressed. When she didn't react, he stretched his arms and gave her a casual flex of the biceps. His body was probably in better shape now than when he'd played pro football; he said he worked out three hours a day at the gym that Colette had built for him, and the evidence was right in front of her.

"Fine."

"What's wrong, princess?"

"I hate when you call me that." She cocked her head, stuck her right earring through her ear, and felt the backing slip from her fingers and fall onto the cheap motel carpet. "Damn it."

"Guess who I saw last night?" Red asked.

"Who?"

"Your old boyfriend from back in the day."

Sonia looked up from where she was trying to find the missing piece of the earring. "Scott and I were just friends."

"Guess where I saw him."

"Thrill me."

"At my house." Now his smile looked both rueful and bemused. "Talking to my wife."

"Oh?" Sonia tried to sound disinterested and glanced at Red to see how successful she'd been. But his face, while smiling, was almost neutral, as if he were looking to her to put what he'd seen in perspective. "Did you say hello?"

"They were coming out as I was coming in."

"They?"

"He had the kid with him. You know, his nephew."

"Henry?" Sonia frowned. She was thinking about Owen, the way he'd staggered and stumbled through the overgrown grass as Scott had walked him across the yard and inside the house the other night. It was hard to imagine anyone in that condition being able to take care of *himself*, let alone a five-year-old; Sonia knew from experience how bad Owen could sometimes get. When she was tending bar, the only way to get him to slow his drinking down was to ask questions about

Henry, turning his thoughts back to the responsibilities at home. And sometimes it worked.

"Henry." As he often seemed to do, Red had read her mind. "That's Owen's kid, right? Scott's brother."

"Yeah."

"Whatever happened with you two anyway?" Red asked, scratching his thick patch of chest hair as he gazed up at the cracked ceiling. "You and Mr. Greeting Card, I mean. Sounds like back in high school you two should have at least had a friendly little roll in the hay . . . or whatever you people roll around in, in these parts. Snow? Maple leaves?"

"Is there a point to any of this?"

"Hold up." He pushed himself up on his elbows, looking at her. "Did Scott and Colette ever . . . ?"

"What?" Sonia shrugged. "I never asked."

"Owen told me you guys almost hit it off until you kicked Scott to the curb."

"Meaning what?"

"Maybe it was because you caught him and Colette bumping uglies."

Sonia looked at her watch. "You're a poet."

"See, that's what I love about you," he said, climbing out of bed, still naked, half erect, coming over to the open door to plant a kiss on her cheek, almost chastely, his stubble rubbing against her chin. "Some days you're the saddest little girl in the great state of New Hampshire."

"No," she said, "that would be your poor neglected wife. Why don't you go home and make her some waffles?"

Red laughed. "You off tonight?"

"I'm working."

"Then I'll see you at the bar."

"I'll be counting the seconds," she said.

The sound of his laughter followed her out to her car.

SCRAPS OF SNOW LAY on the ground, soggy confetti from some long-gone parade. The granite sky was flat and cloudless, clear back to the mountains. She shivered inside her coat, starting the engine and blasting on the heat. Her brain felt foggy from not enough sleep.

Red had started out as a diversion, a friendly face at the bar. Given his NFL history, she had expected machismo, a surfeit of overconfidence, but to her surprise, he was understated, a good listener with a genuine sense of humor. There was a worldliness to him that attracted her, and a soulful quality that she thought had come along with everything he'd gone through in New York. Just the fact that he'd chosen to marry someone like Colette McGuire, at this point in their lives, had—in and of itself—almost made him interesting enough to pursue on its own merits.

Now, though, she wasn't thinking about him at all but about Scott, and why he and Henry would have gone over to see Colette.

Research, she thought. *For his book. It could have just been research, but why wouldn't he mention something like that?*

And a better question:

Why do you care?

"I don't." She found an old Motown CD, the Supremes, and put it in, turned the volume up loud. It was wrong for the moment, and she tossed it aside, fishing through her CD wallet until she found Billie Holiday's *Body and Soul.* Moments later, Lady Day was singing "Gee Baby, Ain't I Good to You." Spread underneath the winter New Hampshire sky, her voice filled the car with almost unbearable hurt, but Sonia let it play anyway.

Her cell phone buzzed. Red. She turned the song down.

"Yes?"

"Take a look in your glove compartment."

She opened it. An envelope fell out. Fat and heavy, bristling with twenties, and a couple of hundreds tucked in at the back. "Red—"

"It's for your dad."

Happy to be your whore, she thought, with such sudden, jagged viciousness that it startled her, as if she'd just swallowed a chunk of broken glass. Red would have been hurt if she'd ever said anything like that to him. In spite of everything, he had an unexpectedly sweet streak, an almost childlike eagerness to please, and had told her on multiple occasions that he'd continue to give her money for the medical bills even if she stopped sleeping with him. He'd just never understand how it felt opening an envelope of cash when she could still feel his semen dried on her thighs.

"Thanks," she managed.

"And I'll still see you tonight, right?"

"Tonight," she said, and hung up, putting the pedal to the metal, driving away from there as fast as she could.

BACK IN TOWN, Sonia drove past the partially renovated Bijou Theatre on the left side of the street and slowed down, even though she was already running late. There was a blackened pit in the middle of the wreckage, and she watched the workmen carrying out wheelbarrows of burned debris, old theater seats, and mounds of broken brick. One of the workers climbed up on an aluminum ladder rising from the hole in the ground, rubbed his hands on his pants, and started running toward the trailer that served as the office. The man wove his path through the debris with a combination of urgency and hesitation that Sonia found very familiar, and when she finally caught a glimpse of his face, she realized it was Owen.

She beeped and slowed down, but he didn't even look up at her. He was already storming up the wooden steps to the office as fast as he could. As he turned to knock on the door, Sonia saw he had some round flattened object tucked under his coat. It looked like some kind of narrow wheel or oversized serving plate, but Owen was cradling it in both arms, hunched over it as if he'd just unearthed a relic from some lost civilization.

She stopped the car completely, traffic bulking up behind her at the intersection as she craned her neck back and to the left. Before she could get a better look at the relic, the trailer door had already swung open and he'd vanished inside, the door clapping shut behind him.

Behind her, the blast of a horn she'd initially confused for Lester Young's saxophone on the car stereo snapped her back into the moment. Pulling ahead, Sonia made a mental note to ask Red when she saw him about what exactly had motivated the McGuire family, after ignoring the ruined remains of the Bijou for all these years, to choose this moment for what was surely a complicated and expensive renovation. It was a problem she wasn't aware had been preoccupying her until very recently. Seeing Owen scurry from the pit to the mobile home with the object under his arm had crystallized it for her.

Red will know.

If Colette McGuire had an angle, Red would already be playing it.

Whatever else Red Fontana might have been, Sonia sometimes thought of his opportunism as a pair of glasses that allowed her to see clearly into the town where she'd grown up, a place whose byzantine complexity—people doing things they didn't want to do, people doing things they didn't know they were doing, people doing things for the wrong reasons—often left her baffled. She saw too much. Red saw only what he wanted to see, what he could take. He slept with her because he liked it, and Sonia was willing to trade on that for a little outsider's insight into Milburn.

Who's the opportunist now? she mused. *Maybe we're more alike than I thought.* And for the first time that morning, the almost unbearably sad voice of Billie Holiday pouring up through her vehicle's sound system actually sounded like music.

CHAPTER SIXTEEN

SCOTT STARED AT THE LAPTOP screen and heard his stomach growl.

He hadn't eaten all day—had last ventured into the kitchen for coffee sometime in the afternoon—and without the punctuation of meals, another entire day had slipped by. When he turned to look out the large, not-quite-rectangular windows, he was startled to see that it was dark. That couldn't be true, but it was.

He got up and stood by the window, gazing out across the yard, where bare tree branches enclosed the grounds. The sense of pure isolation was absolute.

He knew that if he were to put on his coat and gloves and walk outside with a flashlight, crossing the grounds to where the trees took over, he could go for a long time without encountering anything. He could stand out there and scream as loud as he wanted and no one would hear. There would be only the great sprawling house out here in the middle of nowhere, a house that had no business being this far from town, and the woods that kept it secret.

I won't go out there, he thought. *It's too late, and I still have work to do.*

But standing up and going to the window had distracted him. His thoughts swung back to his great-grandfather H. G. Mast and the painting of Round House that hung on the other side of the first floor. It seemed to Scott that the painting and the story were all about the same thing, not just the house but something in it that all the Mast men had seen and struggled in their clumsy dreamers' way to understand. Apparently part of that struggle involved losing track of time, whole quantum lapses at a stretch.

He went back to the laptop and sat down. The drive to understand was powerful now, a constant and provocative itch. Some part of him understood that his discontinuation of the drugs was part of that poignancy, but there was another aspect of it too, not so easily explained.

Creative visualization.

I am Faircloth, he thought again. *I'm Faircloth, and my wife is dead, and I still have these files in front of me.* Of course there *were* no actual files about Rosemary Carver, but hadn't that helped him before, that element of self-hypnosis, closing his eyes and seeing the story?

He closed his eyes and imagined piles of reports about the disappearance of the girl, the way that his protagonist would have seen them. Something in there, a handle that would allow him to continue where he had left off the story.

The girl, yes, and the painting, but something else besides.

The man.

Rosemary's father.

Scott opened his eyes and typed:


```
Faircloth couldn't sleep.
    The people in town had already started ask-
ing about Maureen. Always the dutiful husband,
he had told them that she'd gone down to Boston
to visit her mother. An extended visit, perhaps
several weeks--the poor dear was quite sick,
lumbago, a chronic affliction that only got
worse this time of year.
    At night while he sat here in the huge, empty
dining room of the house and fed stick after
```

stick into the fire with a steady hand, Faircloth
thought about how long it would be until concerned townsfolk started asking more direct
questions. Shouldn't she be back by now? Was she
all right? How long had it been since he'd spoken
to her? And then the whispers behind his back,
followed inevitably by a visit from the sheriff,
the estimable Dave Wood. The polite inquiries
followed by the not so polite, the first unspoken
accusation, and ultimately the search of the
premises, the abandonment of all pretense of
politeness. They would be looking for a corpse.

It would take a dozen men as many hours to
search every room of Round House. Like the man
in the Poe story, Faircloth would invite them to
tear it apart beam by beam if they so wished. To
marvel at the strict and stringent commitment
that its original architects had made toward
avoiding every straight line, blending and
smoothing every corner. And in doing so, they
would find nothing. It went without saying. No
body, no corpse, no trace of poor Maureen, who
had died confused and strangling on her own
blood, with a single bullet in her forehead,
while Faircloth stood over her.

No clue.

Rosemary Carver had taken care of that.

Faircloth turned from the woodstove fire to
the piles of paper that he had collected here,
amusing old historic documents and affidavits
with signatures long since faded. He began sorting through the relics. Since he killed Maureen,
his interest in Rosemary Carver had galvanized
into something like obsession. He wanted to
know everything possible about the girl in the
blue dress, the thing that had welcomed him
here and taken care of his problems with his
whorish, drunken lout of a wife. He wanted--

Here he stopped, looking down at the item he
had just uncovered. It was an old daguerreotype
of the sort manufactured after the Civil War,
and it showed a tall man in a black suit with a
tall black hat looking steadily back at the camera. The shadow of the hat's brim eclipsed the
man's features except for the bright sickle of
his grin. His long arm hung around the shoulder
of a small girl. The girl was Rosemary Carver.
Faircloth knew that the man was her father.

There was a sudden *thud*, and Scott sat up with a jolt, jerking so
hard he almost knocked the laptop from his knees, crying out "Oh
Jesus!" His vision of himself as Faircloth—Faircloth's research spread
all around him—was so clear and compelling in his mind that he was
actually surprised to look around and find the room empty except for
his computer and the fire in the woodstove. He had *seen* the paperwork
here, stacked around him, just as Faircloth had seen it in the story. In
that regard, at least, the act of self-hypnosis had been utterly effective.
He was both awed and a little frightened by how successful the tactic
had been.

His heart was pounding. He held his breath.

Another noise resonated through the dining room, a single unmistakable *thump*.

Scott felt the small hairs stiffening over the back of his neck, down
his forearms, an absolute alertness to the particulars of this moment.
All the solitude that came from being out here, miles from town, miles
from anyone, arrived back with him now, the knowledge that in this
dark pocket of the country, he was all alone.

And yet he *wasn't* alone.

He sat listening, waiting to hear it again.

When it came, it wasn't a thumping sound. What he heard now was
a series of plaintive scratching noises, like an animal trying to claw its
way through the walls. His mouth was sucked completely dry, so arid
that his lips felt glued shut.

Looking up from the computer, he realized that the scratching
noises were coming from behind the door on the other side of the din-

ing room, the door that—in his father's novel—led to the black wing, where Faircloth had stashed his wife's body.

But of course there's nothing back there, because that place only exists in this book. If I open that door now, all I'm going to find is an empty closet with some dead flies on the shelves.

Very carefully, determined not to tremble as he moved, he placed the computer next to him on the settee and stood up. More than ever, the floor felt slightly angled beneath his feet, the corners of the room even more rounded. He walked across the dining room to the door and rested one hand on the knob. It was cold, as cold as the keys that he'd found in the front door.

He turned the handle.

The door swung open.

What he found himself looking at was not an empty closet. Instead, the space that was revealed was a long black corridor full of darkness and frigid air, giving way to a profoundly blank and open passageway, as if there were some entirely separate house hidden within this one. There was a noise like a gasp from deep inside.

Releasing the doorknob, Scott started to walk into the corridor.

As he set foot in it, he felt something slide off his lap. With a jerk and a grunt of surprise, he reached down instinctively, groping at it. The whole world rotated sideways on its hinges like a magician's stage prop, and Scott realized that he was still sitting on the settee, the laptop on his knees.

He had never stood up at all.

He had been sitting here the whole time.

Writing.

Looking down at the screen, he read:

```
    Faircloth put his hand on the knob and opened
the door. It was completely dark in there, and
he couldn't see any end to it, as if he could walk
in and just keep going forever. A noise came
from somewhere in the very back, a noise like a
gasp or a sigh or a very faint laugh.
    Faircloth started walking inside.
```

CHAPTER SEVENTEEN

"HOW LONG HAVE YOU BEEN OFF your medication?" Sonia asked.

It was the next morning, and Scott was in the kitchen of the house, talking to her on the phone as he poured coffee into the biggest cup he could find. "Who told you about that?"

"I'm only asking because I'm concerned. Last night you called and told me you thought you were cracking up."

"It was just a figure of speech." It wasn't, of course; at the time, he'd meant it as literally as anything he'd ever said in his life. The experience of finding himself back at the computer, writing about an encounter that he'd felt absolutely certain he was experiencing, had knocked the legs out from under him. Saying so out loud, just speaking the words, had granted him a peculiar relief that had allowed him some exhausted version of sleep. Truly crazy people didn't think they were going crazy—or was that just a misconception?

"So?" she said. "How long has it been?"

"Since what?"

"The meds."

"I don't know. A couple weeks, at least."

"What were you taking?"

"Lexapro," Scott said. "Why, are you a pharmacist?"

If she noticed his tone, she ignored it. "How long have you been on it?"

"About three years."

"Ever gone off like this before?"

"No, but—"

"Why did you stop?"

"I didn't anticipate being out here for so long. I ran out and just never got around to getting a refill. I guess I thought I was doing all right without it." He wavered, debating whether or not to continue. "And the writing is going really well too."

No reply. He looked up, staring out the window. He pictured her staring back at him with a gaze that could outlast a glacier.

"Really," he said.

"I don't see this as being a good thing for you, Scott."

"I got my sex drive back. That's a bonus, right?"

Sonia didn't laugh. "Eudora Gordon is our local pill pusher. Go see her."

BUT HE DIDN'T, not just yet. He felt much better this morning, stronger, and there was simply too much of Round House that he still wanted to explore. His recent success with the writing had emboldened him, stoked his curiosity, and now there was an entire ring of keys that he hadn't tried yet, doors to be opened, whole unseen rooms to be investigated.

At the end of the second-floor hallway, he found the stairwell that he knew he'd have to stumble across eventually—a bare, unassuming set of steps that led up to the heretofore unseen third floor. Oddly, there was no railing or banister, as if the builders had never intended visitors to go higher up in the house than the second story.

But there's always another story, right? he thought, and barked a laugh. Was that funny or just insipid? Back in Seattle, they would have known the difference.

He carried his coffee cup with him, feeling the temperature drop with each step. Invisible spiderwebs traced schoolbook cursive across his scalp and neck. At the top, he paused and sipped from the cup as he stared down the long hallway that took form in front of his slowly adjusting eyes.

The third-floor corridor was as wide and long as the concourse of an old-fashioned ocean liner from the Gilded Age. Flocked scarlet wallpaper rose in hundred-year-old patterns on either side, a winding floral print that made him want to reach out and caress it. At one point, he stopped walking, momentarily certain that he'd heard the faint sound of music, like an old, scratched 78. He put his ear to the wall and listened, vaguely aware of the distant, canned-sounding crooner's voice warbling:

> *We don't want the bacon,*
> *We don't want the bacon,*
> *What we want is a piece of the Rhine . . .*

Scott opened the door in front of him. The room that it revealed was empty. Stopping in his tracks, he listened again and heard nothing. The music was gone. Had it even been there in the first place? He thought about what Sonia had said about his medication. No question that the world without it had become more tactile, deeper, revealing whole layers that he hadn't noticed before. It was as if a protective veneer had been stripped away and now everything came at him with heightened texture, including the continuously smoothing nature of the overall design. He took another step, dragging his hands along the wallpaper, feeling the patterns intertwine against his fingertips. What would it be like if all of a sudden he awoke to find himself sitting at the laptop again, describing this scene?

I don't see this as being a good thing for you, Scott.

"But I'm *fine*," Scott said aloud. And he was. He was here, that was for sure, and he felt clearheaded, no depression, better than he had felt in a long time.

And writing. What more can you ask for?

The next three doors he tried were already unlocked, and each of the rooms was empty. The knob of the fourth wouldn't give. He put one of the keys in it. It turned halfway and stopped. Scott tried the next key, and the next. The process was already going to require more patience than he could muster. He was getting ready to give up, or at least go down for more coffee, when the lock clicked and the door swung open.

He entered what was definitely the biggest of the rooms he'd seen up here so far. In the middle stood a bed in a rough-hewn oak frame, neither masculine nor feminine. Old partially melted candles in brass candlesticks and bookshelves surrounded the bed, with an old hand-cranked record player standing on a nearby wooden cabinet. His first thought, that this might have been the source of the music he'd heard earlier, proved false—there was no record on the turntable, and the device was buried under so much dust that he doubted it would work even if it had been cranked up. Dried flowers that looked as if they'd turn to dust if he touched them stuck out of a chipped porcelain vase in the corner. More books. The smell of the room was faintly familiar, redolent of some faded old cologne or hair pomade that men might have worn back when they listened to music like the kind he'd heard earlier.

Scott glanced at some of the books and saw that they were poetry: Elizabeth Barrett Browning, Pablo Neruda, Shakespeare—love poems. He looked from the bed to the candles, then back at the books. His glance caught on a slightly open door in the corner of the room.

It was a closet. Inside, hanging on a hook, he found a fuzzy green sweater with a hole in the sleeve. Scott brought the sleeve up to his nose and inhaled, and some buried part of his limbic system registered the cologne as one of his father's, though he didn't consciously remember the man wearing any kind of manufactured scent. He lifted the sweater off the hook. There was something heavy in the pocket, and he took it out, a pack of Lucky Strikes and a monogrammed gold lighter, with the initials *FLM*. He'd never known his father to smoke. Frank Mast had always referred to cigarettes as coffin nails and the people who smoked them as gaspers.

He opened the pack of Lucky Strikes. Only three left. Scott took one out and, on impulse, inserted it between his lips just to see how it would feel. Even the paper tasted stale; the dried-out crumbs of tobacco that landed on his lips and tongue had no flavor left at all. He flicked the lighter, testing the flame, and as it illuminated the closet, he saw something hanging on the wall.

It was a painting. It wasn't large, perhaps twelve by fourteen, an original in a wooden frame with curved corners. The subject was the house itself. The artist had painted it from the perspective of the woods at dusk. Represented here, Round House looked even bigger than it did in real life, sprawling and tall, with lights in the upper windows gazing back at the viewer.

Scott took a step closer. There was a shadow in one of the upper windows, he thought, a semitransparent blur of gray against the dull yellow, a figure peering out from inside. It made him think of Sonia's father looking out at him, and Colette's Aunt Pauline, people so close to death that they hardly seemed part of this world at all. Scott reached up toward the canvas and touched the brushstrokes that had laid the image out, felt nothing but the dust that had accumulated over the decades, a slithery filthiness that made him retract his hand with a grunt of revulsion as if he'd accidentally touched a dead rat. Still his gaze stayed riveted to the shape painted in the window as if he expected it to move.

He thought of the painter, his great-grandfather, Great-Uncle Butch's father, H. G. Mast, the one who had hanged himself in Paris. In his family, talent might not have been quite synonymous with madness, but Scott thought the commonality between them must have been sizable, at least as big as the house staring back at him from the canvas, and the thing leering inside its window.

It's me, he thought with a start. *It's my face.*

From elsewhere in the house, somewhere downstairs, he heard his cell phone chiming, drawing him back to the present. Hard to believe how well sound traveled in here. His mind flashed to Sonia. He started to leave the room. The hallway was colder than ever, and he put on the sweater without thinking about it, headed for the staircase, wearing his father's ghost.

CHAPTER EIGHTEEN

"I WAS GONNA DRIVE out to the cemetery," Owen's voice said, sounding as foggy and remote as the frozen gray vapor gathering outside the windows. "You want to come along?"

Scott looked at the date on the phone display. A straitjacket of realization tightened over his chest, compressing his lungs and heart. With everything else that had been going on, the novel and the house and the medication that he hadn't been taking—

"You there?" Now his brother's voice was faint, echoing from the far side of some distant harbor. "Scott . . . ?"

"I'll meet you there." Without knowing why, or even realizing he was doing it, he put his hand against the kitchen window and pushed. Some subconscious part of him was wondering how hard he could press before the glass shattered and sliced into his palm. "Greenfield Cemetery, right?"

But Owen had already hung up.

SCOTT DROVE THROUGH TOWN looking for flowers to bring to his mother's grave. The closest he could find was a fake sweetheart bouquet from the convenience store outside of Milburn, and he started plucking off the little heart-shaped ribbons and sequined appliqués from the green cellophane as he drove. In the end, what remained looked so bad that he threw the whole thing out the window, where it caught on a barbed wire fence, a chintz remnant flapping in the breeze. He stopped the car and got out. The northeast wind carried the smell of the coming blizzard they were predicting on the radio, and he felt the barometric changes ringing through his skull like some archaic navigational tool.

He walked along the road back to where the flowers hung, took off his gloves, and put both hands around the stiff plastic petals, squeezing until he felt the sharp metal barbs piercing his palms. The harder he squeezed, the better it felt, until blood trickled from his clenched fists and he finally let go, leaving the crushed fake flowers dripping on the fence. The congestion was gone; he could breathe again.

HIS MOTHER WAS BURIED on a barren hillside that looked even worse under the gunmetal armada of low-hanging clouds. Scott's fingers throbbed in the iron air as he gazed through the gate. The grass hadn't been mowed for months, and the stones were half buried in dead leaves. On the other side of the fence, he saw Owen leaning on his truck. He took off his sunglasses and regarded Scott with raw and glassy eyes.

"Fuck, man," Owen croaked as Scott approached, "what happened to your hands?"

"Don't worry about it."

"You cut them all to shit."

Scott pulled out a pair of gloves from his coat pockets and put them on, squinting across the landscape. "This place is an embarrassment."

"The bank foreclosed."

"On a *cemetery*?"

"It happens around here more often than you'd think." Owen's red eyes disappeared behind the sunglasses again. "They're calling for two feet of snow by nightfall. Let's get on with it."

Scott thought they were going to walk to the grave, but Owen got back in his truck, so he climbed into the passenger seat. Henry was sitting in the middle in a dirty coat and mismatched mittens, looking as if he'd missed breakfast. He had a soot-colored smudge on his cheek that Scott wanted to wipe off, but he didn't want to remove his gloves and scare him. He settled for putting one arm around Henry's shoulder and promising himself he'd take the kid out for lunch when they were finished here.

Owen drove over the narrow cemetery road, stopped again. "Hold on," he muttered, got out, kicking leaves and weeds away from the stones. He shook his head and climbed back inside, and they drove again, stopping, getting out, looking around again, and pulling aside more leaves. The third time, after he'd driven clear around the far side of the cemetery, he just got out and walked to the nearest cluster of graves, standing there. When Scott climbed out, he was holding his face in his hands and breathing deeply. He recognized the expression of his brother trying not to throw up.

"Is she out here?"

Owen didn't look up at him.

"Maybe we should just go home," Scott said.

Owen mumbled something and sniffed. Clear liquid dripped from the tip of his nose.

"What?"

"Our family," Owen said, "is so fucked." He wiped his nose on his sleeve and frowned at Scott. "Where'd you get that sweater?"

"I found it back at the house."

"Ours?"

"Round House." Scott shook his head. "The one out in the woods."

"What are you doing out there, anyway?"

"Same as always, finishing Dad's story."

The embalmed pallor in Owen's cheeks made his eyes look even redder and glassier, like an amateur taxidermist's idea of verisimilitude. "Dad didn't start it."

"What do you mean?"

Owen didn't say anything. Scott reached into the pocket and pulled out the old pack of his father's Lucky Strikes. He took one of the two remaining cigarettes and gave the other one to his brother, who accepted it in silence. They both sat on tombstones smoking while Henry watched them from inside the truck.

"Shit, man." Owen spat. "How old is this thing?"

Scott shrugged but didn't put it out, even though his eyes were watering and he was trying not to gag. Owen threw his butt into some dry leaves, and Scott watched as a thin flame appeared, rising tentatively over somebody's grave. He imagined another fire, this one starting in the graveyard, spreading west in the wind to swallow up the whole town in one all-consuming conflagration. The possibility held a certain fatalistic appeal. He wondered what Owen might think of it.

"Why don't you move away from here?"

Owen looked at him. "Where? And do what?"

"I don't know, start over."

Snorting, Owen walked over and watched the flame rising like a spectral hand from the ground, fingers lengthening as it clawed its way upward along the edge of the old stone. He ground it down with one dirt-caked boot. "Still running away," he muttered.

"What?"

"Nothing."

"What did you mean when you said Dad didn't start the story?"

Owen gazed up at him. "Grandpa Tommy."

"What?"

"He used to sing me songs."

"Wait, you actually *met* Grandpa Tommy?" Scott thought back to the theater poster he'd found for the play *One Room, Unfinished*, written by the relative that his father called the city man, the one with holes in his shoes.

"When we were little," Owen said, scraping the burned leaves from the bottom of his boot onto a gravestone. "You weren't around. I think you were out of the house with Mom or something. Grandpa Tommy was up from New York, and he got his guitar out. I was probably five years old. I'd never seen anybody actually *play* guitar before. I thought the music just came from some magical place or some shit, I don't know. Anyway . . ." Owen shrugged. "He played a whole song for me, like five times. That's how I learned it." Was there a glimmer of pride in his voice? "That's when I started to play guitar."

Scott couldn't remember ever meeting his paternal grandfather, the failed playwright and evidently a musician as well. Like many of the details about his family's past, it could have meant something but didn't. Looking out at the graveyard, he realized that he'd never really tried to have any true connection with the men and women he called relatives. Now they were almost gone, like a matched set of delicate objects, crystal or bone china that had been recklessly dropped and smashed throughout the generations until he and Owen were the only two adult Masts remaining. The most misleading thing about his family had been the illusion of durability: In the end, it turned out the only thing you had to do to invalidate your family was ignore it. While Scott always somehow held himself above Owen because he'd escaped town and gone on to get a high-paying job, Owen had been the one who was more connected to daily life and whatever remained of the Masts. Owen was the real person; Scott was the anecdote, the Christmas card from the coast.

He forced himself to suck down what was left of the cigarette until it burned against his fingers, and then held it there. Owen was still looking at him, wiping his lips.

"I could use a drink," he said. "You want to go back to town?"

Scott shrugged. "Sure," he said. And then, "Let me take Henry out, buy him lunch."

Something ugly twisted over Owen's face, a spasm of dislike. He shook his head. "Forget it."

"Hey, look, I didn't mean—"

"Go get your hands bandaged up," Owen said. "And get some more of those pills while you're at it. You look like you could use them."

"Owen, wait."

"You're not some shining example of something, you know. You're not some great success story. You're just as fucked up as I am. Shit, you're worse. You can't even see it."

Scott nodded. It didn't seem to make his brother feel any better. Owen walked back to his truck, got in, and drove away, leaving Scott to walk back through the graveyard to the gate, where he'd left his car. The wind was rising, howling across the barren terrain. He was almost to the gate when he saw the stone behind a snow-choked pile of leaves.

ELEANOR MAST

LOVING WIFE AND MOTHER

"IN MY FATHER'S HOUSE ARE MANY MANSIONS."

Scott realized he had nothing at all to leave here. After standing in front of the grave for a long time, he took off his bloody gloves and laid them on the pile of leaves in front of her stone, a fitting monument in some way he couldn't describe.

He tucked his hands under his arms and walked back to his car.

CHAPTER NINETEEN

WITHOUT ANY REAL SENSE of where he was headed, Scott found himself pulling up in front of the Milburn Regional Hospital, a beige brick building that sat by itself beyond the northern outskirts of town. As a child, he'd been here only once, when Owen had fallen off the roof and broken his arm. His most lingering memory was the poor reception on the waiting room television. Today there were fewer than a dozen cars in the parking lot and an ambulance sitting in front of the main entrance.

Walking in through the sliding glass doors with his wounded hands still jammed in his pockets, he approached the desk where a heavyset man in a scrub top was checking his email. "Can I help you?"

"I don't know," Scott said. "Do you know if there's a nurse here named Anne Tonkin?"

"Anne's an X-ray tech. Let me see if she's here." He checked a schedule taped over the phone, picked up the receiver, and dialed. "Hey. Is Anne back there? There's somebody here to see her."

Scott walked over to the gift shop and browsed through greeting cards and balloons.

"Hello?" a voice said. "Were you looking for me?"

The woman in front of him was in her late twenties. She wore blue hospital scrubs and a white jacket; her face found its center in gold-flecked brown eyes so dark and intense that for a moment, as unlikely as it was, he thought she must have recognized him from somewhere.

"My name is Scott Mast—you might know my family."

"Your father was Frank?"

"That's right," Scott said. "Actually, I wanted to ask you about a distant relation of yours. A man named Myron Tonkin?"

Anne frowned, then smiled, as if realizing she'd been the victim of a sly practical joke. "Oh my." At this distance, Scott realized, she smelled like tobacco and butterscotch. "You've been talking to Pauline McGuire, haven't you?"

SHE TOLD HIM THAT SHE had been on her way out for a cigarette, and they stood outside the hospital while she turned her back to the wind, cupped her palms, and expertly touched the tip of the flame to a Camel 100.

"Whatever that delightful old bat might have told you," Anne said, "my great-great-grandfather Myron was the genuine article—the original bad seed. People in my family still talk about the time they caught him peeping at his own little sister, and this was a hundred and some odd years ago." Anne lifted her gaze to examine Scott's expression. "I'm not saying he deserved what happened to him, but everything I've heard about him, he was on his way to a bad end regardless."

"How old was he when he went blind?" Scott asked.

"Let's see." Anne bit her lip, summoning up data. "Thirteen or fourteen, I think." She inhaled again, held, and released a perfect smoke ring. It hovered between them for a split second and then vanished. "Let me guess—Pauline McGuire has you convinced that his old schoolteacher Mr. Carver struck him blind."

"I wouldn't exactly say I'm convinced."

"There's absolutely no proof of that. This was back in the dark ages, though, when people around here still sacrificed rabbits and crows' eggs for a good harvest. I'm not kidding—you and I grew up in a very superstitious part of the country. Although I'm sure I don't have to tell *you* that."

"So you don't believe the stories?"

Anne smiled. "I'm not going to deny it makes a good story. But do I think that some old nineteenth-century warlock used black magic to school disobedient kids? The fact is my great-great-grandfather went blind in childhood, probably due to some kind of optic neuritis or macular degeneration, and as cruel as it sounds, it probably saved him from a life of crime."

"What finally happened to him?"

"Nothing particularly interesting. From what I've heard, he lurked around home for the rest of his life, rarely left the house, never really learned to function without sight. Died relatively young, buried in the family plot."

"What about the others?" Scott asked.

"What, you mean the girl who developed a speech impediment and the boy who got polio?"

"Pauline said he was trampled by a horse."

Anne smiled again. She made it seem as if nothing pleased her more than standing outside a small-town hospital on a twenty-degree day, smoking and debunking family myth. "I'm sure she's not above adding drama to the story where it might be required." She looked at her watch. "I have to get back to work. Are you sure you don't want me to get someone to look at your hands?"

"It's nothing," Scott said, and realized it was true. The pain had stopped a long time ago. In fact, during the course of his conversation with her, he had forgotten about it entirely.

CHAPTER TWENTY

FROM THE HOSPITAL, he drove east, circumventing town without really thinking about it, to Colette's house, all without passing a single car. Although the threatened nor'easter hadn't yet arrived, everyone in the area seemed to have already gone into hiding. The snow-swept emptiness made him think about one of those end-of-the-world movies in which the hero wanders down vacant streets peering through windows, looking for evidence of where it all went wrong.

Pulling up to the McGuire house, he was already beginning to feel the parasite twisting in his guts, a kind of hunger but not for food, the urge for something else. The possibility made him shudder. Thirty-four was an ominous age to be acquiring new appetites.

Colette's convertible wasn't in the driveway. He went up to the porch and knocked on the door, rang the bell, and waited. After a minute, he walked along the sloping, landscaped hill to the granary, half expecting to find her back there. But the grounds were deserted; even the iPod-wearing groundskeeper with his black knit cap was nowhere to be seen.

Scott opened the door to the granary and looked inside at the heaps of grimy books and disorganized boxes, all at once unsure of why he'd come. How much more did he expect to find? He took his swollen, bloodstained hands from his pockets and stared at them, the stippled cuts and punctures looking, despite their lack of pain, as if they should have been steaming in the cold air. *You idiot,* the Himalayas of paper shouted at him. *Go home.* But which home exactly? He ought to have insisted on taking Henry out and buying him lunch first. But he was in no frame of mind to insist on anything right now; his psyche felt as formless and unsteady as a bucket of water, given shape only by the thing that held it back.

Out of sheer desperation, he began sorting randomly through the piles, lifting them up and setting them aside into some kind of chronological order, a pathetic attempt to establish organization. The damp mildew smell grew more intense as he dug deeper, wrenching away whole heaps of old books, their water-damaged covers permanently adhered; he dropped them in one corner. Newspapers went into a different stack. There was an astonishing volume of loose papers, some shredded as if Dawn Wheeler's rats had been making nests in it. But from the sound of it, he was the only living thing out here, and he worked with the steady, mindless concentration of a man compulsively avoiding his own thoughts.

Two hours later, he came across the blueprints.

AT FIRST, HE DIDN'T recognize even them. Holding the age-stained sheets of paper up to the light, he traced the outlines of hallways and rooms and doors with one finger, following them across the discolored and tattered pages until, all at once, a flashbulb burst in the back of his brain. He dropped the papers to the floor, stepped back, knelt down, and stared.

They were the architectural designs for Round House.

The plans deviated in peculiar ways from the finished product—the structure described in the blueprints was both familiar and uncanny. From what Scott saw here, there was much more to it than met the eye—hidden passages and whole subchambers that he'd never seen. It was as if this house had eaten a smaller one and was still digesting it a room at a time. Details that the contractors had decided not to exe-cute; or maybe the builders had run out of money using plaster to cover up all their sharp edges.

Or maybe you just haven't seen it all yet.

The old pine boards creaked behind him, and Scott jerked upright with a start.

"Hey," Colette said in the doorway. She looked bright-eyed and apple-cheeked, slightly out of breath, as if she'd just come back from a long run. Oddly, it suited her, made her seem younger and more vital. "What are you doing here?"

"Just looking around." He put his hands in his pockets. "Sorry. I should have waited until you were home. I just thought—"

"Relax. I just got back and saw your car out front." She craned her neck to look at the drawings on the floor. "What's that?"

"Some kind of architectural designs, I guess," Scott said, uncertain as always as to why he felt compelled to withhold information. For the first time, he noticed that the hunger in her eyes matched his own.

"Come on into the house."

"What?"

"There's something inside I think you ought to see."

"I really can't." He thought of the aunt shriveled up in her bed-room, surrounded by old posters and glamour shots, enshrouded in imported tobacco smoke and local murder lore. "Actually, I should probably get going."

"Why are you always in such a hurry?" Colette's smile was vulpine but genuine; she looked as if she were on her way to a cannibal barbe-cue. "Come on, you jerk. Can't you see I'm trying to help you here?"

INSIDE THE HOUSE, someone had thrown all the flowers away. The funereal reek of cloying blossoms that had clogged the air the last time he'd been in here was gone, replaced by the even worse stench of old burned things—fabric, stone, skin, hair. Once you burned it badly enough, did it matter what it used to be?

He stopped in the doorway of the living room and looked inside. Colette had set up a movie screen on one side of the room with a sixteen-millimeter projector pointed at it, the kind he remembered from elementary school phys-ed movies on the dangers of unprotected sex and drunk driving. Somewhere in the bathysphere of his consciousness, he felt the murk of his unease thickening into dread.

"Take a seat," Colette said. "Make yourself comfortable."

He pointed at the projector. "What is all this?"

"Today's the anniversary of the Bijou fire."

"I know what day it is."

"Pull those curtains for me, won't you?"

"What *is* this?" Scott repeated, aware that his voice was sounding a little strained, not just around the edges but everywhere, and thinking that under the circumstances, it might not be inappropriate. The kinds of movies that Colette McGuire-Fontana might want to show him weren't necessarily the kinds of movies that he wanted to watch.

"See for yourself."

She flipped a switch on the projector, and its sprockets started making that familiar whirring crackle, like a fan with something caught in its blades. A beam of bright light flared up across the room. On-screen, Scott saw the big white sans serif title HELPING HANDS come up along with a canned-sounding orchestral score. He realized that on some level, he'd been expecting this, exactly this, because, in a sense, it was what he deserved.

"Your great-uncle Butch's movie," Colette said loudly enough to be heard over the sound track. "The one you never got to see."

"Where did you get it?"

"The Bijou. Your brother found it the other day under some debris up in the projection booth. It was almost completely intact."

"*Owen* found this?"

"It is a part of the town's history." Her voice had a singsong tour guide's inflection that made him feel a little sick. "Of course, Aunt Pauline *insisted* we acquire it for our town archives."

On the screen, the camera was playing over rows of low-income housing that missionary teams headed by Scott's great-uncle Butch were in the process of rebuilding. Great-Uncle Butch's voice-over came on, quoting Scripture and beginning to describe the importance of hard work and Christian charity. Scott curled his fingers into his own wounds, clenching tight, reopening them; his nails came back satisfyingly bloody.

"Were you at the theater that night?" he asked. "The night of the fire?"

Colette didn't look back at him. From where he stood, behind her and to the right, Scott saw the curve of her cheekbone and jawline changing colors with the shades of gray and white on the screen, a halo of hazy light around her hair.

"And where were *you*," her voice asked from what sounded like far away, "on the night in question?"

"I was away at college."

She turned and speared him with a long, hard stare.

"You couldn't be bothered to come back?"

"You know what?" Scott managed. "Screw this." His voice was shaking; his eyes were hot and headachy, as if he'd been staring directly into a spotlight, burning out his retinas. "I don't need to watch this."

"Then go," she said, still smiling. "I'll tell you how it ends."

But he couldn't move. Colette touched one of his hands, lifted it up to look at it in the dusty cone of the projector's light. "Come on." Her voice was gentle, almost kind. "I'll get you a Band-Aid."

CHAPTER TWENTY-ONE

SONIA DIDN'T NEED a calendar to know what day it was. When Owen stormed into Fusco's and started ordering drinks two at a time, nobody said a word. After delivering his first Jim Beam and Budweiser, she watched it disappear in seconds while the patrons at the pool table looked on in fascination. A man's self-destruction was always a good show.

"Where's Henry?" Sonia asked as casually as possible.

Owen looked at the empty stool next to him as if he expected the boy to be there and shook his head. "Back in the truck."

She got her coat and went out to check Owen's pickup. Heavy flakes of wet snow were tumbling and swarming everywhere, clinging to her hair and eyelashes, smoothing over the edges and seams of the world and rounding off the corners.

"Henry?" she asked. "Hey, kiddo, are you—"

The passenger side door was open.

The truck was empty.

SONIA RAN AROUND BEHIND the bar to where she had parked the
Corolla, under the sign EMPLOYEE PARKING ONLY, and pulled her
sleeve down over her hand to swipe a thick hood of snow off the windshield. Despite the weather, the engine started right up, and she rolled
out onto the street, hoping to catch a flash of Henry's jacket somewhere up the sidewalk.

It wasn't the first time that Owen had left the boy in the truck only
to have him wander off. The last time, back in August, she had found
him standing in front of a closed toy shop window with his nose
against the glass, watching the electric trains. But it wasn't summer
now, it was the beginning of a blizzard, and the temperature was dropping by the minute.

She dialed Scott and got no answer. Then, reluctantly, she called
Red's cell.

"Hey," he said, sounding far away. "What's up?"

"Henry's missing."

"Who?"

"Owen's little boy."

"Oh." He sounded disappointed. "You at work?"

"At the moment, I'm driving around looking for him."

"Who, the kid?"

She felt a sharp finger of impatience prodding in her chest. "Where
are you?"

"Doing a little online shopping. How do you feel about white
gold?"

"Red, the kid's only five," she said. "He shouldn't be out here
alone."

"Uh-huh."

She sighed, realizing she had to spell it out. "You think you could
possibly help me out on this one? Rouse yourself to action?"

"Where's Owen in all this?" Red said, sounding irritated now. "No,
wait, let me guess: halfway between the stool and the floor."

"People were there for you when you needed it." This wasn't exactly
true, actually more the opposite, but she was counting on him being
sentimental enough to let it slide. "I'm wondering if you could at least
call some of your friends in the fire department."

"For Christ's sake, Sonia, he's not some cat stuck in a tree." She
heard a keyboard clicking in the background: at home all right, but

probably Googling himself, a habit that he'd confessed from his New York days. "Call Lonnie Mitchell. Tell him he owes me one. If you don't find the kid in the next half hour or so, let me know, I'll see what I can do, okay?"

"Forget it."

"Wait, princess, hold on a second—"

She hung up on him, turning left at the intersection of Norway and Aickman Avenue, heading back downtown. It wasn't just getting dark out now, it *was* dark, the only light filtering from the few shops that were still open. Snow pounded the windshield in waves. Sonia turned up the car's heater. There was an iron quality to New England darkness this time of year that she could practically taste. A little boy wandering around in this weather wouldn't last through the night.

Red would help her if she forced the issue.

She turned left, heading out to the McGuire house.

CHAPTER TWENTY-TWO

THEY WATCHED THE MOVIE in silence.

There was something profoundly unsettling about sitting here in the McGuire living room with the smoke-damaged remains of the same film that his mother had been watching unspooling in front of him. Colette didn't appear to mind—if anything, the silence seemed to soothe her. She sat beside him on the couch, sipping a glass full of clinking ice cubes and watching the footage wind through the projector.

Helping Hands started out mundanely enough, with grainy, discolored shots of Great-Uncle Butch's missionary teams at work. These tasks encompassed painting and refurbishing old poverty-stricken homes in the Kentucky coal region, replacing roofs, windows, and whole rooms of old row houses whose owners had been too poor or shortsighted to do anything about it themselves. Cheerful, clean-cut young men and women in scarves worked with brushes, ladders, and saws, occasionally glancing up at the camera to smile or crack a joke the microphone didn't catch. Throughout all of it, Great-Uncle Butch's voice-over narration described his team's commitment and the gratitude of the people whose homes they visited. Every so often, a Bible verse appeared on the screen, just in case the audience was unclear on exactly how the mission fit into the larger vision of God's word.

Then, fifteen minutes in, the scene shifted from southern slums to the woods. The trees cleared to reveal another house, this one imposingly huge, sprawling up ahead. Scott had time to think: *Wait a second, that looks like—*

He didn't finish the thought. The air inside Colette McGuire's living room had changed, become thinner, as if the oxygen content had unexpectedly plummeted. Scott was already feeling a little unsteady, and what he saw on-screen now heightened his sensory disorientation to such an alarming degree that he wondered if he was really seeing it at all. The last time he'd felt this profoundly deranged was the endless afternoon that he'd endured his mother's funeral, when he'd rammed his skull into a wall afterward just to clear his head. Now he thought the amount of self-inflicted pain that it would take to achieve those same results might very well kill him.

In front of them, Round House blazed to life on the movie screen.

GREAT-UNCLE BUTCH'S handheld camera traveled up the front steps and into the entryway. The music and voice-over narration had crackled away to white noise, leaving only the occasional scrape or scuff of footsteps as the camera moved into the main hallway; otherwise, the sound track was just a hiss. Scott stared at the screen as the corridor straightened out in front of him. It went back, on and on, ending in a tiny window covered in semitransparent curtains with a radiator underneath it.

When Colette touched his shoulder, he jumped.

"You all right?" she asked.

His voice was thin, reedy. "Is this still the same movie?"

"This is the movie."

Scott thought about the blueprints he'd found, of the image of one house swallowing another. There was the same feeling here, as if his great-uncle's movie had captured some hidden depths to the house, secret, compartmentalized space behind the walls.

This is it, he thought. *This is his version of* The Black Wing.

The camera wandered onward seemingly at random, its disembodied eye trolling the round emptiness in almost total silence. It passed through two small rooms, into the kitchen, lingering on an iron skillet where it dangled from a hook. Then it pirouetted almost drunkenly around, entered another doorway, and went up a flight of stairs and down the second-floor hallway, lined with closed doors on either side. Who, Scott wondered, was controlling the camera? Presumably his great-uncle Butch, but what if it wasn't? What if the camera came upon Butch himself standing in one of these rooms, his great-uncle turning around and staring back at it in black horror? What if the face belonged to Scott himself?

Of course, he couldn't have been in the movie; he'd never set foot in the house until a few weeks ago. He forced his eyes to remain on the screen. The last door on the right led to more stairs, and the camera went down again, moving through the corridor and to the right. It had been tilting ever so slightly, but now the tilt had become more severe, giving everything a slanted, off-kilter angle. At the end of the hall, it turned into one of the rooms.

It was the dining room: Scott's workroom.

He felt as if he'd never seen it from this direction before. The smooth, bare walls looked angry somehow, pulsing with a cold, indefinable hatefulness, and although the room was empty, he could feel the presence of something *within* the space, growing in strength like a static electrical charge. It reminded him of a high school science experiment he'd once done involving a pair of steel plates, oppositely charged, a current growing between them, invisible but undeniably powerful, ominous in its silence.

But it *wasn't* totally silent, Scott realized. If he listened, beneath the whir of the projector, he thought he heard music crackling on the sound track again, warbling and anachronistic:

> *We don't want the bacon,*
> *We don't want the bacon. . . .*

Scott frowned. The old World War I music, faint as it was, didn't seem to be coming from the projector at all but out of the screen itself. He took a step toward it, cocking his head, and stared. Suddenly, a low black shape shot past the camera, too fast to be seen.

"Did you *see* that?" He leaped back, squinting through the tunnel of light, toward Colette. "What *was* that thing?"

"I don't know." Her voice sounded numb, dreaming.

"Can you rewind it?"

She fumbled with the knobs on the projector. Both the music he thought he'd heard and the projector's noise were replaced by a louder, more urgent clatter, and the image on the screen froze, stuttering slightly, showing a plain white wall. Colette twisted another switch, and the footage began to roll backward with a swaggering, exaggerated slowness.

On-screen, the black shape emerged from the shadows on the left, changing positions in between every individual frame. *Of course it is,* Scott thought. That was what gave the illusion of movement, the persistence of vision. Except now, watching the same scene in reverse, he somehow felt as if the black shape were actually *moving* in gaps between frames, as if it were alive somehow within the darkened confines of the film, the parts that they couldn't see.

"Wait," he said. "Hold it there."

"It keeps slipping."

"You have to be careful. If you pause it too long in front of the bulb, the footage starts to get too hot."

"Wait. I think I've got it." She stopped the film again, and he approached the screen, staring at the shape. Pinned down into stillness, it had become even more indistinct, a murky smudge, not even a shape anymore but just a shadow.

Except, he realized, the shape wasn't really black.

It was blue.

CHAPTER TWENTY-THREE

SONIA HADN'T BEEN OUT to the McGuire house in sixteen years. She told herself it was because there wasn't anything else out here for miles and thus no reason to make what was a long and inconvenient trip through otherwise empty country. But the truth was—

Never mind the truth.

But it was too late for that now. The memory came whether she wanted it to or not.

Sixteen years ago, the day before she and Scott were supposed to go to Senior Prom, she had been driving these exact same hills in her father's old lopsided panel truck (EARL GRAHAM—JUNK 'N' MORE!) with a load of rolled newspapers. Her father had always let her borrow the truck every day after school, and she'd drive out to the *Globe*'s regional distribution center, a warehouse twelve miles away, pick up her papers, and drive back, stuffing the plastic paper tubes all along the way until she'd reached the McGuire mansion. It was one of her last stops, and in winter it was always dark by the time she got to it. She'd been pulling off to the side of the road, paper in hand, when she'd noticed the Mast family Country Squire station wagon parked in the McGuires' driveway.

Sonia had recognized the station wagon instantly. Technically it belonged to Scott's mother, but it was the vehicle that Scott always ended up using if he needed a car to rent videos or pick her up for a date. In fact, she and Scott had spent several hours wrestling around its backseat just two days earlier, exploring the mysteries of the universe in the dark along the shore of Clayton Lake. There was nothing remotely flashy or cool about the station wagon, with its sparkly Epcot bumper sticker, broken dome light, and fake wood-grain side panels; the only spectacular thing about it was what happened between them in the backseat, there in the dark.

The sight of it there, in front of the McGuire compound, caught her off guard more than she could possibly have articulated. She remembered jamming down the brakes of her father's truck, newspaper still in hand, and the sinking feeling in the pit of her stomach as her gaze rose up, almost involuntarily, to the light in the second-floor window. She remembered what she'd seen up there.

That can't be him, she'd thought. But of course it had been. Up in the lighted window of Colette McGuire's bedroom, without so much as a drawn shade to obstruct the view, had been the unforgettable sight of Scott, presumably on his knees, eyes closed, in front of Colette, who was lifting her breasts up into his waiting mouth.

Dropping the McGuires' newspaper on the road in front of the box, Sonia had hit the gas pedal of her father's truck and peeled away. She couldn't remember the thoughts racing through her head at the time, but she didn't think it was due to her faulty memory or some suppression of painful events. Looking back on that moment, she didn't believe she had actually been thinking *anything,* but simply reacting, putting as much distance between herself and what she'd seen as humanly possible.

Now, almost two decades later, she was back driving through the snow on this same country road, just a glorified extension of the McGuire driveway. And there—perhaps illustrating her own life's insatiable appetite for redundancy—was the rental car that Scott had been driving, parked in front of Colette's convertible.

For a moment, Sonia couldn't do anything but sit there and try to digest it. It was exactly like sixteen years ago. Seeing this car now only made her realize how little she'd changed since then, an emotionally deadening thought, yet one she was powerless to suppress. What good was growing up, she wondered, supposedly moving forward with your life, having new experiences, if the person you thought you'd become was just a set of Sunday clothes that hardly covered up the desperate, needy adolescent you thought you'd left behind?

The voice of reason, the one that had told her to stay in law school, the one that advised her to steer clear of Scott once she'd heard he was back in town—the one, in other words, she never listened to—told her not to stop here. She got out of her Corolla and walked through the snow-swirling dark toward the main house, half expecting motion-activated lights at any second. They didn't come; there were no alarms or barking dogs or threats to mobilize private security guards. If nothing else, the McGuire family still thought it was invulnerable.

What are you going to do, knock on the front door?

Twenty yards from the porch, she veered right, grasping her way along the outer perimeter, stumbling a little on the low fence that surrounded some kind of overrun garden. Snowflakes clumped in her hair and eyelashes, rendering vision sticky and unreliable. She saw a flickering yellow light hazing in the bushes surrounding a tall window. Shoving her way through the brush, she put her face to the frosty glass and stood there shivering, feeling her hands already starting to go numb. On the other side of the window, the curtains were divided just enough for her to get a glimpse inside.

At first, Sonia didn't understand what she was looking at. Scott and Colette stood in the living room in front of a movie screen. Scott was pointing at something; Colette was just staring at it. The image on the screen twitched and skipped, pinned imperfectly into place, a giant, dying moth trapped on top of a bare bulb. From her place outside the window, Sonia saw a room with the figure of a girl in a blue dress. Behind her was a man in a dark suit, his arm on her shoulder. The girl was smiling. Watching the scene unfold, Sonia realized there was something familiar about the room itself, the doorways and the high ceilings, the *curves,* and after a moment, she realized what it was. The man and the girl on the movie screen were standing in a room in Round House. But why was Scott here watching movies about it in Colette's living room?

Sonia's curiosity faded beneath a kind of dawning horror. There was something wrong with the girl's face—it seemed to be melting from the inside. Still smiling, the girl turned her head and looked up at the tall man in the black suit. At that exact moment, the man's eyes flashed up from the movie screen, staring directly out the window at Sonia with an unmistakable air of absolute recognition, a grin spreading over his face.

He sees me out here, her mind babbled. *He sees me outside the window, and he knows I can see him—*

Her cell phone gave a brief buzz. She jumped, knocking her elbow against the glass.

All at once, Scott spun around and stared straight at her, his face bathed in the projector's light. Sonia had no idea whether he'd seen her or not. She felt the muscles in her legs jump without orders from her brain.

She scrambled from the bushes and fled.

CHAPTER TWENTY-FOUR

"WHAT?" COLETTE SAID. "What is it?"

"I heard something." Scott yanked the drapes aside, using the opportunity to get control of his voice. When he'd heard that thump on the other side of the window, he'd been deathly afraid he was going to scream. As irrational as it was, the notion of Rosemary Carver standing outside in the snow, looking in at him, refused to go away. If anything, the sprawling white emptiness outside the window only intensified it.

"There's nothing there," Colette said.

Scott turned reluctantly back to the movie screen. The footage was beginning to melt against the projector's bulb, the face of the girl in the blue dress contorting, blackening, stretching to become irregular and wrong. Behind her, the figure of her father appeared to elongate until the scene blistered into incoherence. Scott caught a puff of scorched celluloid drifting from the projector's casing just before the picture dissolved in a black cauldron of bubbles.

"Oh shit," Colette said with a high-pitched manic giggle. "It's on fire." She grabbed a blanket from the sofa and tossed it over the projector, where thin tendrils of smoke had already begun to rise. The projector fell over with a crash, swinging the beam up to the ceiling before it flickered and went black. The burst of activity shook Scott from his fugue, and he staggered sideways to find his balance against one of the tall brass lamps in the corner.

"I have to go."

"Wait," she said.

"Colette, I'm not going to—"

She covered his mouth with her lips and kissed him. Scott, caught openmouthed, felt her tongue sweep past his teeth, with the flavor of meat and milk. He drew back, not looking where he was going, only hoping he would be able to find the exit.

"Remember?"

"I'm sorry." It didn't sound like his voice at all, and he didn't sound sorry. Somehow he managed to step over the projector and its cords, the table where it had been standing, circumnavigating furniture and lamps on his way out, wincing every step of the way.

"Where are you going?" Colette asked.

Scott turned and looked back at the darkened screen where he'd seen the last images of the house, knowing only that he had to return there.

It was calling him back.

CHAPTER TWENTY-FIVE

SONIA DIDN'T EVEN BOTHER with the phone until she was back in her car and driving away from the McGuire house, the Corolla gobbling up icy asphalt, fishtailing all over the road. By then, it had stopped ringing. She hit MISSED CALLS, saw Red's number pop up, and stabbed TALK. It didn't even have a chance to ring before she heard Red's voice, breathless on the other end.

"I found him," Red said.

"Henry? Where?"

"The site."

She frowned, talking louder than she had to. "What?"

"The construction site in town," Red said, sounding exasperated. "The Bijou, the old theater, you know?"

Sonia was struggling to steer and balance the phone on her shoulder, not normally a difficult feat, but at the moment, it felt next to impossible. All around her, the winter wind boomed and roared, never going away completely. "What was he doing there?" Suddenly she remembered the trailer that stayed parked behind the chain-link, serving as the office for the project, and how Red once said he sometimes holed up there when he didn't want to go home. He'd even tried to convince her to meet him there for a quickie one night. "Is he okay?"

"Yeah, he's—" Red sounded flustered. "He's fine. Just get here, okay?"

She did, putting the pedal down, disregarding the weather and the slippery roads. Through the flying snow, the storefronts of downtown leaped into her headlights like a series of flat, painted canvases. She shot past them and swung up in front of the remains of the theater, almost skidding out of control, and sprang out and ran along the chain-link fence looking for a way in. On the other side, under its fresh layer of white, the sagging husk of the theater looked like an arctic shipwreck. Over by the trailer, hinges squeaked and a rectangle of light swung open in the dark.

"Sonia?" Red's voice, shouting over the wind. "Is that you, princess?"

"It's me," she said. "How do I get through there?"

"Hold on." He staggered down out of the trailer, wading through the drifts, and Sonia saw that he was carrying Henry in his arms, wrapped in a blanket. The boy was clutching a backpack. "There's an opening off to your left."

They met at the fence gate, and Red passed Henry over to her. "I was in the trailer going over some payroll stuff when I heard a noise. I found him over there. . . ." He nodded vaguely in the direction of the theater. "He was curled up on the ground."

"God." Sonia looked at the boy's face. It was filthy, bruised with ash and dirt, but she didn't see any blood or sign of injury. His eyes were open, watching her, dusty orbs in the night.

"Hey, bud. You okay?"

Henry nodded, hugged his backpack closer, as if he feared she might take it from him.

"You shouldn't have come out here," Sonia said. "It's very danger-ous. We were worried about you."

He blinked and nodded. "Where's my daddy?"

Good fucking question, kid. Sonia felt a wasp of anger fly up from her stomach and plant its stinger in her throat. It didn't matter what Owen had been through—the thought of him abandoning the boy in the truck on a snowy night was enough to make her want to call the police on him and find a better guardian for his son. Shifting the boy's weight to her shoulder, she took out her cell phone and started dialing.

"Who are you calling now?" Red asked.

"Lonnie Mitchell."

"Hold on." He touched her wrist. "Let's not do anything rash."

She gaped at him. "What are you talking about? Henry could've frozen to death or fallen through one of the holes in the theater and broken his neck." She was aware of Henry watching her, following the conversation avidly, and tried to soften her tone. "It's dark out here, Red, and it's freezing cold."

"You're right," he said. "But if you call the police"—he lowered his voice to just above a whisper—"they're only going to take him away."

At this, Sonia felt the boy stiffening in her arms. *That's the idea*, she wanted to say, followed by: *Since when are you such an advocate of Owen Mast?* But neither of these things were what Henry needed to hear right now. As it was, he already looked on the cusp of tears. She could feel him trembling in the Polarfleece blanket that Red had swaddled him in.

"Look," Red said. He stared at her for a long time before continuing. "Let me talk to Owen first. I'll pour some coffee into him, sober him a little, and let him know what it's come to. I'll bring him around. After that, if you still want to call the cops, okay. But I think . . ." Red took a breath, and she could see him struggling to arrange the words in his head. Sonia had seen trial footage of him in this exact state after his first wife's death, a man grown fat on life's cheerful generalities, now laboring hard to find some precision within the depths of his five thousand–dollar suit. "I think taking his kid away from him might be the last straw."

"What if it's the wake-up call he needs?" Sonia asked.

"You said people were there for me when I needed it, and you were right. Owen and I have had our differences, but I owe him this much. At least I have to try."

"I don't get this. Why are you sticking up for him?"

"If I don't," Red said, "nobody will. I guess maybe I know how that feels."

Sonia felt all remaining argument vacuumed out of her in the form of a silent sigh. An earlier version of her—the individual she'd thought she was before seeing Scott's car parked outside the McGuire house tonight—might have put up more of a fight, but at this point, she just didn't have it in her.

Admitting that to herself, though, was harder than she'd anticipated. And in the end, she just walked away.

CHAPTER TWENTY-SIX

ASLEEP IN THE STOCKROOM of Fusco's, sprawled out between cases of beer and liquor, Owen dreamed of the Bijou fire.

The dream was vivid enough to send his heart racing, even as he slept. Everything was slowed down, the details sharpened: He could see his mother's tired face reflecting the colors of the movie and smell his father's Aqua Velva mixed in with the gassy smell of the old man digesting another dinner. From here and there came the soft crackling of the audience munching popcorn. His father stifled a yawn. Emotionally it was all clearer too, Owen's anger at having to be here when Scott was free at college, his loathing for this town and his parents and Great-Uncle Butch. Everybody knew that Great-Uncle Butch was a fraud. All missionaries were frauds and leeches; they sucked up money and claimed to be doing God's work, and if you believed them, well, then you were just another sucker too. Not that there was any shortage of them here tonight, he thought—sheep lining up to be sheared, one after another.

Somewhere in the audience, a kid started crying. Owen tried to ignore it at first, concentrating on his own rage, squeezing it down into a hard black ball in his chest. The pain gave him a perverse thrill, like biting off his nails and pushing the parings up into his gums until they bled. But as the crying got worse, became screaming actually, Owen realized something was going on behind him that maybe didn't have to do with the movie.

He was going to turn around when he noticed what was on the screen. Instead of missionaries painting houses, there was the figure of a pale girl in a blue dress, standing there with her arms spread wide. Somehow Owen found this seemingly innocent image totally unnerving—and he wasn't alone. Several rows back, the kid's wails rose up a notch, as if he were being tortured. All at once, Owen started seeing stars, his mouth filled up with nauseated saliva, and he knew he was going to be sick. Either that or he was going to start crying. To his right, he saw his father covering his eyes, and was he screaming too—or was he yawning again? It didn't make sense.

I'm only feeling this way because I'm drunk, he thought remotely. *It's the anniversary of the fire, and I got drunk; I'm having nightmares, some kind of fucked-up posttraumatic flashbacks like those Vietnam veterans, except instead of a war, I got this. I'll wake up shivering in a puddle of piss and everybody will be laughing at me, but at least I'll be awake.*

Except that, more and more, with every passing second, the nightmare was becoming real. Between the screams of the kid and the image on the screen, some third event was taking place. In chemistry class, they'd learned how certain compounds, inert in themselves, came together to form lethal mixtures, but what was mixing together here? Owen became aware of a boiling cloud of explosive energy, as if the theater were filling with natural gas.

Buried in the dream, the sense of impending doom was more than he could take. He jumped out of his theater seat, shoved past his mother, who scowled at him—"Where do you think you're going?"—and fell into the darkened aisle, smashed his knee on the armrest, and started scrambling for the red EXIT sign. A few other heads turned at the commotion. Owen ignored them all. He took three steps, and that was when he saw the kid who had been screaming. He was a beautiful blond boy, three or four years old, wide-eyed. He looked more scared than any child had any reason to be. He stood on his seat with his arms outstretched to Owen, the message plain: *Get me the hell out of here, mister.*

Not even thinking, teenage Owen scooped up the boy, while adult Owen, paddling helplessly through the drunken dream, thought immediately of his son, Henry. Of course, the boy in the theater seat *wasn't* Henry—on the night of the fire, Henry wouldn't even be born for another fifteen years—but the resemblance between them was more than accidental. And the last thing Owen heard the boy say just before the fireball came rippling through the theater, tearing the child from his arms, was the helpless, unfinished cry that came from the boy's lips, a single word that changed everything:

Daddy.

CHAPTER TWENTY-SEVEN

SONIA BUCKLED HENRY into the back of her car and drove to Fusco's, slowly and carefully, feeling her back tires slither and twist across the packed snow. In her rearview mirror, she watched as Red followed her in his pickup. When they arrived at the bar, Henry had fallen asleep in his harness. She waited until Red got out and came over.

"We'll wait here while you go in and talk to him," she said.

Red nodded and trudged dutifully into the bar like a man going to the gallows, an act he seemed to have perfected just living here in this town. Watching him even now, Sonia felt an errant twinge of genuine affection for him and labored to suppress it. She didn't need any more emotional attachments, certainly not to married men.

So what's your next move?

Henry's chin sagged low to his chest. She didn't particularly want to take the boy back to Earl's house, although her options were narrowing by the minute. She tried Scott's cell phone again, and this time he answered.

"Where are you?" she asked.

"I'm back to the house—Round House." His voice sounded hollow and hoarse, not like himself at all. "The house in the woods," he said, and then added: "I'm writing."

Before she could stop herself, she blurted, "I saw you over at Colette's tonight."

There was a long, deep silence. Then: "How did you—" He stopped. "Was that you at the window? Were you spying on us?"

"What were *you* doing?"

Scott didn't answer. Neither of them spoke for what felt like whole minutes. In the ensuing silence, Sonia felt that vertiginous slippage between past and present, as if they could just as easily have been talking about what happened sixteen years ago, when she'd seen him at Colette's house, up in the window. She had the uncanny sensation that he was feeling the same way: that they'd both stumbled into the exact same chronological wormhole that returned them to the day before the prom. In front of her, snow smacked the windshield, temporarily eclipsing the entire street in front of her. *Time is rolling backward in Milburn, New Hampshire,* she thought. *If you don't watch out, you'll get rolled up with it.*

She broke the spell first. "I-I came out looking for Red. There was an incident."

"What happened?"

Thinking of Henry, she lowered her voice. "Owen left Henry in the truck while he came into the bar to get drunk, and Henry ran off. We found him at the old Bijou Theatre, where the renovation's going on."

"Henry was *inside* the theater? Is he okay?"

"He's all right now," she said, "but I really don't want to send him home with Owen tonight."

"Do you need me to come get him?"

Activity flittered in her peripheral vision: Sonia turned and saw the front door of the bar open and Red lumber back out again, his boots already caked with snow. "One second." She pressed the tip of her thumb over the cell phone's tiny mouthpiece and waited for him to come up to the driver's side, rolling down the window. "Well?"

"Owen's completely blitzed," Red said. "I'm talking totally comatose. Lisa had a couple of the guys haul him into the stockroom to sleep it off." He shook his head. "I'll talk to him in the morning."

"I'm on my way," Scott's voice was saying through the cell phone as Red turned and started to walk away.

"Hold on." Having seen what she did through the curtains at the McGuire house tonight, she realized she didn't feel comfortable turning Henry over to Scott. He didn't even sound like himself now, over the phone. His voice was stilted and mechanical, as if he were reading lines off cue cards only he could see.

"What's the matter?" he asked.

"It sounds like Owen's drunk himself into a coma."

"Goddamn it." Scott made a noise that sounded almost like an animal's snarl. She'd never heard him sound like that before. "Let me get my fucking keys."

"Wait, Scott. Are you sure—"

"He's my nephew, Sonia."

"I've got Henry with me," she said. "I'll bring him to you."

"You know how to get here?"

"I was there with you the first time you saw the place," she said. "Remember?"

"Oh, right." He let out a breathless little laugh, more of a nervous chuckle, some of the tension easing from his voice. "I'm sorry. I don't know what's wrong with me. You sure you don't want me to come out there? I don't mind."

"I'll just bring him. We can talk then."

"Great." Scott said. "I'll be waiting."

CHAPTER TWENTY-EIGHT

COMING BACK FROM COLETTE'S, the last thing on Scott's mind had been writing. It was late, and the headache had become a hallucinogenic marvel of pain so rarefied that it felt like a kind of religious trance, the kind that Dostoyevsky described before his visions of God. Maybe it wasn't a migraine—he'd never had one before—but it had to be close. If anything, he'd anticipated popping some ibuprofen and lying in a dark room with a cool washcloth over his eyes to wait it out.

But the moment he stepped inside Round House, his headache disappeared.

It was almost as if the house had eaten it. In its place he discovered an idea for a new scene in *The Black Wing*—effortless, again, it had appeared in his consciousness, fully formed. Was this how real writers did it? Maybe sometimes you just got lucky. Or maybe this was what they meant about good writing stemming from pain.

Bypassing the ibuprofen entirely, he switched on his laptop, not pausing to bother with the lights, and sat down at the settee and jumped right in:

Chapter 21

The sheriff knew.

Faircloth somehow knew that he knew. It was in the polite but inquisitive way that the lawman asked about Maureen's absence and changed the subject and then came back to it with exaggerated casualness. He was trying to catch Faircloth in a lie.

The sheriff, a genial fellow named Dave Wood, had dropped by a half hour ago. The conversation had started out in the entryway, and after a few minutes, Faircloth had invited him back to the kitchen for a cup of coffee. Sheriff Wood had admired the house, its size, and the way the hallways turned without angles, creating the peculiar sensation of moving even when you were standing still. Had Faircloth actually found that feeling disquieting at one point? He couldn't imagine a time when he hadn't thoroughly enjoyed it.

He gave the lawman an obligatory tour, showing Wood all the little side rooms and corridors as they came along in a clockwise direction throughout the first floor.

They were standing in the dining room when Faircloth decided he would have to kill him.

"Well, this is quite a place," Wood was saying into his empty cup, and then he raised his head upward. "Not a sharp edge in the whole house."

"That's right," Faircloth said. "Even the electrical outlet covers have rounded-off corners. They had to be specially constructed."

"I bet you've got a lot more room up there too, don't you?"

"Sure," Faircloth said. "More than we'd ever need. It's a big place." He chuckled. "I haven't even looked in some of the rooms."

They both laughed, and then the sheriff turned and looked at him. His face was calm and without expression.

"Which one is she in, Karl?"

"I beg your pardon?"

"Your wife."

Faircloth smiled. "Oh, she's not up there."

"No?"

"No." He allowed the smile on his face to widen. "I put her in the wing."

"What wing?" The sheriff frowned, his mouth starting to form a question, when Faircloth swung his

"Scott?"

He jumped and shot a look over his shoulder so hard that something popped in his neck. There were footsteps coming down the entryway. Standing up, sliding the computer from his lap, he saw Sonia at the far end of the foyer with a bundle in her arms. The bundle was Henry.

"You scared me," he said.

"I've been out there knocking, but you didn't answer."

"It's a big place." He was aware that he'd just spoken a line of dialogue from the book, Faircloth's line to the sheriff. "I was just . . . working." He tried to smile, but it felt ridiculous, so he quit. "It's going really well."

Sonia was looking at him expectantly, as if awaiting permission to come closer. In her arms, Henry groaned and shifted, one small hand clutching her jacket in his sleep, the way an infant would reach for his mother.

Scott forced his voice to sound normal. "Thank you for bringing him over. Is he all right?"

"He's fine. He could use a hot bath and a meal, but that can wait until morning."

He nodded and smiled. That was what people did when they were agreeing, he told himself, they nodded and smiled—the normal behavior patterns were returning slowly. "Listen, Sonia, I really appreciate what you've done. Here." He reached for his nephew and felt her hesitating before she passed him over. "I've got an air mattress and a sleeping bag. . . ." He carried Henry into the dining room and laid him down, the boy wrestling with something inside himself on his way into the lowest levels of sleep. "You want a drink or something?"

"No thanks."

"Listen," he said, "I wanted to tell you, that thing at Colette's—"

"None of my business."

"She had that movie that Great-Uncle Butch showed at the Bijou the night it burned. They just found it in the wreckage. Owen found it, actually. It was . . . I didn't understand it." The light of the laptop screen caught his eye, a rectangle of pure, expectant blue—a swimming pool waiting to be jumped into. "Tonight of all nights."

Sonia was still looking at Henry, fast asleep on the air mattress. "Red was the one that found him there."

"Red Fontana, the football player?"

"He's overseeing the construction project. It's a McGuire project, so . . ."

"Right, right. I get it." Scott felt himself itching to get back to the scene that he'd been writing. It was as if Faircloth were still right there, frozen in space with the cup he was going to smash down on the sheriff's head, just waiting for—

"Scott?"

"Yes?"

"Is something wrong?"

"No, why?"

"You keep staring over at the computer screen. It's like you're not even here."

"Where else would I be?"

Her eyes flicked at the laptop.

"Sonia . . ." Before he could stifle it, that same dry, tired laugh escaped. It seemed to startle her. "Look, I'm sorry if I seem distracted. It's just— If you had any idea the kind of day I've been having . . ."

She came closer, blocking his view of the computer screen. "Did you pick up your medication from the pharmacy?"

"I told you I'm fine without it." He almost told her about how he'd conquered the headache and the electrical feeling in his head, but it would mean explaining them in the first place, and he was fairly positive that would be a bad idea. "It's actually helping not being on it. Look." He faced her straight on and held up his hands, perfectly steady, as if that proved anything. "Let me finish the scene I'm working on, okay? Then we'll talk, I promise."

Sonia was looking at him as if he were a stranger.

"Sure, Scott," she said without inflection. "Whatever you say."

CHAPTER TWENTY-NINE

The sheriff frowned, his mouth starting to form a question, when Faircloth swung his cup down, smashing the man's skull. The handle broke off and good old Dave Wood looked at him with a dazed expression. Did you just do that? the lawman's expression asked. Did that just happen?

Faircloth was both surprised and gratified by the ferocity of his response. He grabbed the sheriff's throat and squeezed until his thumbs popped through something just above the notch between Dave Wood's collarbones. With a tiny gasp, the man dropped to his knees and then onto his side. A small trickle of blood ran from the corner of his lips. But Faircloth could still hear him breathing, or struggling to breathe.

For an instant, the sound startled him and he looked down, unable to believe his eyes. What had come over him? He had committed murder, but he wasn't a murderer. He was just a normal man in an extreme situation. He had gone to war and come home to a hero's welcome. He had gotten engaged and put money in the bank. Someday he hoped to go back to college and start his own business. Now all those plans lay smashed before him on the floor. What in God's name had he done here?

The sheriff's eyes gazed up at him, lips moving, trying to speak. Faircloth heard words, hoarse, whispered. " . . . not too late," the sheriff was saying. " . . . help me . . . hospital . . ."

Faircloth bent down and lifted the cop's hand, then paused at the rustle and creak of something in the corner of the dining room.

When he looked up, the girl in the blue dress was standing in the entryway to the black wing. She wasn't alone. The tall man behind her wore a black suit. Her father.

Together they smiled, as one.

Faircloth smiled back. He understood.

" . . . doctor . . . ," the sheriff said in a mushy voice.

Still smiling, Faircloth picked up the coffee cup, now without its handle. He swung it down, smashing it into the sheriff's face. Something shattered, but it wasn't the cup. The sheriff made a squeak, hardly audible. Faircloth hit him again and again, beating the man's face in with the cup until finally it broke in his hand. His arm was very tired and sore, but he felt good, as if he'd accomplished something worthwhile, the way a pile of wood warms you three times--once when you stack it, once when you chop it, and once when you burn it. Hard work is its own reward, as his father sometimes said. Faircloth had never truly understood what he meant until now.

He looked down at the palms of his hands and
saw that they were dripping with

Scott stopped typing. He'd been working very quickly in an effort
to get the words out fast enough. It wasn't until he'd felt his fingertips
sticking to the keys that he'd stopped, shaken from the spell that the
story had cast, and looked down.

There were red blotches all over the keyboard.

Sticky scarlet whorls and dabs and smears were everywhere, spread
across almost every key. It was as if a mouse, its feet dipped in red
paint, had gone dancing across the horizontal surface of the laptop.

He took in a breath, held it for a five count, and let it out. Very
deliberately, he told himself: *This isn't happening. I will turn my hands
over and I will see that they are clean, and then I'll look back at the keyboard and it will be clean too. Maybe I'll get one last brain zap in the bar-
gain.*

But there wasn't any brain zap.

He turned his hands over.

They were still covered in blood.

He sat motionless, staring at them patiently, waiting for the illusion
to go away. That was how you dealt with tricks of the eye and mind,
wasn't it? You waited for them to go away, and eventually they always
did. Because if they didn't, then that meant—

They're real. Or you're crazy. Or both.

But the longer he stared at his hands, the more real the illusion—
assuming it was an illusion—became. At this point, he realized that he
could actually feel the blood drying in the webs between his fingers
and becoming tacky in the lines on his palms. Worse, his joints and
knuckles felt hot and sore, the tiredness spreading clear up to his
arm—but only his right arm. The feeling of fatigue went all the way
up to his shoulder and down the muscles on the right side of his back.
He had done something vigorous and taxing with that arm, and
recently. Like chopping wood, it warms you not once but—

"Scott? Are you all right?"

He looked up over his upraised hands at Sonia, and she stared back
at him in confusion.

Scott put his hands over his eyes, scrunched them shut. In the self-imposed darkness, he heard her coming closer, felt her hand on his shoulder. The room tightened, sloping inward along a vortex of intensifying pressure. An eternity of time passed as he floated in a void and then heard her voice ask:

"What did you say?"

He took his hands down, opened his eyes, and looked at them. His palms and fingers were clean again. Of course they were. They had always been.

"You said, 'I killed them all.'"

Scott opened his mouth and shut it again. He felt a sudden pressure in his throat. "*He* killed them," he said. "He killed them all."

"Who?"

"I don't know."

"Scott?" She touched his cheek. "Are you sick?"

Scott looked over at the boy on the air mattress. Henry's sleeping shape gave him a measure of solace in a way he couldn't describe. His pupils flicked toward the window at a shiver of activity off to the left, just a flicker, as if something inside the wall had shifted. "What's that?"

"Snow," Sonia said gently, walking out. "It's snowing again."

"Where are you going?"

"Just out to check my car. I'll be right back."

Following her toward the foyer, he caught himself running his fingers along the wall and through the sloping curves of the doorway, brought up short by how it was impossible to tell where the hallway began. The plaster walls flowed outward, unto themselves, without demarcation or boundary, in unspoken mimicry of living tissue. There was no question that it had become rounder since he'd arrived here.

He killed them all.

CHAPTER THIRTY

"MY CAR'S ALREADY BURIED," Sonia said, returning from outside with white powder glistening in her hair, more white powder clumped onto her shoes. "I think the roads are only going to get worse." Glancing back to the door that led into the dining room, where Henry still slept: "Maybe I should stay here for the night."

"That's fine," Scott said without much strength. He had just come back from the kitchen, sipping hot tea with lemon, the cup trembling in his hands. He'd hoped that holding on to the mug tightly enough would settle his nerves, but instead, the whole thing was shaking, almost splashing on his knuckles. "There's a bed upstairs. I haven't used it yet."

"Maybe there's a couch in one of the other rooms down here. I don't think I'd want to climb into an old bed anyway. Who knows the last time the covers were changed?"

After evaluating the alternatives—of which there were none—Sonia crawled under the unzipped sleeping bag on the air mattress next to Henry. Scott turned out the lights, leaving a single lamp burning in the hall, then returned to his place on the settee, where the laptop sat with its screen saver whirling. He could sense Sonia observing him in the monitor's blue light.

"Scott?"

"Yes?"

"Am I allowed to ask what's going on?"

He looked up. "What do you mean?"

"With you, tonight."

He paused and then shook his head. "I don't know. Like you said, I think I'm getting sick—a fever or something." Just saying it aloud made him feel better, and he thought of a phrase of his mother's: *Fake it till you make it.* "No big deal."

"Because I was thinking . . . maybe you're putting too much pressure on yourself to finish this book. If it's stressing you out that much, it's not worth it."

"You were the one that wanted me to finish it," he said. "I thought you'd be happy."

"Seeing you like this doesn't make me happy."

"I'm fine," he said. "Really."

"I saw the movie she was showing you, you know."

He tried to look at her, but even with the monitor's glow, he couldn't make out her face across the darkness of the room.

"It was this house, wasn't it?"

"Yeah," he said, tightening his grip on the teacup.

"Did he live here too? Your Great-Uncle Butch?"

"I don't know."

"Scott?"

"Yes?"

"Is it my imagination, or are the corners of the rooms . . ." She didn't finish the question, and Scott didn't answer it. He stared up at the corner, thinking of what she'd once said about how the edges wouldn't meet properly in a dream. Somewhere a clock ticked in the house. Had the ticking noise been there before? It was possible, but not likely. He focused on the soft, measured pace, steady and constant. It should have been reassuring, but it wasn't. For some reason, it reminded him of a finger tapping patiently at a pane of glass, over and over, a hand that wanted to come in.

"I saw something," Sonia said. Her voice sounded different now, younger.

He turned around and looked at her. "What?"

"In the movie you were watching earlier at Colette's house. The man, the one in black . . . This is going to sound really stupid, but—I could tell he was looking out the window at me from the screen."

"*Looking* at you?"

Sonia nodded. "Right before I ran. I swear he was looking me in the eye." She blinked once. "That's crazy, isn't it?"

Scott walked over to the air mattress and lay down beside her, front to back, on the opposite side of Henry. He could feel her pressing herself closer to him, shaking a little as he held on to her, back to front, her hair sliding against his cheek, still cold from her most recent trip outside. On the other side of the mattress, Henry groaned in his sleep.

"Do you think he's going to be okay?" Sonia asked.

"Physically, you mean? I think so."

Sonia didn't seem entirely comfortable with the answer; she seemed to be holding her breath and finally let it out in a slow, resigned sigh. "He belongs with you."

"That's not my decision."

"It could be."

"What are you suggesting?"

"Henry is a sweet little boy," she said, "and he's got brains to burn. But if you leave him with Owen long enough, he's going to turn into Owen. You know that as well as I do."

"So what am I going to do?" he said, "Call social services? Hire a lawyer? Testify against my own brother in court?"

"I *know* Owen"—Sonia's voice seemed to be coming from far away—"maybe better than you do. And I know that Henry brings out the best in him. But Henry deserves better than that."

"He's not my son," Scott said. "As much as I wish he was, he's not."

"I know," she said, and they lay there for a long time, neither of them talking. Sonia's breathing had become deeper and more regular, and he thought she might have fallen asleep until she spoke again:

"Do you realize this is the first time we've ever actually spent the night together?"

Scott nodded, even though she wasn't looking at him, knowing she would feel it. He wished that he could see her face. Something in her voice, its intonation and inflection, made her sound so much like the teenage girl he'd left behind that he almost wouldn't have been surprised to find that sixteen-years-younger version of Sonia lying next to him in the dark.

"I'm still cold." She rolled over, sleepy-eyed and stretching, and nuzzled her face into his chest. Scott kissed her forehead, and she held on to him tightly, shivering, and then pushed him away.

"I don't want to disappoint you," she said. "I'm not ready for anything just yet."

"Neither am I. I wasn't even thinking about that."

"Liar."

"No, I'm serious. Plus, I don't know if you noticed, but there's a kid in the bed."

She laughed a little. "Bed?"

"Air mattress—we'd probably deflate it. And I've got to write anyway."

"Right." That laugh again, like a faint echo, fading. "Spoken like a true . . ." But the last word was lost somewhere between her hair and the pillow. It didn't sound like *writer*. If anything, it sounded like *Mast*.

HE CONTINUED TO HOLD on to her. Eventually her breathing leveled out, became deeper and more rhythmic, and he got up again and carried the laptop to the kitchen and switched on the lights. He considered the gin before opting for bottled water. Better to stay clearheaded, or as close to clearheaded as the house would allow him to feel, if he was going to do this.

Do what? What exactly are you doing—and, by the way, why? And while you're at it, did you really just attribute some kind of anthropomorphic qualities to a piece of architecture?

He chose the easy question first. He was going to finish his father's novel. He could see the ending coming from a mile away. It all had to do with Faircloth and the girl in the blue dress. As the skein of Faircloth's sanity came unraveled, her ghost would become more powerful. Eventually, on the brink of madness, he would discover that his own presence here in the house was not an accident but exactly the opposite, a consequence, the inevitable cause and effect of New England gothic. Twelve-year-old Rosemary had spent her final, horrible days here in Round House's black wing, and somehow Faircloth was connected to it. But how? Rosemary had died in the 1880s, and the book was set in the 1940s. According to the timeline of the book, Faircloth wouldn't have been born for almost forty years. And what about her father? How did he fit into all this?

Scott closed the laptop.

That was when he saw her.

Rosemary Carver was standing in the doorway of the kitchen watching him. The light on her face showed the waxen pallor of her skin, and he could see where it had been eaten away, peeled back to show the underlying cheekbone. There was nothing spectral or illusory about her, no sense of her being a "ghost" in any sort of traditional way. She stood before him with weight, depth, and odor, the sour, soiled smell he remembered from the night that he thought he'd been holding Henry, only to see the boy playing on the other side of the room.

His first conscious thought upon seeing her here was that her body must have continued to grow after her death; the bones were warped and twisted to fit the confines of her pauper's grave. The remains of the blue dress hung from her body like rags of flayed skin. She began wobbling across the kitchen toward him, and it was clear there was something deformed in her pelvis. In the silence where the sound of his breathing ought to have been, Scott could hear the scrape of broken bones grinding and clicking together in their dry sockets.

I can close my eyes. And when I open them, she'll be gone.

But he couldn't make himself close his eyes.

The girl was coming at him more quickly now, moving with a kind of clumsy eagerness. Scott could hear the floorboards creaking under her weight, could feel the still, stale air moving to accommodate her passage here. She moved closer, filling his vision, blocking out everything else. Her smell was very bad now, rich and overpowering, a smell like human waste and grave dirt, flooding his mouth and sinuses and making him sick. Soon she would be so close that her cold face would press against his like clay. And would he kiss the thin, cold ridge of her lips? He had an awful feeling that he would.

Scott's entire body filled with a scream that he was physically incapable of letting out, any more than he was able to take a step back. She moved into the spot where he was standing.

When he looked again, she was gone.

CHAPTER THIRTY-ONE

"*HOW* LONG?" DR. FELDMAN'S voice asked through the cell phone.

"Only a week or so," Scott said, pulling up in front of the drug-store, "more or less." It was definitely *more,* closer to a number of weeks, but judging from the psychiatrist's tone of voice, he wouldn't be happy to hear that, and Scott kept it to himself.

"The electric shock sensations you've been describing are one of the most common symptoms of SSRI antidepressant withdrawal. Have you been experiencing any other reactions? Headaches, fatigue, insomnia?"

"Headaches, yes," he said. "Hallucinations?"

Feldman made a not-too-discreet harrumphing sound. "With this kind of discontinuation syndrome, yes, there may be any number of somatic, mood, and psychomotor reactions involved, including visual or auditory disturbances."

"How vivid are we talking about here?"

Papers shuffled on the other end. A continent away, Scott's cell phone captured the noise perfectly.

"This kind of reckless irresponsibility isn't like you, Scott. I'm call-

ing in a prescription to the local pharmacy. I strongly suggest you get
it filled."

"All right."

"And, Scott?"

"Yeah?"

"When were you planning on coming back to resume our ses-
sions?"

Scott thought of dropping Henry off at kindergarten earlier that
morning, the boy clutching his Finding Nemo backpack as he ran.

"Soon," he said. "As soon as I can."

IT WAS A WHITE, round, scored pill with the letters *F* and *L* imprinted
on either side of the scoring. Scott stood outside the pharmacy looking at it where it lay in the palm of his hand like a perfectly formed
snowdrop, contemplating the symmetry of the thing that he was about
to ingest. At last, he popped it into his mouth and tried to swallow it
dry. The pill got caught in his esophagus and, for a moment, he could
only stand there half gagging, eyes watering, finally scooping up a
handful of snow to help it down.

There was nobody around to watch him struggle. The streets of
town were almost empty, with only a handful of citizens wandering
around, bundled up like Eskimos in the cold midmorning sun. No
snow fell, but the wind was relentless. He started heading back to the
car and surprised himself by walking past it to the next intersection
and looking three blocks down at the Bijou. The demolition site
appeared to be completely quiet, even though it was a Monday.

He walked over, bending into the wind, and when he reached the
fence around the burned-out theater, he saw that all the equipment,
the backhoe and bulldozer and crane, had been removed. Still no
workers in sight, no noise, nothing but the sagging, blackened beams
of the theater behind the chain-link fence, looking strangely sated, as
if it had somehow eaten them all up.

Scott followed the fence to the gate. It was closed but not locked,
despite the big NO TRESPASSING signs. He ducked through it, thinking
of what it must have been like for Henry wandering around out here
in the dark. What had the kid been looking for?

In the daylight and bracing temperature, the events of last night felt even more distant and dreamlike. Since awakening this morning, Scott had told himself repeatedly that what he'd seen in the house had been nothing more than misfiring neurons, a logical conclusion that his conversation with Feldman had backed up. Visual disturbances, hallucinations, could happen to anybody. At the time, it had felt real, but that was why he was back on the Lexapro, wasn't it? To take care of that problem.

He picked his way through the debris, past the mobile home office to the half-collapsed structure where his mother and Great-Uncle Butch had died. Great sagging black walls, a ruined family-eating husk that didn't seem real either. Was the medication already starting to work?

Looking up at the wall, shielding his eyes against the hard sun, Scott noticed a hole where the bricks had fallen in. A pile of rock and dirt rose up alongside it, and without thinking, he began to climb. Little bits of mortar, wiring, and pipe crumbled beneath him.

This kind of reckless irresponsibility isn't like you, Scott.

Yet apparently it was. He looked down. A stream of sunlight slanted through the hole, like a finger pointing out the path he would follow if he lost his balance and fell all the way down to the partially demolished floor and basement, one more Mast family casualty. A trapped circuit of moving air cycled low and mournful through the open space, powdery ash mixing with snow over charred rubble, mostly unrecognizable—a twisted row of theater seats and a jagged, oblong slab of flooring.

Scott looked deeper into the bottom of the pit, thirty feet down where the excavation looked newer, more freshly overturned. Someone had placed a blue plastic tarp over half the exposed flooring, flapping in the wind, held in place with cinder blocks. It was a familiar shade of blue—blue paper, blue fabric, something about it stimulated the connection, the way a random noise on the street might unexpectedly remind you of a song.

There was a loud crash inside the trailer behind him. Scott jerked around, expecting to see someone, maybe Red Fontana, coming out bawling at him that this was private property. But the door stayed closed. Scott climbed down and walked over to the trailer. He looked through the window, rising up on his tiptoes for a better view.

He opened the door.

It was dark inside the trailer, the curtains drawn, with just the green glow of the computer and telephone emanating from the corners. It took him a moment before he noticed the body lying on the floor. It was a man, motionless, sprawled on his back with one arm over his eyes, his leg tangled in a telephone cord. When daylight from the doorway fell across his face, the man moaned and rolled over, opening his eyes to foggy, agonized slits.

"Owen?" Scott asked.

"Oh, man," Owen said. "Turn off the lights. God, please, Jesus, turn out the lights."

"What are you doing here?"

Owen made a groaning noise without enough consonants in it. Scott noticed that the drawers of the file cabinets were open and papers scattered on the floor. *Blueprints*, Scott thought, architectural designs, suddenly remembering the ones that he'd found in Colette's granary. More papers were clutched in Owen's hands, as if some kind of halfhearted snatch and grab were in progress.

"What are you doing?" Scott repeated.

Owen made the same sound again, like a long, drawn-out attempt to say his own name—*ooohhhnns*—and clutched his forehead, trying to curl his body away from the light and cold air pouring through the open door. He wondered if Owen had even considered what might have happened to Henry last night. The thought made him angrier than he'd expected.

"Come on," Scott said, bending down to lift him. "Let's get out of here." He caught a better look at the blueprints, not for the house but for the Bijou, original designs from the 1950s, it looked like.

Owen made the sound again.

"What?"

Owen resisted, yanked his arm away, staring at the floor but speaking clearly enough now: "Bones."

"What are you talking about?"

Ruined red eyes came up to meet him like two reflections of a polluted chemical sunrise. "There were more down inside the theater"— Owen stopped and wiped his mouth—"that they never got out when they cleared the other bodies."

Scott tossed the old blueprints aside, unexpectedly struck by the notion that his brother might actually be telling him something important, or trying to, an association that might change everything if he could just make it stick. He thought of that single white pill washed down with a handful of snow, all that condensed whiteness spreading diligently through his brain like steam, keeping his thoughts from cohering.

"More what? More bones?"

Owen nodded and burped, gulped, then went limp, still clutching the papers he'd dug out of the file cabinet.

"How do you know?"

Owen just shook his head. "Doesn't matter."

"Tell me."

His brother looked at him. "I got wasted last night—drunkest I've ever been. I just kept drinking. Finally I woke up in the back room of Fusco's this morning. Let myself out. Walked over here to the theater and started looking around."

"Why?"

"Last night I dreamed about the fire," Owen said. "Except it wasn't just a dream . . . it was like . . . . . I *remembered* things about that night. Things I forgot I knew. Like on *Oprah* when people get hypnotized and remember shit that happened to them when they were kids . . ."

"Retrograde amnesia?" That wasn't even the correct name for it, but Scott was having difficulty finding the right words, the white cloud in his brain absorbing them before his very eyes. Why had he taken the pill? But Owen knew what he was talking about; he was already nodding.

"I ran out," he said. "That night, at the theater, I just ran out of there."

"What about Mom and Dad?" Scott said. "Weren't they trying to get away from the fire too?"

"The fire hadn't even started yet."

"Then why were you leaving?"

"I just— I knew somehow," Owen said. "*I knew something bad was going to happen.* There was this little kid in the theater behind me, and I could hear him screaming and crying, and I knew whatever it was, it was going to be bad, so I got up and ran out. Mom looked at me and said, 'Where do you think you're going?' but I didn't even answer her. I just started running."

Scott wondered how accurate this dialogue was. A morning-after memory of a booze-fueled dream hardly constituted gospel truth. But Owen was repeating it for him now with a kind of heartfelt sincerity that Scott could not remember seeing in his brother's eyes throughout recent memory, if ever.

"I got halfway up the aisle," Owen said, "and I saw the kid, the one that was crying and screaming. He was just a little younger than Henry is now—he even *looked* like Henry—and he held out his arms for me to pick him up. I grabbed him on the way out."

"You took him from his parents?" Scott asked.

"He called me daddy."

Scott felt another realization trying to come together in his mind, tantalizingly close to joining up and forming a bigger picture, then withering away in the pale antidepressant mist.

"How sure are you that all this really happened?"

"Like I said, I didn't remember it until last night," Owen said. "But it happened. I know it did."

"So . . ." Scott felt his hand being drawn up to the raw spot between his eyebrows, a pressure valve where the cloud might escape, allowing his thoughts to come together properly. Creative visualization. He rested his thumb on the spot, feeling the familiar salty sting, and heard Feldman's scolding voice again. *This kind of reckless irresponsibility isn't like you, Scott.*

"Why were you looking for his bones here?"

"The kid didn't make it out," Owen said.

"How do you know?"

"I dropped him. When the fire started."

Henry's voice, out of the blue: *She said I already was a ghost.*

"They never found his body," Owen was saying. "He's still down there. For some reason, Red and Colette are covering it up."

Covering it up. Scott thought of the blue tarp, the blue dress, the blueprints, all things you used to cover things up. He wished he could see through it, beyond it. Yet there was still so much whiteness in the way. He pressed harder on the spot between his eyebrows, as hard as he could, working through the skin, as if the pressure alone could make something happen.

He heard a sharp chiming sound. He glanced up. Owen was fumbling in his pants pockets, taking out a cell phone. Scott had never known his brother to carry one, but here it was, Owen flipping it open as if he knew what he was doing.

"Yeah?" He paused, listening, a slackness coming over his face. "Yeah, it's me." Another pause, longer, and Scott heard a tinny voice on the other end, before Owen said, "Okay, all right. I'll be right there."

"What is it?" Scott asked.

"Accident at school," Owen said. "It's about Henry."

CHAPTER THIRTY-TWO

THE LITTLE GIRL WITH THE BAND-AID on her forearm sat holding her coat on her lap like a small pink pet that she was afraid might run off. Bunches of wadded-up Kleenex lay around her everywhere, on the bench and on the floor. Sitting next to her, a woman in an outmoded brown suit and thick glasses sat patting her knee. She looked up at Scott and Owen with a kind of startled alarm.

"Mr. Mast?"

Both men answered "yes" simultaneously, and the woman looked momentarily confused. "I'm Principal Vickers," she said, standing up and turning. Scott saw a run in her left nylon, from ankle to calf. "Henry's in my office. Would you come with me, please?"

"What happened?" Owen asked as they walked.

"I think at this point I should just speak with the father."

"That's me."

Principal Vickers stopped with her hand resting on the doorknob, her lens-distorted eyes sweeping from Scott to Owen, back to Scott, and then, with what appeared to be genuine reluctance, to Owen, where they stayed. "We've never had any sort of trouble with Henry in the past," she said. "He's a very sweet little boy, always plays with the other children. That's what makes this kind of thing all the more . . . confounding." Scott realized he'd misjudged the scowl; it wasn't severity but profound, almost heartfelt dismay. "Frankly I'm at a loss."

"I don't understand," Scott said. "What did he do?"

Principal Vickers let them both in.

ON THE WAY HOME Henry sat in the backseat of Scott's rental car, silent, his shoulder belt twisted across his chest. He hugged his backpack in both arms, the same way he'd held on to it when Scott had dropped him off this morning, like a paratrooper about to jump out of a plane.

"You know who bites people?" Owen asked, staring at his son's reflection in the rearview mirror. "Animals, that's who. Are you an animal? Huh?"

Henry picked a dust mote in the air and stared at it.

"That principal said the girl might need stitches. What if her parents decide to sue us? You think I've got money for lawyers?"

The wrinkles in the backpack deepened.

"Fuck this shit," Owen said. "I've got half a mind to lock you up inside the house where you can't hurt people. That's what you do with wild animals that bite, you lock them up in cages. Did you know that?"

"Or set them free," the boy mumbled.

"*What was that?*"

"Owen—" Scott began.

"When we get back to the house, you're going right upstairs. I don't give a shit, you understand? You can stay up there all day and rot. Think about what you did. And hope and pray that kid's dad doesn't decide to take me to court."

Scott pulled up in front of the house. There were no vehicles here, and he remembered Owen's truck still parked outside Fusco's from last night. Owen got out and stormed across the sidewalk, slowing down among the piles and heaps of snow and almost falling over on his way to the front door. Scott looked in the rearview mirror at his nephew's face.

"Uncle Scott?"

"Yes."

"Are rats wild?"

"No. I don't know. Henry . . ." He turned around. "Why did you bite that girl?"

"She wanted to look in my backpack."

"Why didn't you let her?"

"It's private."

Scott looked at the pack in the boy's arms, black smudges and streaks across the side. *Ashes,* he thought. It had been in the back of Sonia's car this morning, meaning . . . what? The backpack had been with him last night when Red found the boy in the theater's wreckage.

"Can I look?" Scott asked.

It took several seconds before Henry reluctantly opened his arms, allowing Scott to take the backpack. He found it to be surprisingly heavy, as if packed to the seams with wet sand, and he realized he'd never actually touched it this morning—Henry had held on to the backpack, all the way to school. He started to open it; the zipper got stuck on something inside. Scott tugged harder, and it sprang open with a little puff of black dust. The burned smell came out, filling the car with a stench worse than simple ash. The backpack was bulging with cinders.

"What is this?" Scott asked.

Henry didn't answer. His eyes gleamed and two big tears welled up and fell, cutting clean tracks over his dirty cheeks. But when he spoke, his voice was clear, almost defiant.

"It's my brother."

CHAPTER THIRTY-THREE

HE DROVE TOO FAST TO COLETTE McGuire's house, taking the curves recklessly, overextending the car's center of gravity. When he got there, the driveway was empty, buried under half a foot of snow. He ran up to the front door and knocked three times—hard—pounding, really.

"Colette?" he shouted through the door. "It's Scott. Open up." His voice seemed to be floating down from some distant corner in the winter sky, up where it was totally disconnected from the rest of him. "I need to talk."

Still no answer. He was about to call her on his cell phone when the door creaked open. On the other side, he saw Aunt Pauline sitting in her wheelchair.

"Scott," she said. "How nice to see you."

"Is Colette here?"

"Of course, dear. Come in out of the cold."

He ducked through the doorway. The olfactory preponderance of flowers was back, and heavier than ever, swirling almost visibly in the bands of sunlight that spilled across the floor. Following the wheelchair past the spiral staircase, Scott tried to catch a glimpse of the woman's face, but she turned the corner into another hallway. For the first time, he realized that the first-floor layout of the McGuire house wasn't entirely dissimilar from Round House. True, these walls, floors, and ceilings all met square and true. But other than that, both houses might have been designed by the same architect. He had another random thought: The black wing somehow connected them.

"How do you like living out in the woods?" the old woman asked.

Scott flinched. Had he been speaking aloud?

"Sorry?"

"In that lovely old house." Now she turned, eyes twinkling from her tiny, prunelike face. "So peaceful out there, don't you think?"

"I'd really like to talk to Colette."

"Have you been out to the pond?"

"Aunt Pauline—"

"It's behind the house, through the trees—the pond, I mean." Aunt Pauline touched her ear. "I left my hearing aid up in my bedroom. Would you mind going up to get it for me? It's on top of the mahogany bureau next to the door."

Hardly thinking of what he was doing, Scott climbed the stairs. *Recovered memory*. That was the term he'd been searching for earlier with Owen. Despite everything else, he was relieved to have thought of it. Perhaps more of his brain was working properly again.

He stepped into the old woman's bedroom, found the hearing aid, a small pink thing in an otherwise empty silver dish, and took a moment to look around at the theater memorabilia on the walls, images of pretty young Pauline from back in her Barbara Stanwyck years. His gaze settled on a framed poster for a play called *One Room, Unfinished*. Familiar from somewhere, but the white pill blotted the memory to a sulky blur. Scott got close enough to read the small print. Opening soon at the McKinley Theatre on Twenty-third Street.

The play's author was Thomas Mast.

"Looking for something in particular?" a man's voice asked behind him.

Spinning around, Scott saw Red Fontana staring at him from the doorway in his bathrobe. The robe's belt hung loose, and the robe itself was open just enough that Scott could tell Red was naked underneath it.

"I came over to talk to Colette," Scott said.

"Then you got the wrong room."

No small talk this time, and Scott was glad for it. "What's going on at the Bijou? Why did you shut down the demolition project?"

"What?" Red smiled. "Is your brother bitching about his paycheck? He barely lasted a few days on the job."

"He said you found something down there."

"That movie?"

Scott shook his head. "Something else, down in the pit."

"The only thing *I* found was his little boy, scrounging down inside the foundation, digging around in the ashes. Sonia wanted to get social services involved. Good thing I like the guy."

"So there wasn't anything else down there?" Scott asked.

"Like what?"

"Something that would cause you to stop work."

"Zoning ordinances," Red said, and his hands disappeared into the pockets of his robe, searching around as if he expected to find something down there. "We're just waiting on the permits, that's all. Red tape. You know how it is—or maybe you don't." With a shrug, he stepped out of Aunt Pauline's doorway, and Scott walked past him, close enough to read the embroidery on the robe: *Holiday Inn*. Red's hand reached out and touched Scott's arm, applying slight pressure on a nerve just above the elbow.

"What exactly did your brother say?" Red's voice asked from behind him.

"He said you found another body down there—a child."

"Unbelievable." Red sounded genuinely awed at Owen's imaginative capacity. "What bottle did he pour that one out of?"

"He sounded pretty convinced."

"Sure he did. If we did find a body, why would we cover it up? Don't you think we would have reported it to the cops?"

Scott didn't know what to say. He was thinking of what Owen had said, about grabbing the boy on his way up the aisle. *He looked like Henry.* Who had Owen taken him from—the boy's mother? Another thought: *What if . . .* But it was already gone.

"One thing's for sure," Red said, "guilt surely is a bitch."

"What do you mean?"

"Well, look at it this way, if it weren't for your great-uncle showing his movie there on that particular night, all those people who died in that fire would still be alive." He must have seen the expression on Scott's face and added, "No offense, but that's the truth of it, right? That's a lot to carry around, especially for a guy like Owen. Could be that finding those old reels of film sent him right over the edge."

"You make it sound like Butch's movie killed all those people."

"Of course it didn't. It was just a fire. I mean, they never did find out what caused it, but . . ."

"I thought it was a wiring problem," Scott said. "In the projection room."

Red shook his head. "It started at the front of the theater, by the screen."

"But there were wires up there too, right?"

"I'm just saying the mind can be a mysterious thing," Red said. His smile was both thoughtful and enigmatic. "Especially when it comes to guilt."

Downstairs, Scott could hear the softly trundling squeak of Aunt Pauline's wheelchair moving restlessly from room to room, waiting for him to deliver her hearing aid.

"Hey," Red said, "you dropped these."

Scott looked back and saw Red was holding the bottle of pills, reading the print on the label. "Brain candy, huh?" He pursed his lips. "Funny, I didn't pick you for the type."

"There's a type?"

"Sure," Red said, and shrugged. "But maybe not."

"Red, honey?" A small, hesitant voice floated down the hall, a woman, but not Colette, familiar from somewhere. He couldn't place it, but he didn't have to—she was coming out of the room now with a sheet wrapped just above her breasts. "Oh, I didn't realize . . ."

Scott immediately noticed the little brown birthmark at the corner of her bubble-gum mouth. He was looking at Dawn Wheeler, the town librarian. Upon recognizing Scott, she blushed but kept her chin tilted slightly upward, embarrassed but triumphant, as if she'd proved something to him just by being here. *I finally got to sleep with the quarterback.*

"Get dressed, baby. And *you*"—Red patted Scott on the shoulder—"Tell your brother I said hi," he said. That poker player's smile was just as unreadable as ever. "Tell him I'll be in touch."

"AUNT PAULINE?"

The old woman sat with her back to him, slumped in her wheel-chair in the kitchen, gray head cocked to one side, knotted hair resting on one shoulder. Scott's first thought was that she was dead, had suffered a heart attack or a stroke, scant seconds before he'd returned.

But she was only fixing tea and rotated around to look at him, almost playfully. "My hearing aid?"

He gave it to her. "I saw the poster in your room for a play called *One Room, Unfinished.*"

"Yes."

"You remember it?"

"Of course I do. I was going to be the star. It would have been a breakout role for me, a little past my prime." She smiled, almost saucily. "But once you get past thirty, who's counting?"

"What happened?"

Some of the pleasure dimmed from her expression, as if an invisible hand had reached in and adjusted her rheostat, dialing it down. "It was never produced," she said. "When Tom couldn't finish writing it—oh, the investors were *furious.* They threatened to sue him for every penny he had, but by then it was too late, of course, and there was nothing any of us could do."

"What was the play about?"

Aunt Pauline blew on her tea, brought it to her lips, sipped, and winced. "A house."

"Why couldn't he finish it?"

"Writer's block." She folded her hands and squinted up at Scott, until he could almost feel himself blurring in and out of focus in her eyes. "He said he couldn't write in New York—too many distractions. So he came back here to that house in the woods, Round House, out by the pond. It's so peaceful out there, you know, so secluded. He wrote for a while, but the closer he came to understanding what truly happened, the more . . . difficult things became for him. When the time came for him to write about her, things started to change for him, and . . . well, he just never recovered."

"What do you mean, things started to change? 'Her' who?"

A door slammed upstairs, and Scott looked around to see Dawn Wheeler charging down in a flood of tears, bumping him out of the way on her rush to the front door. A moment later, Red followed, not hurrying, humming softly and reeking of freshly applied cologne. In the foyer, he hesitated over a dozen species of outerwear before selecting a gorgeous camel hair coat and sliding it over his mountainous frame.

"I'll be back later, Auntie," he said. "In case anyone asks."

Keys rattled faintly, and the door clicked shut behind him. In the wheelchair, Pauline clutched her tea and rocked slightly back and forth in silent but palpable delight. As Scott returned his attention to her, he had the uncanny feeling that Aunt Pauline had not only followed exactly what just happened but had been waiting patiently for the outcome throughout the entire encounter.

"What happened to the playwright?" Scott asked.

Pauline bowed her head, clucked her tongue sympathetically. "He met with a bad end."

"He died?"

"Not before he went completely insane."

"But he couldn't finish the play?"

"*No.*" She held up one root-gnarled finger, correcting him as carefully as a Latin proctor making a slight but critical distinction in verb conjugation. "The play was *why* he went crazy—it runs in your family."

"What?" Scott asked.

"That play was inspired by an incomplete story that *his* father had written. What Tommy discovered in it drove him over the edge. He began to see things in the pond behind the house . . . bodies sunk to the bottom, poor darlings, wrapped in chains to keep them from rising back up. In the end, he simply couldn't stay away from it."

From what? Scott wondered. *The pond, the bodies, or the unfinished play?* "But these things he saw," he said, "they weren't real, were they?"

"Given his lineage, real is in the eye of the beholder, isn't it?"

"What do you mean, his lineage?"

"Well . . ." Pauline raised two tiny, upturned hands and smiled, as if this simple gesture explained everything: "He was a Mast, after all."

"I'm a Mast," Scott said.

The old woman smiled. "Of course you are, dear."

CHAPTER THIRTY-FOUR

SCOTT DROVE BACK THROUGH TOWN and north. The old highway was plowed and clear, but twenty yards after turning off onto the dirt road where his father had met his death, passing those old metal gates, the car hit a drift it couldn't handle and sank into a foot of snow.

"Shit." He climbed out and felt his leg disappear to the knee in a mantle of smooth, unbroken white. The wind seethed and fretted over the plain, sifting restlessly through dry powder as if searching for something irretrievably lost. Midafternoon had begun to turn the shadows blue all around him.

Make your move.

Without actually making a formal decision to continue, he started following the road deeper into the woods. It felt much farther on foot. Twenty minutes from here, people were watching cable TV, reading *Harry Potter*, and surfing the Web, but out here it was still 1956.

Or 1882.

Why had he thought of that particular year? Of course he knew exactly why—it had been the decade of Rosemary Carver's disappearance. He remembered that now. What if time had somehow stopped then, and the same woodland animals that were alive then were alive now, watching him from the edge of the forest?

The woods are lovely, dark and deep. But I have promises to keep—

The cliché of thinking about Robert Frost in a New England forest brought him a fleeting moment of comfort, but the wind was there immediately to wipe it away. Up ahead, the road curved into its final turn, trees retreating into snowy openness, everything so different when he experienced it like this, larger and more immediate. He could've sworn the road hadn't gone this far, that the forest wasn't quite as thick here. But that wasn't possible, of course—there was only one dirt road off the old country highway. This had to be it.

He came out of the trees and saw the house. *Eyeless.* A peculiar adjective, since there were plenty of windows, and since—

Even from this distance, it seemed to be staring back at him. It made him think of the painting he'd found, and it occurred to him that this was the exact angle that it had been painted from. He wondered what it would be like to see a shadow moving inside the house, past the windows and behind the curtains.

There are other ways of watching.

"Stop that shit," he said, hating the way his voice shook.

Fresh tire tracks marked the snow around him. Someone had been here recently. He pulled out his cell phone and dialed Fusco's.

"Scott," Sonia's voice answered. She must have recognized the number on caller ID because her greeting was a statement, not a question. In the background, he could hear glasses clinking, men's voices, the brisk snap of a cue ball.

"Is Owen there?"

Dark and deep.

"Not yet," she said, "but he'll probably be."

"What about Red?"

Long pause. "What's this about?" Sonia asked, and when he didn't reply: "Listen, I'm working till midnight. Why don't you drop by and we'll talk?"

Promises to keep.

"Sounds good." As he spoke, he was still making his way toward the house, careful steps, never taking his eyes off the door. Less than twenty feet from it now and the only sound in the world was the powdery scrunch of his boots through still-fresh snow. "But I've got some things I need to take care of out here first."

"Where are you?" Sonia asked, seeming to realize something as she spoke. "You're not— Scott, I don't think it's a good idea for you to go back into that house right now."

He stepped up onto the porch. "I'll be fine."

"What happened last night? We never talked about it."

"What happened sixteen years ago?"

She fell silent again but not for as long as he'd expected.

"We can talk about that too," Sonia said quietly.

"I'll see you later," he said, reaching for the doorknob.

Before he could touch it, it turned by itself, the door swinging open to reveal the face of the woman standing just behind it, grinning at him.

CHAPTER THIRTY-FIVE

BEER. WHISKEY. BEER.

Sonia wasn't happy with the way the phone call with Scott had ended. Truth to tell, very little about the conversation pleased her, though some part of her realized the last thing he'd mentioned—what happened sixteen years ago—had been inevitable. Getting it out in the open would be a relief, but it would be painful, lancing the wound for the therapeutic value of it. And there were always other types of therapy.

Beer. Beer. Tequila shot.

She poured them all, plus one for herself, Old Grand-Dad, throwing it back before loading up the tray, feeling the hungry stares as she lifted it up, her breasts rising beneath her T-shirt, all part of the show, tips for tits, and wasn't she proud?

"Thanks, Sonia."

"Lookin' good, baby."

"Keep the change, doll."

From over by the pool table: "Yo, sweetheart, can we get another round over here?"

"You got it," she said. Beer, beer, whiskey. Most of them weren't even particular about the brand, and those who were, she already had their preferences down pat, either Budweiser, Miller, or Molson Canadian, if they were feeling exotic. Her whiskey drinkers were all Jack Daniel's or Jim Beam men, except for—

"Macallan, light rocks," Red muttered, easing out of his coat as he took his seat beside an empty stool. "And a drink for my friend."

Sonia's retort—*You've got one?*—stuck in her throat when she saw Owen Mast coming through the door with Henry at his heels, the boy looking even more lost and forlorn than usual. Sonia felt the sunburned sting of fresh rage moving from her spine outward toward her scalded skin, and Red must have seen it too, because he reached out and touched her hand with his, covering it.

"I'll take care of this," he said, holding her stare. "Okay?"

"He shouldn't be in here," Sonia heard herself growl, like a caged cat. "Not after what happened last night. I don't want to see him here."

"Relax, princess."

"I hate it when you call me—"

"Hey, gorgeous," somebody called out, "how about a stiff one?"

Uproarious laughter greeted this never-before-heard witticism. Sonia nodded, distracted, but Red was already raising one hand, beckoning Owen over to the bar. "Hey, there he is, alive and well. Come on over."

Owen hesitated suspiciously, his boy waiting behind him, an acolyte before his father's hesitation. Sonia knew that his next move would be straight to the stool next to Red's, where the three of them—Red, Owen, and Henry—would line up at the bar like some weird diagram of manhood in reverse.

"What are you drinking?" Red asked. "Let me guess: Budweiser with a Jack Daniel's back."

But Owen didn't answer, and he didn't take the stool next to Red's. For an instant, he seemed conflicted about which way to go, and then he turned and walked up to the little stage in the front of the bar, where the three-piece country bands sometimes played on Friday and Saturday nights. Tonight there was just an acoustic guitar up there, property of a local troubadour named John Austin, currently parked at the other end of the bar nursing a Maker's Mark over crushed ice. The singer wasn't even watching as Owen climbed up onstage, but Sonia was, and so was Red.

"Whoa, buddy," Red said, half smiling, approaching Owen slowly, like an animal he didn't quite trust. "I don't think you wanna do this, do you?"

Owen ignored him and looked out at the crowd of curious faces gazing up at him. The pool game had paused, and the players were watching with morbid curiosity as Owen picked up John Austin's guitar and leaned in toward the mike. He tapped it once, satisfied that it was live, and took in a breath. Sonia, who had seen Owen humiliate himself in the bar too many times to count, experienced the nearly overwhelming urge to cover her eyes, or at least shield Henry's view, but she knew it was too late. Even Red had stopped trying to prevent Owen from whatever he was about to do. There was no other choice now but to hope he kept it short.

"Tonight," Owen said, "I'd like to play a song I learned from my grandpa Tommy."

He struck a single chord on the guitar, and the entire bar fell silent. There was nothing ragged or reluctant about the sound: It was perfect. Sonia had never heard Owen play before—had no idea he even could play—but the chords poured effortlessly from the guitar, one after another, Owen rocking slightly forward with the strings under his fingers as he put his mouth to the microphone.

When he sang, his voice was a rusty croak, worn-out and reed-thin:

> *Tall man, tall man, dressed in black . . .*
> *Come to take his daughter back . . .*
> *Walkin' down that lonely road*
> *Walkin' down that lonely track . . .*

He picked out a few more notes on the guitar, fingers moving nimbly now, not missing a lick, coming back to sing:

> *Cross him once, you'll learn the way*
> *Cross him twice, you'll rue the day*
> *He's the man, the devil's own*
> *Come to take his daughter home . . . .*

There were more lines to the song, but the guitar overwhelmed them, and Owen hung back from the mike, croaking words that Sonia couldn't hear. When he finished, the bar was utterly silent. Then somebody started to clap. Another patron joined in. A moment later, the bar was full of the sound of applause and cheers. Rather than acknowledging any of it, Owen just stepped down to the bar, back to where Henry sat on his stool, gaping at his father in total disbelief.

"Listen to that," Red said. "You hear that, Sonia? Get the man a drink."

"Red," Sonia said, "I don't think this is—"

"Just one. Whatever he wants."

"Not unless he wants coffee," Sonia said.

"What?" Red's smile wilted a little in disbelief. "You're denying us service now?"

Sonia realized that she was. Maybe it was the thrill of hearing Owen get up onstage and hammer out a song that set them all on their ear. In any case, it felt good to deny Red something. Why hadn't she started earlier? "Bingo," she said.

"All right." Suddenly the former football player's cordial expression looked painted on and already beginning to peel. "Fair enough," he said, no longer looking at her, dumping a pile of bills on the counter. "Come on, Owen, there's friendlier places to get shitty, even in this shitty town."

"Owen," Sonia said, "wait."

Red was still counting out crumpled ones and fives, but Owen paused and glanced up. Whatever had possessed him to get up onstage and play the song seemed to have fled. Now he only seemed bewildered, as if he'd been asked to choose his allies in a skirmish where moments before he'd thought everyone was his friend. Underneath it, though, buried not very deeply, she saw a low species of degraded need. None of those emotions reflected in the boy's face. Now, as ever, Henry just seemed to be drowning in an ocean that only he could see.

"You sure you don't want that coffee? On the house."

Owen opened his mouth, and Red said something she didn't catch.

"At least let Henry stay here. I've still got that bed in back. I'll make sure he gets home all right."

"Sure, kid." Red ruffled the boy's hair. "Have fun." Then, to Owen: "You ready, compadre? 'Cause Uncle Red's buying, all night long."

"Owen," she said, "you don't have to do this."

This time Owen didn't even look back.

CHAPTER THIRTY-SIX

THE WOMAN IN THE DOORWAY of Round House stood absolutely still. Shadows from inside the house obscured the upper part of her face, but he recognized her voice at once, and even if he hadn't, he would have recognized her smell.

"Hi, Scott," she said.

"Colette?" His foot, the one that had been raised to step inside, came back down on the porch. "What are you doing out here? I didn't see your car."

"I parked around back, out of the snow."

By the pond, he thought, remembering what Aunt Pauline had said. Colette stepped aside and he came in. From somewhere in the house, he heard a soft, steady tapping sound like water dripping on a cymbal, echoing outward, louder than before.

He took off his coat and draped it over the banister, knocked the snow from his boots, and saw Colette watching him from the entryway. Standing motionless next to the wall of the foyer, she looked as if she could've been part of the house herself, a wooden carving or figure engraved into the mantel—a permanent addition to the place. She was smiling, a distant, almost sleepy smile, with hooded eyes, and she was holding something, a long cardboard tube.

"I brought you something."

Scott took the tube and opened it, sliding the brittle contents into the palm of his hand. "Blueprints?"

"I found them out in the granary," she said. "They're for this house."

"Thanks."

"Don't you want to look at them?"

I already did, he almost said, but something inside stopped him. Without a table to spread the pages across, he squatted on the floor and opened them up, Colette bending down opposite him to hold her side flat. She was wearing a low-cut blouse, unseasonably light, particularly given the lack of heat inside the house, and, as she bent down, Scott couldn't help but notice the surgically bolstered swell of her breasts, their curvature accentuated even more with the help of a red push-up bra. Her nipples were erect, plainly visible through the flimsy veneer. Despite everything, their appearance had exactly the desired effect on him. Colette reached up with one hand, tucked a strand of fallen hair behind one ear, and looked at him.

"Did you see this?" she asked, pointing at the corner of the page. Scott read:

Final Approved Layout—Round House
Designed by Zimmerman, Vesek, Lister & Lynn,
Architects, Manchester, N.H.,
for Mr. Joel Townsley Mast,
1871

A page he hadn't seen before, or a detail he'd overlooked. Scott read it over three times and looked up at Colette. "It must have been my great-great-grandfather," he said. "He built the house?"

"It was always in your family."

"Then what were you doing with these?"

"I'm the town historian now." With a shrug, Colette lifted her fingertip, allowing her side of the blueprints to scroll up. "I'm glad you're back, Scott. You never should have left." She started walking down the hall, and he realized where she was going—the dining room. "You've been a busy boy."

"What . . . ?"

"I've been reading your book while I waited. I hope you don't mind."

In the makeshift dining room office, Scott saw the pages of his father's manuscript neatly stacked on one side of the air mattress. On the other side was the laptop, its screen bright, half full of text, where she'd come to the end of what he'd written. Next to them, a glass and the bottle of gin stood in what looked like the final dying ray of afternoon sun.

In the corner of the dining room, the oak door stood ajar. He went over and, very carefully, pushed it shut, hearing the bolt click.

Colette watched him. "Your father had quite an imagination."

"Apparently it runs in the family."

"Maybe I can help you get all this figured out. The McGuires have always supported the arts, and I've got a soft spot for lost causes." Now she was turning around, her hands slipping out to find him closer than he'd expected to be. "Being one myself."

"Colette . . ."

"Hush."

"Listen—"

"Remember the night you brought over my prom dress?"

"Stop it," he said thickly.

"This is our last chance." Her tone had changed from effortless flirtation to something more desperate. "It might work this time, you know?"

"What m—"

Her lips were already on his, covering the last of the words, licking them up with soft, spruce-flavored flicks of her tongue. As they stumbled backward across the room, Scott felt himself responding thoughtlessly, a clumsy man falling into a dream. He could feel her fingers gliding expertly over the topography of his body, and then they were sliding back on the air mattress, papers spilling sideways, the glass falling over with a clink, out of the sunlight.

It wasn't right. It didn't matter. Now a wholly different part of his brain was in control, some animal element that something, maybe the medication, had numbed for years. She was already on top of him, heat and weight sloping forward to envelop him, his own body making decisions he couldn't control even if he'd wanted to, and he didn't. What he wanted to do was pin her down and maul her, yank her hair, abandon all pretense of uncertainty for one remaining thing that was hard and strong and uncompromised. And it was already happening. Even now their clothes seemed to be dissolving between them, falling away on their own, leaving nothing but the heat of her flesh brushing against his in an intoxicating rhythm of friction. Scott put his hand down between her legs, instantly aware of how wet she was, and slipped himself inside of her. She felt slick and tight, gripping him with the perfect amount of tension. Rocking his hips forward, he pushed all the way in.

"Oh God." Colette locked her ankles around his hips and dug her nails into his back. "Oh my God. Deeper—come on. Do it. Hurt me."

Her grasp on his shoulders was almost unbearable. He shoved her flat against the floor and thrust harder, ramming forward and down with all his strength. Moments later, naked and sweating in his arms, both of them slamming into each other, breathing hard together, she began to scream.

It caught him off guard and he stopped, but she grabbed him and pulled him on top of her even harder, the heat pouring up from her skin now like something beyond fever—almost as if she were going to burst into flames. When Scott finished, she lay back, gasping, staring at the ceiling. The house lay silent around them, listening.

"Burn it," she said.

BURN WHAT? THE HOUSE? The book? The whole damn town?

Scott realized he'd been in a daze, perspiration drying cold across his chest, when she'd spoken. Feeling the air mattress bulge, he sat up and saw Colette sitting naked with her back to him, clicking through pages on the laptop, the milky purity of her skin showing the delicate shadow-knobs of her spine.

"I think we've had enough burning around here, don't you?"

Click. Click. She kept scrolling upward without a backward glance.

"I talked to Red about the Bijou demolition project." He stood up and started getting dressed. "Owen's convinced that your people found something there."

Click-click-click. "Did he say what it was?"

"A body," he said. "Bones."

The clicking noise stopped. Scott felt a breath of cold air winding through the room from the door in the corner, touching every inch of his still-damp flesh, and felt suddenly vulnerable, exposed. The cold was followed by a terrible smell, nauseatingly sweet, like a box of rotten chocolates. On his forearms, the hairs stood straight up. He was abruptly aware of his own breathing, an in-and-out relationship with life that could end at any moment, for any number of arbitrary reasons.

"That night of the fire," Colette said, "I was there."

Scott blinked. His eyes were watering. "At the Bijou?"

"I saw it all." Colette turned around, legs bent, calves crossed, hugging her knees, and shivered. Had she felt the cold blast too, smelled that rancid smell? "The whole thing."

"What happened?"

"With Henry's mother," she said. "I never told anybody this."

"You knew her?"

"She was just a local nobody—small-town trailer trash from the ass end of nowhere—but her mother worked at our house as a maid. She and Owen had known each other for a long time. And the two of them . . . They must have found some time to be alone with each other, pretty early on."

"What do you mean?"

"She and your brother had another child years before Henry, a son, back when Owen was only sixteen."

Scott opened his mouth and couldn't say a word.

"The girl herself was underage. Supposedly she had a brain tumor in her pituitary gland that had caused some kind of, I don't know, precocious puberty at age thirteen. It didn't matter. Owen was all over her. When he got her pregnant, her parents took her away to have it taken care of."

"Abortion?"

"That was the rumor, but she must have changed her mind. A couple of years passed and I saw them in the theater that night, her and the kid. Owen didn't know until he started running up the aisle. He grabbed the boy, but . . ." She shook her head. "He stumbled, lost his footing in the rush. The boy slipped away—fell from his arms. . . . Owen lost him in the fire. He just kept running."

"And you saw all this happen?" Her explanation felt incomplete, almost like an alibi. "Were you friends with this girl?"

"Are you kidding?" Colette snorted. "Her mother worked for my family—I treated her like shit. She was just like a toy to me, a cheap thing I could break and fuck with and nobody would even know, let alone care."

"What happened to the girl after the fire?" Scott asked.

Colette licked her upper lip. "She disappeared again. From what I've heard, nobody in town saw her until five years ago, when she came back to Owen and he got her pregnant a second time . . . this time with Henry. That was the last anybody saw of her." Colette shook her head. "You know what I used to remember most about her? She always looked exactly the same age she was when he'd first knocked her up. She was tall for her age. Gawky, with breasts and hips. I remember how she used to walk, like she was pigeon-toed or something. And she was always wearing the same cheap blue dress."

Scott felt vertigo take hold of his inner ears. It rose up so fast that he almost fell over. "Blue?"

"Yeah, total Salvation Army special."

"What was her name?"

"Enough talk." Colette shook her head. "Let's do it again," she said, reaching over to touch his thigh. "Come on. It'll be even better this time. I bet I can even make you scream."

He pushed her hand away, never taking his eyes off her. "What was her name?"

For the first time since the conversation started, Colette dropped her gaze, tightening her grip on her legs as if she might somehow curl into a ball and disappear altogether. She was rubbing the inside of her wrist with her thumb, pressing down on the ugly little scar that Scott had noticed the first time he'd talked to her.

"Please don't," she said. "It'll just ruin everything."

"Tell me."

"You don't understand." She was starting to cry now, and it was ugly, tears and snot running down her nose. "I can't . . . If I do—"

"What was her name?"

Colette's attention turned to the laptop next to the pile of manuscript pages spilled indiscriminately across the dining room floor. All the life had gone out of her. It happened just like that. "You already know."

"How would I know?"

"Her name was Rosemary," she said. "Rosemary Carver."

CHAPTER THIRTY-SEVEN

OWEN LOST COUNT OF HOW many drinks Red bought him after the fourth round. The two of them were huddled in one corner of the Studio Lounge, Milburn's other bar, where the gender ratio wasn't quite so skewed and the drinks often arrived pink and sweet with a slab of pineapple dangling off the rim, if not an actual umbrella. At one end of the bar, a two hundred–gallon aquarium bubbled, and Owen found himself wondering drunkenly how it would be if that fish tank were your whole entire world. The treasure chest at the bottom of it, he wondered, would you think the gold was real?

"You ready for another one?" Red asked, tapping the empty glass.

"I ought to . . ." *Get going* was how that sentence was supposed to end, a simple enough sentiment, but Owen got lost somewhere in the middle of it. What he found instead was a fresh tumbler of bourbon, a sight and smell that he normally equated with pleasure, now making him feel slightly queasy. It looked as if the bartender had filled it up to the rim.

"Bottoms up," Red said.

Owen shifted his focus from the aquarium to the ruddy blur of

Red's face in the foreground, smiling companionably, watching the Patriots slaughter the Redskins and occasionally flicking his gaze over at Owen. Right now Owen felt just drunk enough to ask about the demolition site, to confide in Red about what he'd remembered from the night of the fire, but—

But maybe he *wasn't* drunk enough, because something stopped him, something in his gut told him not to raise the subject. Why? Wasn't Red his friend? Owen thought he probably was, but at the same time, he sensed some hidden agenda in the evening, Red getting him drunk to find out how much he knew about the Bijou.

Why?

Owen didn't know. Something to do with his wife? Crazy. Colette would never have said anything to Red. But he particularly didn't like the way Red just kept feeding him drinks, watching how fast Owen put them away and making sure the bartender—a gangling corpse of a guy whom everybody called Old Vincent—kept them coming. When they'd first walked in, Red had passed Old Vincent a Visa Platinum card, put it down on the bar, and opened a tab. At the time, Owen had been sober enough to see that the name on the card was Colette McGuire.

No surprise there. Ever since he'd gotten remarried, everything that Red had, in one way or another, belonged to Colette, which meant that it belonged to the town. That was what people talked about when they talked about Red—how he'd been ass-deep in debt by the time the coroner's reports came through on his first wife, how he'd come up here with Colette because he didn't have a penny to his name. His truck, the house, the clothes he stood up in—all had strings attached to them, leading right back to Colette . . . and Milburn. Losing that would mean losing whatever he had left of the good life.

Like the Bijou Theatre demolition job.

"One more?" somebody asked, Red or Old Vincent, Owen wasn't sure, and the glass magically refilled itself before his very eyes. When precisely had he drained the last one? He could sense what was happening, but it was foggy, like a reflection in the mirror after a long, hot shower. Owen caught a glimpse of the paperback that Old Vincent was reading behind the bar, a *Star Wars* novel featuring a stormtrooper's severed head on the cover. The title of the book appeared to be *Death Troopers*. Owen wondered when the world had become all about death.

The world was spinning. Ice cubes tinkled in the glass, something with a paper umbrella in it. Everything tasted like bourbon. One more and it would be time to roll.

"Easy," Red said. "I gotcha."

"Where we going?"

"Take a drive."

Owen tried to nod, but the swivel mechanism in his neck wasn't working: His head held still, and the rest of the world wobbled back and forth on faulty ball bearings. Cold air chewed a hole in the bourbon fog, and he saw Red leading him out of the bar, snow in the parking lot looming up fast, and Owen was staggering on roller skates, groping for something to hold on to. He found Red's shoulder, as big and solid as a barn door.

"You're my friend, right?"

Red just chuckled something that Owen didn't understand, directing him into the passenger seat of the pickup. Before he got in, Owen caught sight of the gun case in the backseat, the lantern, and the rope. Suddenly every mistake that Owen had ever made in his life—from his first stolen pack of bubble-gum cards to his decision to follow Red out the door—seemed to be building up to this moment.

"Where are we going?"

Now Red's reply was plain enough. "Walk in the woods."

CHAPTER THIRTY-EIGHT

SCOTT TRIED OWEN'S CELL PHONE twice and both times was sent straight to voice mail. He hung up and dialed his next best guess.

"Fusco's," Sonia's voice said.

"It's me," Scott said. "Is Owen around?"

"He left an hour ago," Sonia said. "Maybe longer. With Red."

Standing in the foyer with the phone, Scott could feel Colette's eyes watching him from the dining room doorway, eavesdropping on the conversation. He expected that she would still be naked with her arms across her chest. But when he turned around, the room was empty.

"Where's Henry?"

"He's here at the bar, asleep in the back room," Sonia's voice was saying from the other end. Glasses clinked, conversation rumbled, along with a sibilant hissing he didn't recognize, like the oscillating basket-of-snakes static you sometimes encountered on imperfect transcontinental calls. "What's going on?"

"I'm not sure," he said. "If he comes back, tell him to call me right away."

"Scott?"

"Yes?"

"Are you calling from inside the house?"

"Yeah, but—"

"Are you alone?"

"Yes. Why do you ask?"

"Do you hear that?"

Neither of them spoke; they both just listened, and Scott realized the background hissing noise had become slightly louder, shaping into recognizable sound. It was whispering, the words slipping out too quickly to be recognized, its cadences underscored with choppy little inhalations and pauses as if whoever it was couldn't draw a full breath. Moving again, Scott crossed the dining room, walking toward the door in the corner. It grew even more distinct until he could almost make out what it was saying—*house, help, hope*—and more urgent at the same time—*him, hurt, hit*—bursts of language rushing together. *Hate, hack, heart.* He reached out with his free hand and pressed it against the cold surface of the door.

"No!" The voice inside the cell phone became a deafening shriek. *"No, please . . . DON'T—"*

Grunting with surprise, Scott dropped the phone and withdrew his hand quickly from the door. The cell landed on the bare wooden floor next to his right shoe. He took a step back and regarded it with dull dread, like some enormous, revolting insect that had just crawled out from under a rock. Although it sounded as if the crackling, hissing sound had stopped, he didn't think he was going to be able to pick the phone up again, at least not anytime soon. Kicking it away from himself as hard as he could, though—now there was a possibility with some real promise.

He looked back across the dining room. It remained empty, with no sign of Colette anywhere. Apparently his lie about being alone hadn't been a lie after all.

"Colette?"

Alone in the house; that couldn't be right. She had been here with him two minutes earlier. Scott walked through the entryway to the hall leading to the kitchen, thinking she might have come here looking for another drink.

"Colette?"

The kitchen was also empty, a bare white oblong with its smoothed shelves and round counters undisturbed, all the cabinets closed, the sink polished and shining.

He closed his eyes.

Inside his eyelids, he could make out quite clearly the figure of Faircloth standing at the kitchen sink after his most recent murder, whistling softly to himself as he washed the cop's blood from his hands. Faircloth was holding some bright object under the stream of cold spring water—a tin star, the cop's badge, turning it over in his hands, scrubbing the red stain off the engraved letters with a child's toothbrush. Scott saw Faircloth picking up a hand towel and patting the badge dry, pinning it carefully to his flannel shirt, and then lifting a frying pan to admire his reflection in the makeshift mirror. A dull, ugly grin spread over Faircloth's face, seeping into his expression like mold in time-lapse photography. In Scott's mind's eye, he saw Faircloth's lips twisted around the words.

Howdy, partner.

Satisfied, he took the badge off and . . .

The image trailed away, leaving Scott staring into the empty cabinet of his own imagination: an audience member staring at a blank screen. *The Black Wing,* and the character of Faircloth, had already turned out to be much more real than he'd initially thought. He wondered now in an abstract way if that was who had been in his mind while he'd been thrusting into Colette, the stranger, the other who had enjoyed the sound of her screams.

Abandoning the kitchen, he went back down the hall to the dining room, where the laptop and manuscript still sat waiting by the air mattress. He sank down on the air mattress and settled the laptop on his knees. It was an awkward position, and the computer wobbled back and forth as he typed, but he didn't even notice.

```
Faircloth stood over the kitchen sink, hold-
ing the frying pan like a hand mirror, admiring
the badge on his shirt. He thought about how it
had been riding on Dave Wood's uniform just an
hour earlier--poor, unsuspecting Dave who had
come out here thinking he could trap Faircloth
into confessing to the murder of his wife.
```

"Who's wearing the badge now, Sheriff?" Faircloth asked. "Who's wearing that old tin star now, <u>partner</u>?" He began to sing the song he'd been whistling earlier, out loud and with great gusto. "We don't want the bacon. . . . We don't want the bacon. . . ." And for some reason, the very fact that he was here singing struck him as hilariously funny. He burst out laughing.

When the laughter subsided, he unpinned the badge and reached down, opening a kitchen drawer. It opened heavily, catching a little, already quite full. Faircloth pushed aside the pink hair clips, ribbons and bows, a lipstick, a compact, a torn-off button, a lollipop that had been licked only twice. It was stuck in the hair of a Kewpie doll, the kind you won at the state fair for tossing balls into milk bottles. A pretty pearl necklace. Bright and shiny things.

In the back of the drawer, two baby-food jars clinked together, one full of nail clippings, the other stuffed with hair--blond, brunette, black. Dave's hair was reddish brown. Faircloth decided he would trim a strand of that for the jar too.

Scott stopped and reread what he'd written. Although it wasn't at all what he'd intended for Faircloth's character or the novel as a whole, he knew intuitively that this was exactly what had to happen. Faircloth's true purpose had surfaced at last, like a splinter working itself out of the skin. In the end, Scott realized, Faircloth wasn't the victim of his wife's infidelity, an innocent man driven to murder. He was— had been—something much darker, perhaps from the outset. For the first time, it occurred to him that it wasn't the house that had done this to the man, but—

"But what?" he muttered.

You killed them all.

Scott stood up and looked at his hands, half expecting to find them covered once more in a layer of partially dried blood. They were clean but shaking badly, the palms slimed in sweat.

My great-great-grandfather . . . He built the house—

It was always in your family.

He felt his eyes drawn inexorably, terribly, back to the door in the corner of the room.

You said, "I killed them all."

No, I said—

The door was open again, just a crack.

He was a Mast, after all.

Her name was Rosemary Carver.

It was always in your family.

He was a Mast.

I'm a Mast.

Scott walked over to the door and slipped his fingers around the edge, now so smooth it felt almost shapeless. As always, he found a closet, nothing more. What had his father seen? An ocean swell of black feeling tumbled over him, so powerful and abrupt that he didn't have words to describe it. *Rage, confusion, dread*—all those different terms came close, but none quite captured the immediacy of what he felt. The sensation was like being buried alive, overwhelmed by the weight of his true inheritance. With an involuntary cry, he cocked his fist and thrust it forward with all his strength, smashing it into the back of the closet, drew it back and swung again, hard, fast, unhesitating.

Crash.

He hit it again and again.

Back, forth, crash. Back, forth, crash. It felt good—great, actually—sharp and hard, knuckles popping, smearing blood across the white wall, harder now, a solid thing, something he could beat against.

It was always in your family.

Whatever was missing from his family should have been back here. Whatever he should have inherited from his father, whatever manhood or understanding, this was where it should have gone. Instead, it was just a bare wall for him to beat himself bloody against, over and over, until—

Thump.

Scott stopped. Awakened from a daze of violence, he drew back his throbbing fist, gasping for breath, his arm already going numb to the shoulder. The room, perhaps the entire house, revolved dizzily around him.

He stared at the hole he'd knocked in the back wall, the thin plaster crumbling away. Leaning forward, he peered into the hole and the space beyond it but could see nothing.

The space on the other side was solid black.

CHAPTER THIRTY-NINE

OWEN PRESSED HIS FOREHEAD against the window, watching the snowy woods. The glass felt good against his face. Red was driving them down the snow-covered highway outside of town. It was very dark, and every now and then the truck's wheels would skid a little across patches of black ice. But it was okay. Red was a good driver.

"Where are we going?" Owen had a feeling he'd asked that question before, perhaps more than once, but Red just nodded patiently at the spotlight and the guns stowed behind them.

"Jack a deer," he said. "There's a ton of 'em out here."

"Too cold."

"Bullshit." Red made a mild scoffing sound in the back of his throat. "It's all instinct. You've done it a million times."

"Sleepy."

"Here." Red swung off the highway through the trees and lunged into the whiteout of an unmarked country road. Owen saw an iron gate. It reminded him of the gates of the cemetery where his mother was buried and something else too—he couldn't think of what it was. Twenty or thirty yards down the road, the engine shuddered to a halt.

Red flicked a switch and the headlights disappeared, drowning them in darkness. There was a rustling sound as Red's arm brushed past him on its way into the backseat, followed by another click, one that could have meant anything. Owen felt a chill having nothing to do with the temperature spreading up and out from his pounding heart, and he felt himself waking up and becoming sober, which only made the panic more acute.

"Watch out," he said. "I'm gonna puke."

"Take it easy," Red's voice said mildly, from somewhere in the void. Under the heavy canopy of pines, in the middle of the New Hampshire woods, it was so black that Owen couldn't see his hand in front of his face. *The dome light,* he thought, with sudden hope. *It'll come on if I open the door. All I have to do is—*

He found the latch and tugged on it, the door clicking open, but something was wrong and no light came, only freezing air, sawing straight through his jacket and skin into his bones, making him cough and splutter and shiver like an old man.

"Hold on." Red's whispering voice was no longer to his left. Now it was in front of him, outside the truck, mingling with the icy wind. "You're going to hurt yourself."

Owen's hands groped vacancy. "Where's the lights?"

"I turned 'em off. They scare the deer away." A hand clamped on to Owen's forearm, the pressure just shy of painful. "Take it easy. Your eyes'll adjust." The hand pulled him out of the truck, and Owen stumbled, nearly falling into the snow. He found his balance at the last possible second, felt the snow piled thick and fluffy up to his knees, so dark. A penlight winked up, and Owen saw the planes of Red's face floating in front of him, Red's eyes examining him, flat and expressionless.

"Let's talk about my wife," Red said.

Owen swallowed hard. Somehow, even up till this very minute, some part of him had hoped that he'd been wrong about why they were out here, that he'd just been paranoid. Now he realized he had been right all along. *He knows,* Owen thought. *He knows everything.* "Please, don't . . ."

"I loved you like a brother." Red's voice was mellow, unhurried, the words rolling off his tongue. "Nobody else in this whole town treated you that way, not even your real brother. They all think you're just a worthless drunk, but I always stood up for you. No, you've got him wrong, I always said."

"I'm sorry," Owen whispered. "Look, Red, you gotta believe me, it was—"

"Never mind me." Red's expression hardened even further in the penlight's minuscule glow. "Let's talk about Colette."

Owen swallowed, tasting bourbon, snot, and dirty snow. The urge to throw up was almost overwhelming now, but he was afraid if he started, he wouldn't be able to stop. He could already hear the next thing Red was going to say: *I know all about what happened between you and her, so don't try to lie about it.*

"You know," Red said, "how important that Bijou Theatre project is to her."

Owen blinked and stopped swallowing, wondering if he'd somehow misheard. He found himself able to meet the other man's eyes for the first time.

"What?"

"Don't play dumb—the demolition project, the theater. I know your family's all tangled up with that fire, and there's a lot of, what do you call it, hurt feelings there. But do you have any idea what it's going to do to her if word gets out that you and your kid have been finding bodies down there, corpses that she's covering up?"

Owen could only shake his head.

"You talk too much, Owen." Now Red sounded regretful, almost sad. "Delia was the same way. I loved her, God knows, but in the end, she just didn't know when to shut up. Come on, let's go." The penlight dimmed out, blackness returning to engulf the scene and Owen felt his whole body liquefying, becoming formless as a rustling noise filled the night. Red grabbed his arm, practically dragging Owen along. "If there's one thing I can't stand, it's a—*ow!*" There was a dull thud and Red's voice broke off with a grunt of pain. "What the hell?"

The penlight winked back on. Very dimly, Owen saw Red standing in front of a car, half buried in the snow. Even in his current drunken stupor, Owen recognized it. It was his brother's rental car, the Saturn . . . but what was it doing out here in the middle of nowhere? All at once, Owen remembered the old house Scott was renting. He had never been out to see it, for reasons he would never be able to articulate past the old recurrent nightmare of the thing outside his window, shouting his name in the night.

Red crouched down, shining the light inside to make sure there was nobody in there. When he was satisfied, he turned to look at Owen.

"They say these woods are haunted," Red said. "Colette's old aunt told me they're full of unquiet spirits, the walking dead. So I thought, what better place to take the least quiet guy I know?"

"I don't get it."

"You will."

"Red?"

"Yeah, pal?"

"You aren't gonna hurt me, are you?"

Red just smiled.

THE TRUTH WAS, Red had *never* meant to hurt the dumb bastard. Lashing out at a guy like Owen would have been redundant anyway—he was his own worst enemy. All you had to do was stay out of the way and let him do all the damage himself. Case in point: his entire life. But Red did intend to throw the fear of God into him, make good and damn sure he didn't forget who was in charge.

Red had the whole thing planned out. On the way home from the woods, he would pat Owen on the back and say, *I don't ever want to hear any more loose talk about bodies in the basement of the Bijou Theatre again, you get me? Or next time, you're not coming back from the woods.*

Because . . . Well, dammit, there *was* something else that Red hadn't mentioned about the Bijou project: It was his last chance with Colette. A few weeks ago she'd noticed how much cash he was withdrawing from the joint checking account. The bitch *never* looked at bank statements when they'd first gotten married. And she'd started asking some increasingly uncomfortable questions about where he'd spent his time, and with whom—specifically Sonia Graham.

The weird part was how cool Colette had been about the whole thing, almost as if she'd known all along. Red had said he was sorry, begged her for another chance, promised he'd turn himself around—take charge of the Bijou project and get serious about the family business. And Colette had just stood in her corner, a White Russian in her hand and a maddening little half smile on her face, probably already mentally calling her lawyer. At that moment, Red was visited by a painfully vivid glimpse of his future—divorced, broke, thirty-eight years old, living in a one-room apartment somewhere in Dorchester with his newspaper clippings and a bunch of old glory days stories nobody wanted to hear.

I won't blow this, he'd promised her, forcing a loving sweetness into his voice that he didn't feel. *I'll make it right, baby, I promise.*

And she had just nodded, still holding her drink with that mocking little quirk of a smile. Two ways to wipe that away, a kiss or a slap, and Red trusted himself with neither. Instead, he'd taken a deep breath and mentally promised himself one more roll in the hay with that little librarian—Sonia Graham was becoming *way* too much trouble—and the thought calmed him down enough to just walk away.

So here they were, he and Owen, out in the woods, taking the first step toward making things right. Although Owen hadn't even seen the house yet, he was standing here looking sufficiently scared. In fact, he looked *terrified,* pissing in his boots, as if he really thought Red had hauled him out here to shoot him. Red thought about that, and the little smile on Colette's face, the combination adding up to something bigger, but what?

Then, out in the woods, in the dark, something crackled.

"Jesus Christ." Owen spun around, his eyes huge, looking everywhere at once. "What was that?"

"Just a deer," Red said, but even he had to admit that it sounded much too big to be a deer. His thumb fumbled for the penlight, but it slipped from his gloved hand and plunged deep in the soft snow below them. "Hell." The penlight had been brought along for effect; why hadn't he carried a normal flashlight too?

The crackling of branches grew louder and closer, and then abruptly fell silent. Only the wind was moving now, a low, uneasy moan that rustled the trees. Red realized whatever was in the woods had either stopped its advance or entered the road ahead, which meant it was looking right at them from somewhere very nearby.

Except no animal would do that.

Red dropped to his knees and began feeling around for the penlight, cursing himself for not bringing the spotlight or the rifle. He'd only wanted to scare Owen, but—

"It's coming," Owen whispered. "Red, I hear it! *It's coming toward us!*"

"Shut up," Red muttered, more harshly than he'd intended. For the first time since Delia's death and the subsequent investigation, he felt a tickle of true fear in the pit of his belly, sickly and humiliating.

In the darkness, Owen screamed.

CHAPTER FORTY

THIRTY SECONDS—THE AMOUNT of time it took Scott to get back to the kitchen and find a rusty teapot that he could use as a hammer. Anything could be a tool, or a weapon. In the right helping hands.

Whose hand is holding on to you?

Wham. *Crash.* The hole grew slightly bigger. As a bludgeon, the kettle was hardly ideal, but at least it had a handle and a sharp edge to pound against the shattered plaster at the back of the closet, widening the opening that he'd begun with his fists.

Wham. *Crash.* Bigger.

Now the hole was large enough—a crooked oblong like the giant outline of an old man's misshapen head—and Scott reached in and started clawing out whole chunks of dusty white material, tearing down the wall in slabs. It came readily, willingly, *eagerly* even. Air gushed out, as if he'd opened a dam of invisible water, and he breathed it in—it was as cold as helium vapor. He gasped, his breath ghosting out of him in shades of gray and silver.

The odor hit him immediately.

It was like nothing he'd ever smelled before. Moldy, rotten, fetid—

a heavy physical shape that he could carve from the air and slap down on a petri dish for further study. It didn't belong anywhere near his nostrils or throat or lungs; it felt as if he were breathing in vaporized particles of actual human tissue. Scott gagged into a half-coiled fist, covered his mouth, clung to the hole he'd knocked in the wall.

In front of him, only blackness, with the odd, inarguable sense of vast open space, as if a whole hidden house were inside the walls.

Visibility—none.

Flashlight—no.

Something inside him murmured: *You don't belong here.*

Yet how could he walk away now, when he was so close to finding out what might be on the other side? He thought of the blueprints that Colette had brought over, left somewhere back in the main entryway. But what good would they be if he couldn't see?

I'm not going in there alone in the dark, I'm just not, no way, that's all.

Almost unconsciously, his hand sank in his pocket, found the heavy, rectangular shape of his father's lighter. He brought it out and thumbed the wheel, shooting first sparks and then a high, bright flame, and stared at the flickering space that was revealed.

The long, rounded corridor in front of him seemed to stretch on forever.

It was sparse and plain and narrow, with a curved concrete floor and smooth, almost circular black walls that didn't look as though they'd been painted black but were somehow sculpted out of naturally black material—some substance that literally absorbed light. There were no doors and no windows. Although the passageway appeared to be straight, there was definitely some bend to it, some winding quality just outside the lighter's glow.

Seeing it here in front of him, as real as it was, brought on an entirely new species of self-doubt. It occurred to him that this space, which existed exactly as it was described in his father's manuscript, might have been the last thing that the men in his family had seen before they finally lost their minds. Now he was seeing it too. He'd witnessed it once before and then snapped back to consciousness to realize that it was all a hallucination, but what if that last time had been a final warning, one he should have heeded? If he'd just put the manuscript away then, stopped working on it, and stopped thinking about Faircloth and his relationship to Rosemary Carver and her father—

Faircloth was a serial killer, and this was where he brought his victims.

But it wasn't really Faircloth, was it? No, Faircloth was nothing more than a puppet, a fictional character imbued with something much darker.

Scott pushed his way into the hole he had created, entering the black wing beyond.

He looked around, the corridor broadening so that he could no longer see the walls on either side. His foot bumped into something on the floor, a solid object that he almost tripped and fell over, and he bent down to study it. It was a leather shoe with the laces removed, age-rotted and smothered in dust. How old was it? He had no idea. Just beyond, the widening space slanted leftward. He turned, and a marking on the wall caught his eye—scratched into the black surface at shoulder level.

Scott held the lighter closer and saw that it was a date, eighteen hundred something. The rest was too worn away to decipher, or wiped away, as if someone had attempted an imperfect scrubbing job. As he looked down again to make sure he wouldn't trip, he saw a huge brown stain on the concrete, splattered out in every direction, and knew instinctively that it was a starburst pattern of dried blood as old as the floor itself.

He followed the passageway to the left, stepping carefully, and almost ran into the set of steel bars, like the door of a cell. It wasn't locked, and as he pulled it open, the high creaking sound of old iron grating in his ears, he felt speckles of rust flaking onto his hands. On the other side was the biggest space yet. Within seconds, he grasped the layout, despite the flickering insufficiency of the lighter's flame.

Oh no.

The chamber was divided into stalls on either side, not as black as the walls surrounding them. They had heavy wooden doors equipped with bolts that locked from outside. Inside each stall, Scott saw dirty floor and rusty chains bolted directly into the walls, with heavy manacles at the end of them. Tin bowls and cups, dried out for over a century, lay in the corners in the dust of old straw. One stall had a ragged, colorless shape he didn't recognize at first; upon closer inspection, it became a child's doll. Above it, on the pale wooden wall, was written:

The Lord is my Shepherd I Shall not Want He Leadeth me

The crooked, spidery letters trailed away to nothing.

Scott looked ahead. Up at the far end of the room was a long workbench, its corners carefully sanded off. As he approached it, he began to make out the shapes of tools, carefully organized for convenient access. Here were the sharp edges that he'd found nowhere else in Round House: axes, drills, a whole arsenal of hammers and chisels and clamps, pliers and wrenches, pincers and screws. Beyond that were archaic instruments that seemed to require some new vocabulary to describe—an awl, an adz, things even older and more arcane, items that hadn't been named since their invention a thousand years ago. Tools defined only by the hellish extremes of torment they inflicted on their victims. There was a stove, like a smithy's forge, an array of black rods standing in formation next to it—brands, pokers, and long, clawed metal andirons. A bellows and a sack of something slick and crumbled that he supposed might at one time have been coal. Hanging from a hook above it was a leather apron with thick straps and heavy metal buckles, stained so thoroughly with layers of dried brown that it probably would have stood up stiffly all by itself.

Scott picked up one of the hammers, a blocky thing with a spiked steel head, and looked at the name burned into the wooden handle:

FAIRCLOTH

The lighter flickered and then brightened again. Now the handle read:

MAST

With the hammer still in his hand, he looked back around at the stalls, realizing only now how many there were—how big this room had been made, in order to accommodate all its occupants. Eight stalls with two sets of chains dangling in each stall. He imagined his oldest relative back here, Joel Townsley Mast at the beginning of the family line, tending his secret life by the light of the forge. He would be dressed in the leather apron and perhaps nothing else, illuminated in that hivelike orange glow; sweating as he went about his work amid the screams and pleas and sobs that came from the stalls around him.

Scott's foot clanked over something, and he looked down to see a square trapdoor constructed of heavy wood with an iron ring.

He grabbed the ring and pulled.

It was too heavy. He couldn't lift it, couldn't even budge it.

One last try. He grunted, felt the muscles in his lower back and shoulders aching in protest. Then, unexpectedly, the door popped up, the ancient hinges squealing as the slab of wood was flung open.

Scott squatted down, the trapdoor balanced on his knee, and held the lighter down into the blackness, but it did no good. He saw only the very outer portion of a rusty metal pipe that ran straight down.

It smelled damp down there.

He could hear the soft but unmistakable gurgle of water—some kind of underground well, or . . . ?

It was inspired by an unfinished story that his great-grandfather had written, Aunt Pauline had said—

In front of him, in the last of the stalls, something moved.

He sucked in a gasp. The noise that he had heard was a slow crackling sound, and then it stopped. He thrust the lighter higher in the air, as if raising it might somehow make it brighter. Instead, the flame snuffed out completely.

Oh God.

Hands spread out from the darkness, stroking his face, cheeks, and the back of his neck like bundles of oily feathers. He couldn't scream. The palms smothered the noise before he could make it. Reaching up to pull them away, he felt only open space, as insubstantial as cobwebs. In the blackness, other hands groped at him, sticky, searching, but every time he moved to free himself, he found nothing but empty air.

The lighter—he still had it. He flipped the wheel, sparks flying, and in that instant, the faces flashed all around him, hollow-eyed, starved, stringy hair stuck to their skin, chained in their stalls awaiting further agonies or death. As one, their cracked mouths open to silently shape his name.

"No," he said, shaking his head.

He ran, clumsily, half blindly, one arm outstretched in front of him, rounding the bend where the corridor curved, blundering upward toward the place where the black wing joined the rest of the house.

As the voices of the house grew louder around him, Scott ran faster, his free hand clawing at his skin where he'd felt the hands touching him and, even now, feeling nothing there.

CHAPTER FORTY-ONE

OWEN STAGGERED BLINDLY in the dark woods, tripping and stumbling through the snow. His guts ached and his chest burned, but he kept moving, heedless of where he was going, knowing only that he had to get away.

The touch of the hand on the skin of his neck had been leathery and damp, sour-smelling, edged with ragged nails. He could still feel how the fingertips had lingered under his chin, somewhere between a grab and a caress, tilting his head to expose his throat. Screaming, Owen had twisted around as if to look at the thing, but the night's blackness filled his eyes to the brim.

"Owen!" That was Red shouting out for him. "Get your ass back here!" There was a crash, and the other man cried out in pain and surprise. "Oh shit! What the hell? What the fuck?"

Owen kept crashing along, arms outstretched, swiping aside pine boughs and branches. Whatever was behind him in the woods, he knew he had no real chance of outrunning it—not because he'd gotten a good look at it, even when it touched his throat, but simply because he knew what it was, on some primal level, had always known.

It was the man.

The man from Grandpa Tommy's song.

Tall man, tall man, dressed in black—

Owen winced. A sharp branch speared the side of his face, raked a streak of pain into his cheek and brought tears to his eye. He was thinking about how foolish he'd been, how stupid to pick up that guitar and sing Grandpa Tommy's song.

Tall man, tall man, dressed in black—

I'm the one who brought you back—

Good God, had he invoked the thing by singing about it? He couldn't remember why he'd felt compelled to do that. Something else had just taken over him, and up he'd gone without another thought, but . . .

In the distance, he heard a laugh. He swung around, shoulders heaving, and stared back across the black terrain he'd just crossed. He couldn't hear Red anymore, couldn't hear anything at the moment except his own booming heart and labored breathing. His throat closed, his chest squeezing with panic.

Damn it, this was bad. This was so bad.

Tall man, tall man—

His steps faltered, wobbling and disjointed, knees too weak to propel himself forward. Whatever was behind him in the woods, he could sense it growing silently closer, stalking him, as if it were herding him deeper into the forest. Toward what, and why?

Fear struck a series of reverberating notes down his back. Abruptly he felt as if he were going to lose all control. Remembering the song that Grandpa Tommy had sung him made him feel even weaker and more afraid, a cowering child in an overgrown man's skin. What was wrong with Grandpa Tommy anyway, that he had to sing that song to Owen when he was a kid, Grandpa's face pale and scared like a junkie, stupid old fingers trembling so hard he could barely hit the right chords?

Movement in the trees behind him now, branches crackling. Owen held his breath and was unable to repress a soft, nasal-sounding whimper. The noises got closer. This was it. Giving way to near hysteria, he felt a terrible looseness spreading through his lower abdomen, as if he were pissing himself or bleeding out. Feet shuffled off to his right, the muffled thump of boots in snow.

"Owen—"

Red staggered into him, practically bowling him over. Red's fists found Owen's coat, grasping its collar, dragging him down in a wet snowdrift.

"Red?"

"Stay low. You hear me?" The other man's voice was a shaking whisper in his ear. "Don't move."

"Red—"

"I saw him," Red hissed, "I can hear the son of a bitch. He's back there in those trees."

"We have to get out of here." Owen's eyes felt as big as fishbowls, still not nearly big enough to take in the volume of the night. "It's not human."

Red didn't say anything. He hunkered down next to Owen in the snow, staring hard off at the copse of trees they'd just come through. Owen could feel the wind starting to rise up again from behind him, blowing back in that direction, and thought, *It's carrying our scent back to him. He'll be able to smell us.*

Red elbowed him hard. "That way, over there." He was clutching something that Owen hadn't noticed before, what looked like a pocketknife, pointing deeper into the woods. "There's a slope, the ground goes down into some kind of clearing. I can see lights down there."

Owen looked and saw them too, yellow and white that glimmered through the crooked branches like cheap jewelry. At the same time, the noises in the trees behind them started again, a graceless shambling sound coming toward them. Barely thinking, he pushed off, found his balance, and rose to his feet, swiveling and barreling forward toward the downward slope, in the direction of the lights.

Don't look back. Don't look back.

The snow grew almost instantly thicker beneath him, wetter, harder to navigate. He heard Red grunting after him, the bigger man laboring to cut a path. On level ground, Red would be faster, even in the dark, stronger, more agile, years of professional football making him innately more powerful.

But this ground wasn't level.

Owen heard him fall.

He looked back.

In the second or two that he stood there gaping, he saw Red writhing around in the snow, trying to pull himself up. He'd done something to his leg, stumbled over a rock or root system hidden beneath the double treachery of snow and blackness, and twisted his ankle. He was muttering to himself, swearing, rubbing his leg, and struggling to regain his footing. Somehow he managed to stand and reach into his pocket for his cell phone, only to drop it again in the snow.

"Fuck," he said, and bent down again to look for it, laughing a little hysterically. He was still searching when the soft creaking noise up above sent a wet load of white slush sliding from one of the pine boughs.

The trees behind Red opened up, branches pushed aside. At the sound of snapping twigs, Red jerked his head around, mouth open to say something, and saw it. He tried to get upright, pawing at the snow, crawling forward. His head went up once, eyes meeting Owen's. "Help me," he said.

Then the thing came down on top of him with a thick, wet ripping noise, like muddy carpeting being pulled up. Underneath it, Owen heard the sound of something heavy and lifeless dropping into the snow.

He ran down the slope toward the lights.

He didn't look back again.

CHAPTER FORTY-TWO

SCOTT RAN BACK OUT of the black wing, the lights of the dining room hitting his eyes like blinding daylight. Slamming the oak door behind him, he scooped up the phone where he'd dropped it on the floor. The buttons were the size of pinheads, too small for his trembling fingers. Cell phones were not made for emergencies. He dialed.

"Sheriff's office."

"This is Scott Mast. I need to talk to the sheriff."

"Scott *Mast,* you said?"

"Yes, yes—"

"Can you spell that for me?"

"M-A-S-T," he almost shouted. "Mast, for God's sake. I need to talk to Sheriff Mitchell, it's an emergency."

There was a long pause, tinny music, and he realized he'd already been put on hold. He stood in the far corner of the dining room staring at the door. He needed to get away from here. He'd discovered what he'd gone to find—the wing itself, and the end of the story. Once the sheriff came out to look at the old addition, there would be investigations, perhaps even human remains located in the old stalls, certainly enough to—

"Hello?" said a brusque voice, not one he recognized, though it had to be Lonnie Mitchell.

"Yes, I need to report . . ." *What?* "I'm out here in a house north of town, and I found something you need to come out and see."

"We're a little busy at the moment, Mr. Mast. Or haven't you looked outside lately?"

"This is serious."

"What's going on?"

"It's a long story. Is there any way you could send somebody?"

"We're running a little low on manpower at the moment," the sheriff said. "We've got about two hundred households out there without heat and electricity. I've got every available man helping move these people into shelters before it gets any worse."

"This is an emergency," he said, and his voice must have conveyed what the words could not, because the sheriff sighed.

"What's the problem?"

Scott took in a slow, deep breath, aware that this might be his only opportunity to explain. "Part of this house, my family's old house, has an extra room behind a wall. I found it tonight, and it's very large. I went in and looked through the whole thing, and I think it might have been used as some kind of torture chamber."

Silence from the other end.

"Hello?" Scott asked. "Are you there?"

"I'm not in the mood for jokes tonight, Mr. Mast."

"Wait, don't—"

"Hang tough till morning. Tomorrow, if you're still alive, I'll come out and look at your torture chamber. Okay?"

"No, I—"

Click.

Scott stared at the empty room, the door in the corner, and then out the window into the snowy night. Twelve miles to town on foot, a three-hour walk in temperatures that he wasn't dressed for and a windchill factor of forty below.

Or you can stay here.

He went through the first floor of the house switching on every light he could find. Without any kind of flashlight or lantern, he was going to have to turn the entire house into one big lightbulb and hope it would get him as far as the road leading out to his car. He put on his

boots, coat, and hat, no gloves, thumped through the entryway and out
the door. Fine grains of snow peppered his face as he made his way
cautiously down the steps. He could feel himself breathing it in.

Get used to it. It's a long way to civilization.

From the moment he stepped outside, Round House loomed large
over him, dark despite all its faint illumination from within, a mon-
strous presence whose shapeless outline became even larger and more
imposing from the outside. His feet puffed into the loose white powder. Ankle-deep drifts off the front porch became knee-deep once he
started slogging through them, and he knew the roads would be
impossible to navigate even if he was somehow able to get the car free.

The car—he thought again about Colette. What had she said?

I parked around back.

He cupped his hands to his mouth. "Colette!" His voice impossibly
thin and faint in the night, the surrounding forest consuming it.
"Colette!"

He began walking around the outside of the house. Its great walls
stretched out endlessly, and Scott was aware of the presence of the
black wing, hidden somewhere inside beneath wooden planks and
chimney bricks, pulsing like a hollow poisoned heart. Beneath the
snow, the ground sloped downward. At last he could see the outer
western edge of the building at the border of the night, as if it marked
some final outpost beyond which nothing existed. In the starlight, he
saw something shimmer in the distance, the frozen pond.

His foot dropped into a packed-down spot—a tire track.

He followed it twenty yards to a bare spot in the snow, where the car
had obviously been parked until very recently. It was gone now, another
set of tracks, fresher ones, running in the opposite direction. In the
clear winter air, he thought he could still smell the exhaust, but there
was no sign of headlights anywhere in the distance. He was amazed
that she'd even been able to find the road, but if anybody could do it—

Turning back toward the house, Scott felt something bump against
his shoulder in the darkness.

He stopped and looked up.

It was a foot.

That's not what it looks like, his brain gibbered. *That can't be what it
looks like, because what it looks like is—*

The wind picked up, and Colette's body turned slightly on the rope that connected her neck to the tree branch above, her legs dangling at face level. One of her boots had fallen off to expose a stocking-clad foot. The wind had blown her hair into a snow-strewn tangle that fell over one of her eyes but left the other staring glassily down.

As he looked up at her, Scott felt the ground beneath his feet splintering, shearing off, shifting in two diametrically opposite directions and pulling him with it. On one side was madness; on the other, coherence. He already knew which direction he was tilting toward, and there was nothing he could do to stop it.

Yes there is. Pull yourself together.

That was hilarious. He was losing his mind, skating blindly toward the abyss. It was already too late. Then the wind changed direction, and her face twisted the other way, creaking, though the one revealed eye somehow seemed as if it were still fixed on him. Scott bit his lip, felt his thoughts coming back around, not to normalcy but at least coherence.

Colette, who did this to you?

The wind flipped up the bangs of her tangled hair, flashing her other eye. The rope creaked, shifting.

Or had she done it to herself?

He stared back at the bare spot where the tire tracks led. Someone had been here—had come across Colette and strung her up, left her strangling, and taken her car, and . . . and . . .

The wind blew. She was turning again, coming back around.

He had to cut her down.

Scott forced himself to reach upward toward the body. The rope was knotted just a few feet out of reach. It already looked as if it were coming unraveled, slipping under her deadweight. Without a knife or a saw, and some kind of ladder, he didn't know how he was going to free her. His mind flashed to all the sharp instruments inside the black wing. What about the kitchen? Wasn't there something there he could use?

He put one foot in front of the other and started back toward the house, moving as fast as he could in the snow, and behind him he heard something fall.

He stopped and looked back.

The rope had slipped the rest of the way off. She lay in a heap in the snow, the noose still hooked around her throat. Lumbering back to

her, bending down, he positioned himself to lift her body and heard—
what?

Something. A soft murmur of air escaping from her lungs.

Scott flinched, stared at her.

One of her eyelids twitched.

"Colette—" He started to pick her up again, hesitated—*what if her neck was broken?*—and realized he was going to have to take that risk. If this had just happened, there was a still a chance of getting her back. "Come on, girl. Come on. Hang in there."

Bad choice of words, asshole.

Straightening her out, Scott laid her on her back and touched her throat, but his fingertips were numb and he couldn't feel anything. He had to get her back to the house.

There's no time.

CPR training was mandatory at his job—the company got some kind of insurance break for offering it. He tilted her head back and mashed his mouth against her cold lips, the tissue lifeless, blowing two breaths in, then moved down to her chest, hands together, compressing hard thirty times. Something cracked—ribs. He went back to her mouth. Two breaths. Thirty compressions. He checked the pulse, felt nothing, tried to blame it on his numb fingers. How long were you supposed to continue? *Until help arrives.*

He breathed. Compressed. Checked for pulse. Felt nothing. No signs of life. In the distance, the wind rose up as if taking a special interest in his failure here, firing snow into his eyes before settling again. Colette stared up at him through eyes that were done seeing.

But I heard her make a noise. I could have sworn I saw her eyelid move.

Compressions.

Breaths.

Until help arrives.

That was a good one.

He kept pumping, already feeling the fatigue settling into his joints, and pushed on anyway. Not because it meant anything but because there was nothing else to do. The cold was starting to slow him down. He realized there was no way he could have made the long walk back to town.

After a while, he carried her into the house.

CHAPTER FORTY-THREE

BY THE TIME HE BROUGHT Colette back into the dining room, fetched a kitchen knife, and cut the rope from her throat, he'd already started thinking of her as *the body*. When you took away the pulse and respiration, what you were left with was just *the body*, wasn't it? And all the Red Cross training in the world couldn't turn *the body* back into a person.

He lowered her down onto the air mattress and took out his cell phone. Still two bars left on the battery, but when he dialed Emergency Services, the screen read:

NO SERVICE AVAILABLE

He knelt down and went back to work on her anyway, doing steadily diminished breaths and compressions until his shoulders burned and his muscles felt limp and toneless. In the end, he just stopped. Nobody could blame him for that. There was no longer any question about heart rate or respiration. After a certain point, you simply stopped, because it was just you, you were all alone, and you couldn't do any more.

Covering the body with the sleeping bag, he picked up the phone, dialed 911, and waited.

And waited.

His mind yammered with questions. Who had done this to her? If she'd killed herself, why, and why tonight? What had prompted her to go through with it here at the house? What happened to the car?

NO SERVICE AVAILABLE.

He couldn't stop looking at the purple bruise that had formed around her neck, like the tattoo of a necklace. Finally dragging his eyes away, he walked back to the dining room, where the sleeping bag lay draped over the shape on top of the air mattress. Kneeling down, he lifted the sleeping bag from Colette's face and forced himself to look down at her open eyes. One of her hands had fallen out and lay palm-up on the floor as if in beggar's supplication. Her lips were parted enough that he could see her tongue. The corpse would be heavy, he knew, and he still wasn't sure that carrying her out of the house was the right thing to do. He stayed there for what seemed like a long time listening to the snowflakes tick against the windows, pressing to the glass like a thousand eyes.

Gazing down at the upturned hand, he took his first real look at the scar on the inside of the wrist. He noticed now that the flesh had been cut in the shape of a crucifix, that Colette must have cut down and then made a shorter line across. When had she done that, how long ago? Had that been her first attempt, or were there others that hadn't left so obvious a sign? Who had saved her that time—or had she cut herself and then called the ambulance as soft pink clouds formed in the warm bathwater around her?

Scott touched the scar, found himself tracing the path of it with his index finger.

What if she sat up right now and grabbed me?

He reared back, utterly unnerved by the thought. Suddenly he didn't want to be in the same room with the corpse, not tonight in this house. Standing up, he made a deal with himself: He would walk once around the first floor, considering his options, and if he didn't come up with anything better, he'd wrap her up and carry her out on foot. Maybe cell phone reception would be better once he got closer to the highway.

He backed out of the room, unable to look away from her face. Too late he realized that in his haste to get away, he'd neglected to cover her face again. He could feel the dead eyes on him, their blank and accusatory stare. In the foyer, out of sight, he felt slightly more stable and, almost without thinking, took out the cell phone and hit redial for the sheriff's office, already thinking how he would handle getting her out of here. Bundling her in the sleeping bag would help, he thought. Maybe if he didn't have to look at her face—

The line was ringing. He was connected.

"Sheriff's office."

"This is Scott Mast again, I need to talk to the sheriff."

The sigh from the other end was audible even with the imperfect signal. "I'm sorry, Mr. Mast, but the sheriff—"

"I've got a dead body here."

He could feel the receptionist's voice processing this. "What was that?"

"You heard me."

"Hold on."

While he waited, Scott walked from the foyer to the first-floor landing and looked up the long staircase. He hadn't been upstairs in days. In fact, there were rooms in the house, locked and unlocked, that he had never seen—probably dozens of them. Whatever secrets they contained would remain a secret, at least from his eyes. His mother's epitaph came into his mind: *In my father's house are many mansions.*

"Mr. Mast? What the hell's going on out there?" Sheriff Mitchell's tone of impatience now bordered on rage. "What's this about a corpse?"

"I found her hanging from a tree," Scott said quickly, not minding how the words ran together. "I tried to bring her back, to resuscitate her, but . . ."

"A suicide?" Even Mitchell's anger couldn't hide the distinct impression of a man who'd abruptly found himself out of his depth. "Do you know the identity of the victim?"

"Colette McGuire."

"Oh." Then he heard Mitchell murmur in a low voice, to nobody in particular, "Oh shit. Are you sure?"

"I've got her here," Scott said. "I brought her into the house. I didn't know what else to do. I've been trying to call, but my cell phone couldn't get service in this weather."

"Where are you?"

"Round House, an old house outside of town. If you go north off Highway 12—there's a country road . . ." Directions failed him, and he thought feverishly: "Where my dad crashed his car."

"I know the place," Mitchell said. "And you're all by yourself out there?"

"Yeah."

"All right. I'll come out. It might take me awhile. Just sit tight, okay?"

Scott nodded. "All right." He put the cell phone away and sat down on the bottom step to wait.

CHAPTER FORTY-FOUR

AN HOUR WENT BY.

Without realizing it, he began to pace through the foyer and adjoining hallways, detouring around the far end of the first-floor corridor so that he could avoid the dining room. The dining room was where the body was. He didn't want to go back there unless he absolutely had to.

He kept the cell phone cupped in his hand and opened it every few minutes to make sure the battery still held a charge, in case Mitchell was trying to call him back. But the phone didn't ring.

He realized that along with trying to avoid the dining room, he'd started trying to avoid touching the house if at all possible. As he paced, he stayed in the middle of the halls to keep away from the slightly curved walls, and he only walked through doorways that he didn't have to open. He never stopped moving, never sat down, simply continued to circle and glance over his shoulder, checking his cell phone and putting it down again, reentering through the foyer, the hallway, and the kitchen, wishing he could somehow see all of it at once. He tried not to look at the rounded corners where the wall and floor came together, and he didn't look up.

The end of the hallway was in sight, the dining room, the gray edge of the air mattress just visible in the corner of the entranceway.

He turned away.

It didn't seem to make a difference. He could still feel her in there half covered by the sleeping bag, head cocked to one side with that bruise around her neck, waiting for him. Why in God's name hadn't he simply covered her face?

Do it now. Just go back in there.

Instead, he went back to the kitchen and made coffee, but when the black stream trickled into the pot, it came out thick as syrup, too bitter to drink. He pulled out the filter basket and saw that without realizing it, he'd filled it to the top with grounds, and dumped it into the trash, pouring the dregs down the sink. Behind him, in the kitchen doorway, a shape moved against the wall—the shadow of a tree in the porch light probably. He stared at the wall, waiting for it to happen again. It didn't happen again.

When his cell phone rang, he almost shouted out loud.

"Hello?"

"I ought to kick your ass," the voice on the other end snarled. It was Sheriff Mitchell's voice, but barely—there was some kind of animal inflection to it. "What the hell do you think this is, Mast, April Fools' Day?"

"Sheriff?"

"Tonight of all nights, to pull this shit. If I weren't so busy right now I'd drag you off to jail myself."

"Hold on," Scott said. "I don't know what you're—"

"Telling me you found Colette McGuire's body. You think that's funny? Is that your sick idea of a joke?"

"Sheriff, I'm not lying. I told you, I've got her corpse in my dining room."

"Oh yeah? Then maybe you can tell me what she's doing standing here in my office."

Scott couldn't breathe. He felt the sensation leaving his hands, so that it seemed the phone was hovering next to his ear all by itself. There was a rustle of the receiver changing hands.

"Hello?" a woman's voice asked. "Scott?"

He recognized her immediately, at least with the part of his brain that dealt solely with facts. He tried to speak her name and couldn't get past the first consonant.

"What's going on?" Colette said. "Sheriff Mitchell says you called him and told him you found my dead body out there . . . ?"

Now his entire arm had lost all muscular control. Vaguely, he felt the cell phone slide slowly from his ear. It snagged momentarily on the cuff of his shirt like the prop of some amateur sleight-of-hand artist, then fell to the floor.

From the far end of the hallway, in the direction of the dining room, he heard a thump.

IT WAS FOLLOWED by another noise, quieter but more sustained, like someone dragging a pile of heavy, wet rags and rotten leaves across the floor. Scott felt his tonsils swelling, blocking his airway until he couldn't breathe. Very faintly, from the cell phone that had fallen from his loosely curled fingers, he heard Colette's voice droning on, saying "Scott . . . ? *Scott . . . ?*"

He stayed exactly where he was. He did not want to walk up to the other end of the foyer, through the hallway that gave onto the doorway of the dining room, and find out what that thump had meant. He most definitely did not want to know what the soft slithering sound was, either. And he *especially* didn't want to know whether that oak door in the corner of the dining room had been slightly open when he'd been in there last time. He thought it might have been, but now that he considered, he just wasn't sure.

The house stood all around him, calm, motionless, awaiting his decision.

Scott turned around and slowly started walking back in the direction he'd come. It didn't take long. Twenty steps later, he stood in the doorway looking into the dining room where his laptop and the pages of his father's manuscript still sat.

The air mattress was empty.

The sleeping bag lay on the floor.

The body was gone.

And the oak door in the corner of the dining room, which he had gone through before and come running back and slammed shut upon return, *was* open.

Just a crack.

CHAPTER FORTY-FIVE

HE THREW THE FRONT DOOR open and stumbled outside, not feeling the cold.

On a purely physical level, he felt nothing at all. In fact it felt as though the entire sensory component of his brain were switched off, blown out, NO SERVICE AVAILABLE. All that mattered was the ground beneath his feet and the distance he could put between himself and the house.

He knew the rental car was somewhere up the road, and he was now convinced that he could push it out of the snowdrift himself with his bare hands if necessary. His vision had struck its own deal with the night, swallowing leagues of blackness in exchange for a murky but adequate view of the terrain. He trundled across the landscape like a machine, a thing comprised solely of pistons and levers, incapable of experiencing exhaustion. Even if it cost him some irreplaceable measure of humanity, he planned to just keep running.

Five minutes later, his cell phone rang.

He wavered, gasping, yanking it from his coat pocket, whirling around to look back at the house where it still shone dully through the trees in the distance, all lights on, calling him back to it like a beacon. Fumbling for the baby's fingernail of a button, he wheezed out something that didn't sound remotely like words.

"Scott?" It was Sonia. "Scott, are you there?"

He produced another garbled sound.

"Are you okay?"

He staggered, reeling with the question, the glow of the phone hovering before him like some luminescent deep-sea creature. "No."

"Where are you?"

"That road—by the highway—"

"I'm coming out."

"Road's blocked off."

"Get as close as you can to the highway," Sonia said. "Wait for me, you understand? Don't go anywhere."

And she was gone, leaving him once more to his own devices. The cold was finding its way into his joints now, his shoulders and knuckles and knees, filling them with silver. Scott stuffed the phone back in his pocket, balled his hands into fists, and broke back into the night, disregarding the sandpaper rasp of his lungs, ignoring everything but the path that lay ahead. He told himself he could run forever if it meant being away from the house and whatever was inside.

Up ahead, something crackled in the woods, loud enough that he could hear it even over his parched breathing. Dry pine branches snapped and popped as if the thing might be uprooting entire trees. Scott could make out the rough shape of it, and it was too big to be a deer, standing upright, watching him.

My eyes, playing tricks on me.

As if on cue, his eyes began to water, clearing, and for a stinging instant, he saw with absolute clarity the outline of a figure hunched in the road ahead of him. The man was squatting in the snow like an animal, his pants around his ankles. After a moment, he stood up, and Scott saw that he was a giant, probably seven feet tall. His pants were still down, and his enormous uncircumcised penis dangled between his pale legs like a length of rope, perhaps a foot long from root to head. Scott's mind whirled, coming close to madness, and he thought absurdly of all the legendary penises of history, John Dillinger's, Napoleon's. *Let us now praise great penises,* he thought, and startled himself with a croak of near-hysterical laughter.

The man glanced up at where Scott was standing and grinned furiously, as if sharing the joke. He turned to look down proudly at the enormous bloody pile he'd left steaming on the ground, then scooped up a handful of snow and wiped himself, threw it into the woods and pulled up his pants. As he stood there in the road, his grin did not change. But other parts of him seemed to be in *constant* motion: His limbs, even his trunk and torso, appeared to shimmer and roil as if his flesh were packed with maggots.

Watching him, Scott could feel the outline of the man's form wavering, becoming transparent.

The wind swirled, taking the vision with it.

Beyond it was his car.

IT LAY SLABLIKE and half submerged, a metallic gorgon gone to sleep just below the mantle of white. He opened the passenger door, whooping for air, and fell inside, rubbing his hands together. It was just as cold in here, but simply getting out of the wind was an improvement. The keys were still in the ignition—it took his frostbitten fingers three tries just to take hold of them—but even then, the engine made only a surly growl and refused to catch. Scott kept turning it anyway, flooring the gas until he was afraid he'd flood the engine, and then gave up.

He opened the glove compartment in hopes of a flashlight, perhaps placed there as a courtesy from the rental agency; of course there was nothing, no road flares or even matches he could use to guide him the rest of the way. Once he'd caught his breath and beaten some dull semblance of feeling back into his fingers, he forced himself to climb out again.

He thought about the tall man in the road, hunkered down over the pile of bloody shit, grinning up at him.

I can walk, he thought again. *I can walk FOREVER if I have to.*

He passed the old iron gates, the ones that had first caught his eye when he'd had Sonia drive out to the spot where his father had crashed.

Five minutes later, he was standing at the side of the highway, waiting.

CHAPTER FORTY-SIX

SCOTT LOST TRACK OF TIME. He had absolutely no sense of how long he'd been standing out here with his bare hands clamped under his arms, stomping his feet for warmth, shivering until his ribs ached and the muscles in his abdomen felt shredded by fatigue. No cars passed, and nothing stirred except him and the indifferent shine of dying starlight a million miles away. There was only him and the lonely road, as lifeless as history. After enough time passed, he almost considered going back to the car, trying the engine again to see whether he could at least get the heater going, but he was afraid if he did that, he might miss Sonia.

And he was afraid of what he might see in the woods.

Finally, after what felt like a lifetime of waiting, a pair of headlights scratched the distance, brightness gathering and becoming stronger, making new shadows across the road. The engine howled closer, pulling up alongside him. Behind the wheel, Sonia sat wearing a black knit cap, a few strands of hair sticking out. She stared at him wide-eyed like a woman stopped at an accident.

"Scott? You look awful."

He tried to speak but couldn't—he was shivering too badly and his voice was gone. Dropping into the passenger seat, he felt only warmth, and for that instant, all the night's horrors were eclipsed by a surge of primordial gratitude.

"There's coffee. Here." She took a chrome thermos from between the seats, unscrewed the cap, and poured him a cup. Still shivering, Scott brought it to his lips and sipped until the hot, strong liquid began to thaw the ice from his throat. His murmur of appreciation sounded like an obstinate nail being pulled out by an iron pry bar. Slow, methodical pain had already begun creeping into the joints of his fingers. The dashboard clock glowed 1:14 A.M.

"We got stuck leaving the bar," Sonia said. "I had to get out and shovel us out."

"Us?"

"I had Henry with me. I took him to my father's house. Earl's watching him."

"Where's my brother?"

She glanced at him: It might have been a shrug—her heavy coat made it hard to tell. "I'm really not sure." Beneath the strands of hair, her eyes searched him, their questioning depth breaking something open in him that the coffee hadn't been able to touch. Without further provocation, Scott felt the words spilling out. He told her everything—finding the black wing and Colette's body, and then hearing her voice on the phone. He made his report with a minimum of inflection, a detached unfolding of events whose emotional component was still as numb as his body's core temperature.

When he finished, Sonia said slowly: "What's happening to you, Scott?"

"Isn't it obvious?" He slid his cell phone out. "I'm losing my mind."

"Who are you calling?"

"The sheriff."

Sonia reached out and took the phone from his hand, a gesture so surprising that he just let go of it.

"Wait," she said.

He frowned. "Why?" For the first time, he noticed that they were following the highway north instead of south. "Why aren't we going back to town?"

She took in a deep breath and let it out slowly, over a span of several seconds. When she spoke again, her voice sounded different, the way people sometimes didn't sound like themselves when they were driving at night, their faces not wholly visible.

"There's something you have to see."

"Where?"

"Your father came into the bar one night," she said. "This happened a year or so ago—last winter, when it was just the two of us sitting there. He stayed for hours, and he . . . he told me some things. He made me promise I'd never tell anyone—especially not you or Owen." She spoke with great slowness and almost painful deliberation. "But I don't think I can do that anymore after what you told me."

"What is it?"

"I just have to show you. It's a good distance away."

"How long?"

"Up north," she said. "You should try to get some sleep."

"I can't."

He put his head back against the seat and shut his eyes. Exhausted or not, he thought there was no way he'd be able to fall asleep. Yet somehow, he did.

CHAPTER FORTY-SEVEN

WHEN HE AWOKE, it was still very dark, fat scissor-cut snowflakes spilling through the yellow cones of the headlights. Sonia was driving, talking on her phone in a voice too low for him to understand, and they were pulling up to a large gray building that he didn't recognize.

He looked at the clock. It was 4:05 A.M.

Scott coughed, and his wind-burned hands gave a harsh bark of pain. "Where are we?"

"Pine Haven."

"Never heard of it."

"It's about a hundred and forty miles north of Milburn." She parked and got out. "Follow me."

Back into the cold, but it was much worse, the increasingly northern climate clattering through his unprepared half-conscious mind like a pile of loose tin and scrap iron. Being asleep had made it worse, and part of him longed for the huddled unconscious state of dreamless oblivion that had carried him north, the warmth and mindless vacancy of it.

Instead, he crouched forward against the bitter wind, hands tucked in his coat, following her blindly along the side of the huge building beneath a buzzing sodium arc light. The very length and configuration of the building seemed to make the wind worse, shaping and honing it like a blade until his joints felt as if they were on fire. Through bleary eyes, he saw a button with a sign that said:

PRESS FOR ENTRY

Sonia thumbed the button and waited. After a moment, the gray door unlatched and swung open to reveal a hospital corridor, industrial green walls, and a worn tile floor beneath long fluorescent tubes. Despite the promise of warmth and light, Scott felt himself hesitating, held back by the smell of commercial cleaning supplies and floor wax that barely covered the compounded mixture of body odor, sweat, urine, and excrement that had accumulated inside over the years.

"This is going to be hard for you," Sonia said.

On the other side of a bare metal desk, a towering black man in hospital blues met them without a word and walked in his silent rubberized shoes down the green hall. Scott followed. The hall was very long, and he realized there were echoes here, other voices, perhaps a great many of them—someone crying or laughing, a sudden shout, a groan of uncertain provenance, voices bounding back and forth like noises in a public pool. The space gave the noises a weirdly distorted resonance. Up ahead, another door—this one steel mesh—waited for them. The orderly brought out a key on a long spring-loaded wire, unlocked it, and ushered them through. The door closed behind them with a clang.

Here the orderly stopped, and Scott understood that he meant for them to go forward alone.

"She's down at the end," the orderly said. "Last on the right."

Scott moved forward on feet that didn't feel like his own. He came to a final door, heavy-gauge steel with a reinforced glass window and a slot beneath, big enough to accommodate a tray of food or the passage of small instruments.

He looked through the smeared glass.

The woman on the other side gazed back at him. Her drab gray hair lay flattened against her face; beneath it, Scott could see the puckered scars of old burns from her forehead down to her chin. Her eyes were a watery shade of violet, like broken stained glass—so different, but so familiar. When she saw him standing there, she raised one hand slowly to the glass, her eyes staring out at him in frank disbelief, and touched the window lightly as if afraid that it might break.

Scott felt his airway pinch shut so that he could hardly breathe, let alone speak. "Mom?"

She continued to look at him, the crookedness of her mouth becoming more pronounced, until he realized that she was actually trying to smile but had forgotten how. Scott felt tears welling up in his eyes, helpless to hold them back. As if embarrassed by his reaction, his mother's flicked her gaze above his head, over and around, as if she were following the path of some flying insect that she alone could see. Her finger tapped the window, made a little scribbling gesture.

"Here," the orderly said, reaching past him to slip a pad of paper through the slot in the door, along with a soft-looking black crayon. She took the pad awkwardly in her incomplete right hand and gripped the crayon with her left, like a child, hunching over it to create a series of slow, deliberate lines, then holding it up to the glass:

> *My name is Eleanor*

Scott just shook his head, wiped his tears, but more were coming, a perpetual river, it seemed. Finally he found his voice.

"Mom, what . . . what are you doing here?"

The sad, crooked smile returned as she took the tablet back. The black crayon slithered over the bottom of the page, moving faster in a quick, irregular scrawl. Reading upside down, Scott could already make out the words:

> *Do I know you*

"Yes. Mom, it's me. It's Scott."

She nodded patiently, waiting with the crayon.

"I don't understand." Scott looked around, back to the steel mesh door, where the orderly stood leaning against the wall next to Sonia. "Let her out of here. I want to talk to her."

The orderly shook his head. "She can't speak."

"Open this door."

"I can't do that."

"Why not?"

"For one thing, it's against the terms of her stay."

"The terms of her . . . ?"

"It's a court-ordered program," the orderly said. "You want her out, you're going to need to talk to a judge in the morning." He cast a glance back at Sonia, where she waited at the far end of the hallway. "You're not even supposed to be back here this time of night."

"Mom . . ." Scott looked back through the glass. "Dad said you died in the fire. He told us that you didn't make it—" He wanted to say more, but his voice went hoarse. On the other side of the glass, his mother was writing again, faster now, the page crowded with words, starting out big and shrinking as she ran out of space.

> *I remember you were there in the Theater when the Fire started—is your name Owen?*

"It's Scott," he said. "I'm Scott, Mom."

> *Were you in the Fire?*

"No," he said. "I was away at school. I wanted to come home but I was too busy. I tried to come home, but I couldn't make it."

She was nodding along with him, listening, the crayon moving diagonally across the paper, taking up space and leaving crumbs of wax in its wake.

> *There was a Fire and I couldn't get out. That's why I'm here so they can take care of me and if there's a Fire they can protect your father and Owen and me*

The orderly grunted, reading the note over Scott's shoulder. "She's getting agitated, seeing you here."

"There has to be someone I can talk to," Scott said. "Some way of getting her out until we get some answers." Turning back to the face in the window. "Mom, I—"

She was holding up the same sheet of paper, jabbing at the words *Fire* and *father* and *Owen*, eyes widening, sharper now.

"Dad died, Mom. He died a few weeks ago. That's why I'm here.

Owen's—all right." By force of will, he mastered his voice, drew back his tears. "Did Dad— Is he the one that put you here?"

She nodded beatifically, and her smile held, deepening into a kind of grimace, and one hand came up to rub at her temple, almost of its own accord.

"Why?"

His mother flipped the paper over, wrote:

Safe here

"Safe from what?" he asked, but she just pointed at those two words. "I can take care of you." Even now, he was unable to overlook the massive irony of that statement. He couldn't even take care of himself.

She shook her head, writing again:

I don't want to go anywhere. Please don't make me go away. I like it here. This is my home now. They protect me from

She ran out of space, flipped the sheet of paper over, and discovered that she had written on that side too. She flipped it back over again, increasingly anxious, searching for empty space on the margins, turned it sideways and flipped it back.

Scott looked at the orderly. "Is she on medication? How much do you have her on?"

"You want a list?"

"I want an explanation."

"You'll have to talk to her doctor."

"Where is he?"

"Right now?" The orderly stared at his watch for a long moment. "I'd have to say home in bed." And he added, in a lower voice, "Which is where *you* ought to be."

On the other side of the glass, his mother flipped the page and started a fresh sheet:

Your name is Scott?

"That's right," he said.

For a moment, she stood there looking at him with a little frown, her lips moving slightly. Then:

I have something for you.

Swaying back to the room behind her, she stooped down, digging through a box somewhere in the shadows. When she straightened up again, she was in possession of a flat rectangular object roughly the size of an unfolded newspaper. Through the smeared safety glass, Scott saw that it was some sort of faded handicraft, a brittle tapestry woven from colorful strips of construction paper, apparently assembled a long time ago. It was wide enough that she had to curl the sides up to push it through the slot. He accepted it and held it in both hands. It crackled when he turned it over, reading the handwritten words printed on the back as a kind of reminder to herself:

Give to Scott

"It's a place mat," the orderly explained. "They make them in the activity room on arts and crafts day."

Scott looked at the place mat, a thing a child might have brought home from kindergarten or summer camp, and then back up at his mother. She was still hanging on to the crayon, eyes wide and pleading and blank on the inside. Her hands stroked the grimy glass that divided them, fingers splayed, as if she wanted to touch him. He thought of her here, inside this place, locked away where no one even seemed to know who she had once been—a wife, a mother, someone who had made a difference in his life.

"Why did Dad do this to you? Why did he lie?"

Still smiling, she settled back down and slipped her hand through the slot beneath the window. Scott reached down and touched her fingertips, the ragged fingernails rimed with dirt. They felt cool and damp, as if fashioned from hard clay. Withdrawing them, she picked up the crayon one last time and scrawled:

My name is Eleanor

"That's enough now," the orderly said. "Time to go."

"Mom." Scott kept looking into his mother's eyes. "Listen to me. I'll be back. You don't have to stay here. I'll talk to your doctors and . . . I'm going to get to the bottom of this, okay? I promise. Mom?"

She peered at him, tears welling now. Shaking her head. Trembling. Not sure what to do with her hands. A teardrop clung to her chin, dangling fat and pendulous, and fell.

"Mom? *Mom?*"

He put his hand through the slot again, but she stood back, arms crossed over her chest, staring at him, scared out of her mind, as if she were looking into the eyes of a stranger.

CHAPTER FORTY-EIGHT

SILENCE FOR THE FIRST HOUR, with only the muffled rumble of the road between them. At last:

"Scott."

He stared straight ahead and didn't answer.

"I know not telling you was wrong," Sonia said.

"Wrong." Monotone: "You think it was wrong."

"I know it was. And for what it's worth, it probably doesn't mean anything to you right now, but it's been torturing me from the moment I laid eyes on you again. It's been killing me. From what your father told me at the time—"

"Why?" Iron rods fastened his neck to his shoulders, preventing him from turning to look at her, or looking at anything besides the snow-strewn galaxy of the very early morning in front of them. "Why couldn't you just tell me?"

"Your father said she was . . . beyond help. He said seeing her like this would be much harder on you and Owen—you in particular, because you weren't there that night and he knew you felt terrible about it. He made me promise. He said it would only make you feel worse."

"Isn't that my decision to make?"

"I'm sorry."

Scott didn't bother responding. Raw black emotion was piled up inside him, scalding and ugly, and although he didn't know what he was going to do with it, he could already tell that it wasn't going to go away. He fingered the place mat that his mother had given him, the crooked strips of what he'd realized was nothing more than cheap construction paper woven together, looped and secured with school glue.

"Something happened to her in the fire," Sonia said. "Your father said she was trapped under part of the wreckage for hours. He said when she was brought out, she had just . . . snapped. She wasn't herself. She wasn't going to recover. So he put her there for her own safety."

"Safety from what?"

Sonia didn't answer, just kept her eyes on the road.

"It doesn't make sense," Scott said. "He told everyone she was dead."

Her voice was scarcely a whisper. "He said she would've wanted it that way."

"And you believed him." Scott leaned forward, shoving his fists against his eyes, the dull ache somehow helping relieve the pressure that was building behind his sinuses. "What made you change your mind about telling me the truth now?"

"Tonight, when you told me you thought you were losing your mind . . ." She glanced at him. "I don't know. You're so lost. I guess I was hoping for . . . some answers."

"*You* wanted answers," he said, and shook his head. "Unbelievable."

"My questions were all about you. Whether you were going to be okay about all this. Whether you and I could ever—" She broke off, took a breath, held it, and let it out. "I'm so sorry, Scott, and you don't have to forgive me, now or ever. I just want you to know that I was only doing what I thought was right. Most of all I guess I just hope you won't shut me out."

He didn't say anything. He watched the road and the snow.

"We can fix it," Sonia said. "We can make it better—we can get her out of there. I can help you do that."

They drove for another long stretch without speaking. The pressure in his head felt close to exploding. It was after six now, and Milburn lay up ahead, becoming visible in the first reluctant moments of winter dawn.

SCOTT'S MIND FLASHED to the vision of the man in the woods, Robert Carver, grinning at him from the snow, the figure seeming to writhe and churn. The pressure in his head gave another massive squeeze, and he felt the harsh electric pain drive white-hot shards through his spine. It was far worse than it had ever been before. Without actually meaning to, he made a fist, causing the place mat that his mother had given him to rip at one side, the paper strips splitting apart along the outer edge.

In the glow of the dashboard light, he saw the edge of something tucked inside. It looked like yellow legal paper, several sheets, folded and stuffed into the woven place mat.

Sonia looked over. "What's that?"

"It was inside."

He removed the pages and unfolded them. Four sheets of paper, each one full of the careful cursive handwriting that he associated with his mother, interrupted occasionally by large blocks of text that she'd crossed out so thoroughly that he couldn't read through it. Scott switched on the dome light and held up the first page.

9/21/96

> *Dear Scott:*
>
> *If you are reading this, then it means I have somehow found a way to get through to you, and I am glad for it. Your father says that he has put me in this place for my own safety and protection, but protection from what? I am not crazy. I pose no threat to myself. But from what happened that night at the Bijou Theatre, I believe your father thinks that I am safer here, far away from town and presumed dead. I don't know if that's true or not. I feel like I know very little. There's no question that this is an awful place, full of pain and suffering. At night I lie awake and listen to the screams. But*

Here a thicket of crosshatched pen lines scratched out the rest of the paragraph, rendering it illegible. Scott's eye moved down the page to where the handwriting resumed.

It may be better than continuing to live with what I know now. Because of the security here and the medication the doctors give me, I am afraid that this letter will have to be our only communication. The drugs are very powerful, and they administer them regularly. I am already beginning to forget. This may be a blessing. It is very hard for me to focus, but I have to try.

What I'm about to relay to you, I discovered before the night the Bijou burned. I already had my suspicions, long before that. I researched the Mast family without your father's knowledge. I already knew that some of his relatives had committed suicide, many more of them had gone insane. Knowing that, I began to

The rest of the paragraph was crossed out. It resumed with:

Your father's great-grandfather was a human disease, a walking affliction. There are no words to describe what was wrong with him. He built Round House as a place where he could indulge his very worst desires and urges without fear of being caught. I don't know how many women and girls died within its walls, but their voices still speak to me, so perhaps I am less stable than I initially supposed. Or it may be the drugs, or the voices here in this godforsaken

This godforsaken

Another block of crossed-out text.

The worst mistake your great-great-grandfather ever made was abducting a girl named Rosemary Carver. She was a girl who

Scott, this is very hard for me.
The drugs
The drugs are
Believe it or not, what I've written so far has taken me almost a week to put down, and if I don't
No extra time important things only

Rosemary Carver's father was a witch, not a female kind but maybe a warlock is what he was called. Swore a blood oath of vengeance against the Mast family—a curse is what he called it a curse of madness carried on in stories, plays, paintings. Your father knew but didn't believe it until he started seeing things that made him want to believe it. I tried to tell him about the movie because I could already tell it was too late because he told the story

The rest of the second page had been completely slashed away with such vehemence that Scott could almost feel his mother's frustration in trying to convey what she knew. He started the third page, already alarmed by how much larger her printing had become, slanting blocks that took up too much space.

Scott, the curse is the story. I didn't know the rest until it was too late. Colette McGuire's prom dress. I sent you over to her house with it that night. She had given it to me to alter it for her so she could wear it for prom.
Reason why: She was pregnant.
Owen. Owenowen.
Shared her physical body wifth Owen.
The baby was Owens.
Little boy who died in the fire, baby of hers and Owen wuz Colettes attempt to try to mend things with the Mast family. She may try share herself again I don't know. She may try sharing with you. Maybe she has alredy dun this, I dont know. To stop the curse. She's part of the curse too but on the other side of it. This is what I learned about Colette that you must know scotty.
Rober Carver had two dotters. Not just 1 but TWO, rosemary dyed but the 2nd cotter lived & she marry a man name mcguire & colette
Colette is only living dessedent of rosemary carver

Wait.

I can do this.

Scott laid the third page aside and picked up the final sheet of yellow paper with trembling hands.

> *Colette is bound to our family as we are to hers, by Blood. Possessed by the spirit of her dead ansister. Brought back every generation by The Rosemary story. Or song. Or play. Or painting.*
>
> *When I think about it I can see how that is, our two family tied together with the story, slave to her fathers curse as we are. The haunted and the haunting, with no end ever to the pain and madness and suffring. Having Owns child may have seem like the only way to try to undo the curse but when I saw at the bijoo Fire the movie start. The little boy started screaming in so much pain he died & I know the curse cannot be ended like this but she may try again*
>
> *she may try again & try again but never get free*
> *in the end Scott she always get hungry*
>
> *It is a curse & ther is no way to stop it I am so sorry Scott Mommy is tired but I cant remember anymore because they give us medicin here it makes things softer I am so glad they give me medicin here every day so I can forget but I will never forget yu.*

> *I love you scotty,*

> *Mom*

SONIA HELD PERFECTLY STILL, reading the last pages over again. "That night with the prom dress. I saw you two up in her bedroom window together."

"That's why." Scott looked at her, remembering the night sixteen years earlier, Colette's hands tearing open his shirt, her tongue on his skin, so eager and hungry, her breasts already beginning to swell from the baby that she'd had Owen put inside her belly. "She'd never shown any interest in me, but that night—"

And tonight.

Sonia looked away. Scott remembered Colette telling him how

Henry's mother had been Rosemary Carver, and now he understood what it all meant. Rosemary Carver in her tattered blue dress, restless and yearning to find some peace across the decades, willing to try anything to release herself from the bondage of the curse . . . and failing, failing.

in the end Scott she always get hungry

"We need to find Owen," Scott said, and no sooner were the words out of his mouth than another, more urgent thought dawned.

We need to find Henry.

CHAPTER FORTY-NINE

EARL'S JUNK SHOP STOOD untouched. They walked through the hushed aisles, every item holding its breath as they passed into the house.

"Dad?" Sonia called. "Dad, did—" She paused, touched her face. "Oh my God."

They found him sprawled facedown on the floor in front of the sofa, still hooked up to his oxygen mask, the tube having pulled loose from the tank. In the end, death had shrunk him, diminished whatever was left of his presence, flattening every dimension of his body until he looked like a suit of clothes that had simply slipped off the hanger. Somewhere the tank hissed on and on. Sonia fell to her knees beside him, her shoulders trembling in silence as she wept. Witnessing her silent crying, the old things, the curios and bric-a-brac that had gravitated toward Earl Graham throughout his time here, all seemed to release a long, slow communal breath of resignation.

Scott ran up the stairs, three at a time.

"Henry! *Henry?*"

He checked the bedrooms, the bathrooms, the closets, under the tables, and behind the doors, just in case the boy, frightened, had gone into hiding. He went back through the junk shop and searched under the tables there. He called and called the boy's name until it was only a meaningless sound.

There was no answer.

Circling back around to the front room, he found Sonia still kneeling on the floor with her father's hand pressed between both of her own. She lifted her face up to him, chalk white and empty of expression. She had never looked so lost or lonely in her entire life, an ageless sense of abandonment hollowing out her eyes, making her seem very small.

"Is he here?"

Scott shook his head. "Your father . . . ?"

"No," Sonia said. She spoke very softly, hardly louder than the sound of the oxygen seeping from the tank, but he heard her very well.

"I'll call an ambulance."

"No need," she said. "There's no hurry. Henry first." She cleared her throat without much strength. "Do you have any idea what might have happened to him?"

"Yeah," Scott said. "I do."

CHAPTER FIFTY

OWEN HAD BEEN WANDERING in the woods throughout most of the night and could no longer feel any part of his body. The fear had dissipated, but the temperature and numbness only grew worse, more burdensome, until he arrived at the realization that he was going to die out there. The knowledge brought only a faint sense of regret that he would never see his boy again. Henry was all that mattered. There was nothing else in his life worth missing.

It had all started when he'd slipped the rest of the way down the hillside in the dark, tumbling ass-over-teakettle through the darkened drifts. His head hit a rock, and he'd let out a sharp cry of shock and pain.

He had sat up again, rubbing the back of his skull and eventually groping his way forward through the night, looking for the lights he'd seen earlier and not seeing them. How far had he fallen? He had almost called out for Red, and then he remembered the thing that had emerged out of the trees, a shape that had seemed neither animal nor human but something else entirely, a tall, ungainly thing that nonetheless stood up in humans' clothes and moved on overly long and stilted legs. Witnessing its arrival had made his heart beat faster and reduced his whole body to some kind of quaking percussion instrument, like the kind that stagehands used to simulate thunder.

He thought of Grandpa Tommy singing, playing the guitar with shaking junkie hands, forcing the words out as if he didn't want to sing them but didn't have a choice, singing to Owen about the tall man all dressed in black, come to take his daughter back. When Owen had first heard the song, as a small boy, it had scared him, but what frightened him worse was the way old Tom played it for him, over and over, driving the words deeply into Owen's head. *Gotta learn this*, Grandpa Tommy had said, his cigarette-ruined voice sounding weak and awful and somehow feminine. *Someday this song will be yours, all yours. You'll own it and it will own you, just as sure as your name is Mast, so you better make sure you know all the words and know 'em well. . . .*

IN THE END, Owen had just started walking, trying to find his way back to the road on his own. He went on like that for what felt like hours, staggering, sometimes falling when the snow got too deep, forcing himself to stand up and move forward until every bit of energy was gone. He was tired, lost, out of breath, out of options, out of hope.

Finally he just sat down in the snow, felt how it conformed to the weight and contours of his body, accepting him without question as if it had been waiting here all along. Somewhere in the world, he guessed every person's death was written down for him, waiting to be discovered, and here he'd found his. He'd heard that freezing to death was like falling asleep, that you could just close your eyes and fade out. For the first time ever, he looked back at his life and didn't feel so bad. He only wished that he had a piece of paper and pen to leave a note for Henry. What would he write? *Sorry? Be good? I love you? I tried my best?* All of those things felt true to him now, but he'd never bothered to live up to any of them back when he had a chance, so how much better were they than a bunch of self-pitying drunkard's lies? Better that he couldn't leave any note at all—better still that Henry just forgot he'd ever existed.

His eyes had adjusted to the darkness by now, and sitting there, staring into the night, he noticed a clearing up ahead. Faint yellow lights spilled over the snowy plain, the same ones he'd seen earlier, and Owen realized what it was.

A house.

He stood, having to expend real effort to dislodge himself from the snow and start on his way to the house. Not just any house, but a sprawling fortress that expanded both up and out, as if it had eaten a hole in the surrounding woods and landscape and grown fatter out here all by itself. Owen began walking hastily toward it, invigorated by the promise of survival. All the lights were turned on, and now he could see clearly in what was left of the night.

As he approached the rear of the structure, he felt his foot skidding forward and realized that what he'd initially taken for a clearing was actually a frozen pond. The ice was solid—it didn't make the slightest creak or crack as he hurried over it. Parts of the pond were actually bare, a gleaming sweep of onyx along the opposite shore. On the other side, he climbed up the embankment and stopped.

A big, empty house in the middle of nowhere with all the lights turned on, Owen thought, and the fear that he'd experienced earlier that night came rumbling back through him, bigger this time.

But he was freezing. He needed a place to get warm. And if he could get inside and find some way to make contact with the outside world, get back to Henry and make an escape from here, from this town, from this whole side of the world . . .

He stalked around the outside of the house as quickly as possible, but it still took an excruciatingly long time to reach the front porch, the snow-covered steps—footprints, half full of snow, someone had been here recently—and up to the door. Owen didn't bother knocking. He turned the knob and stepped inside.

"Hello?" he shouted. "Anybody home?"

The entryway stared back at him, gaping and silent and absolutely still. From the first glance, he saw there was something seasick and wrong about the whole thing, and he squinted up at the corners, trying to find out where the wall ended and the ceiling began. Or, for that matter, how you knew you were in the hallway instead of one of the closets. All the spaces oozed together in a blurry nightmare of foolish formlessness. It felt like a drunken hallucination, but Owen knew drunkenness, and even without reaching out to touch it, he knew that this was real.

He closed the door behind him, the door latch resonating throughout the first floor, and looked around. Even from here, he could tell that the rest of the bizarre house would be large and elaborate. Hall-ways ran in every direction, ending in doorways that only seemed to communicate with more corridors, farther back. And that was just the first floor.

But it was all somehow familiar. Had he been out here before? For a party, a long time ago, or maybe some construction job?

"Hello?" he repeated, and the word sounded strange, hanging in the air all by itself. "Anybody home?" His earlier intuition that the house was empty now felt like a certainty. It was as if it had been laid out here just to wait for him. He moved deeper into the foyer, still shivering, wondering why he didn't feel warmer. He listened for the sound of a furnace but heard nothing. There was a main staircase up ahead and some old sheets of paper spilled out on the floor in front of it with drawings on them. Blueprints. The rest of the foyer and the corridors had been cleaned out as if by thieves, and that made them feel even larger.

Owen slowed down and shuddered. He'd inadvertently stepped into an invisible cloud of foul air, so ripe and contaminated that it almost felt warmer than the air that surrounded it. Up on his right was a door leading to what looked like, from the gaudy chandelier that hung above it, some kind of dining room, but—

He spun around and looked back in the direction of the front door. A sudden sensation as if something had moved behind him, very *close* to him, made the hairs on the back of his neck stand up. But there was nothing in the foyer, nothing in the hall, nothing anywhere, except . . .

Well, there was just nothing, that was all.

For the next half hour, he walked the house, upstairs and down. He went as far up as the third floor until it unraveled his nerves too severely and he had to quit. Occasionally he caught another whiff of the bad smell, but it always drifted past him and was pulled away again in a matter of seconds, as if manipulated by some complex circulatory system. Once, up on the third floor, right before coming back down, he had heard very faintly the sound of some old music playing from inside one of the walls, like a scratchy old gramophone wound up and left playing. That had been when he'd turned around and gone back down.

Some of the items that he found in the upper rooms included a box of old clothes; a painting of the house; a thin book called *By Dark*

Hands, apparently self-published, written by one of his relatives, Hubert Gosnold Mast; a box of children's toys; and a box of rocks. Individually these items were random, even meaningless; taken together, they created an unsettling composite in Owen's mind, as if, placed in one room, they might outline the shape of something best left unseen. He decided to come back down, bringing *By Dark Hands* with him. It felt as if he'd been up there forever, yet the darkness outside the windows was as thick and dense as ever—if anything, it felt even *darker.*

Owen cracked open the book. The date stamped in the front was 1860, making the author at least his great-great-grandfather's age. Or did it go even further back than that? It felt brittle, the binding almost falling apart in his hands, and the print was tiny, headache-inducing, the lines of type slanting crookedly to the edge of the page. Even as Owen flipped through the yellow-stained pages, he could feel them loosening in bunches, as if the whole thing were disintegrating. Owen tried to follow the story—something about a father looking for his daughter—and got hung up on the language.

He flipped to the last page to read what was printed there:

> *And when at last, long past the toll of midnight, he chanced to see the figure of the girl spat forth from that damned black place, the shunned house's most infected spot, source of all his unease, the man knew that all of his waiting was not in vain; and he even smiled. For whether or not she might deign to rest her dark hand upon him, whether he might yet live to see the light of morning, he knew that he was destined to spend the rest of eternity within her cold embrace.*
>
> *He stood up then to ask his question: "What shall ye do to me now?"*
>
> *She only grinned at him with teeth that shone like daggers, grotesquely long, and he inclined to listen. But instead of her sweet voice, his ears received the lower intonations of a masculine one, its unfamiliar tone grating like small rocks against a millstone, its laughter rich and hungry. And as he turned to look*

Owen read it again. The book ended there, midsentence. It didn't look as if any pages had been torn out. It just stopped.

Back in the foyer, a child's voice lisped incoherently behind him, from the area he'd thought might have been a dining room. Owen felt cattle prods go off from his spine, running the length of his legs.

"Henry?"

The muffled rumor of footsteps, moving toward him or away from him, he couldn't tell. Owen ran back to their source, boots thumping, heart pounding. He arrived at the doorway of the dining room, took it all in at once—the air mattress, the laptop, the pages sprawled across the hardwood floor. Owen grabbed one of the pages and looked at it, a spray of words assaulting his eye.

This is it, he thought. *This is the house that Scott . . .*

He realized he was still carrying around the old book, the one he'd found upstairs. He looked back at the pages and the laptop. Finally his gaze arrived at the corner of the room and stopped. The closet door in the corner was wide open. Through it, he could see a ragged hole torn into the plaster, revealing a black corridor beneath.

Owen stared at it.

Something was in there.

Something was breathing.

"Henry?" Owen said, coming closer. "Is that you?" He felt his head turning slightly to one side, both hands half raised, as if in anticipation of a blow. "It's Papa. I'm not mad. If you're in there, just come out. Okay?"

Nothing stirred. As Owen grew nearer, he became aware of how agonizingly deep the space on the other side went. It wasn't just a hole in the wall; it was a hidden room, maybe even a whole hallway that had been covered up. The lyrics of the song went back through his head again, too quickly, something about a girl in blue.

"Henry? I love you. Papa won't leave you, Henry."

"Daddy?" a voice from inside asked.

"I'm coming," Owen said. "Daddy's coming." And he stepped through the hole.

CHAPTER FIFTY-ONE

GETTING BACK TO THE WOODS wasn't so easy. It was still snowing, and the roads had gotten worse.

They parked at the side of the road, and Sonia started to get out.

"What are you doing?" Scott asked.

"I'm going with you."

He shook his head. "No."

"Scott—"

"Look," he said, jabbing one finger at the yellow sheets of legal paper between the front seats of the car. "You read the letter. The curse is on my family. It's got nothing to do with you."

Sonia glared at him, red-eyed. "That thing, that spirit—whatever you want to call it—came into my house and killed my father."

"There's nothing to be done. It's unbreakable."

"If it's so hopeless, why even bother?"

"Because of Henry."

"You're throwing yourself into this thing." She sounded miserable and angry at the same time. "Just like your father and your grandfather and your great-uncle and every other idiotic man in your family, you're going to end up just like them. Maybe if I come with you—"

"It's too late for that."

"I'm calling the sheriff then. He'll come out."

"Won't matter."

Sonia looked out, in the direction of the house. "You don't even know she's out there."

Scott peered into the woods.

"She's out there," he said.

CHAPTER FIFTY-TWO

THERE WAS A FAINT CRUNCH of footsteps, and the woman brought the boy out of the woods. Cold daylight fell from the low gray sky. He was bundled in blankets, with thick mittens and warm boots on his feet, and he was no longer afraid.

He was with his mother.

She had told him everything on the way from Earl's house. She spoke with the easy, effortless love of a mother who takes obvious pleasure in being with her son. In the back of her car, Henry listened, frightened at first, then dubious, and finally awestruck by the sheer wonder of what she was telling him. Now he felt the last of his doubt sliding away like a chill in a warm bath. From her purse she had shown him a baby photo of himself with her and told him how she'd watched him grow, loving him from a distance.

"Why didn't you keep me the first time?" he asked.

"I wasn't myself then. Do you understand?"

He shook his head.

"The woman I used to be wasn't prepared for motherhood. She

had already lost one little boy. She thought she was ready for another one, but she was wrong."

"But you're different now?"

Colette smiled, pure, cold brilliance. "Completely."

She told him that from now on, their lives would be different, that the three of them would be together, she and Henry and Owen, the way they should have been from the beginning. She said she was sorry for hiding the truth from him for so long, but now she wanted to make it right.

Suddenly, looking up into the clearing, the boy pointed and said, "What's that?"

"That?" Colette smiled. "Why, that's our new house, dear."

Henry cocked his head. "It doesn't look right."

"It's perfect."

"I don't like it."

"Why not?"

"It's wrong." He shook his head, twisting away from her. She released him, let him climb down into the snow, then bent forward to kiss his cheek.

"Come inside, sweet boy. There's somebody waiting for us."

Henry brightened a little. "My daddy?"

"No," Colette said. "Mine."

As she said that, Henry smelled something sour rising in the air, and he looked up at his mommy. She was different now. The neckline of her sweater looked as if it had been ripped open down the middle by a pair of ragged claws, and she had angry red scratches on her chest, as if some animal had been clawing at her, but the scratches were wide-set, a full finger-width apart. Her face was no longer patient or kind, but colorless, harsh, starved in every kind of way a person could be. Pain boiled in her face, making the muscles twitch and flex.

"Mommy? Are you okay?"

"Yes." She looked at him wanly. "I'm just tired." Tears swam in her eyes. Somehow her pain only made Henry love her more. He wished with all his heart that there were something he could say to make her feel better, but somehow he knew that her problems, whatever they were, were insurmountable; they towered like a black city in front of both of them, a city under a curse. Yet at the same time, in a way he couldn't explain, he *did* understand: He and his mommy were both trapped, somehow, by her father, the man-thing that awaited them inside.

"We can run away," he said.

She picked him up and hugged him so hard he couldn't breathe. More complicated feelings—pain, love, fear—broke through Henry like a kaleidoscope in patterns he couldn't follow. A tiny fraction of the pain slipped from her face, and beneath it he saw the woman who had first come to pick him up from the house in the middle of the night.

"Where would we go?" she whispered.

"Mexico. We can get my daddy, and we can all go together. That man wouldn't find us. It would be okay."

"Oh, honey." He felt her shaking her head, and they were walking again, plunging through deep snow. Henry didn't know what else to say. He wanted to be with her so much, but he had the feeling that she was doing this because she was scared and didn't know how else to proceed. Sometimes his daddy had acted like this, and it always frightened him, because that meant no one was in charge. Henry remembered his father looking at him over a big pile of empty beer cans with a bleary, helpless look on his face, and it was always the worst feeling in the world knowing that no one was the parent, the protector, captain of the ship. Instead, they were all sailing blind in a tumultuous storm over which nobody had control. In his worst moments, Henry understood that this was how the balance of his life was going to be.

She carried him the rest of the way into the house.

CHAPTER FIFTY-THREE

OWEN SAW THE FLAMES from around the corner, an ulcerating orange blaze that sent shifting, uncertain shadows slithering up and down the length of the corridor. He could smell it too, the acrid stench of smoke, coal, and hot iron all crowding the passageway, although it did almost nothing to get rid of the tremors. If something was burning back here, shouldn't it at least generate some heat?

Rounding the corner, he faltered and gaped through the half-open barred door at the chamber ahead. It was like a kind of subterranean barn with half walls dividing the space into separate stalls on either side. Beyond it, directly opposite him, an old-fashioned potbellied stove squatted like a fat man with an open wound, glowering back at him through its grate. Someone had lit a snarling fire, and for a moment, Owen stood hypnotized by the coals seething inside. But he saw no sign of the voice that had coaxed him this far, no trace of the child who had summoned him as father.

"Henry?"

He came closer to the stove, but the heat from within it was stingy, minimal, and provided only the faint illusion of warmth, less a fire than the humid breath of something exhaling its vapors onto his skin.

Then he saw the tool bench.

It was so much more than that, though. Never in his life had Owen come across anything like it, except in the horror movies of his child-hood, movies he could no longer stand to watch. Saws, hammers, drills, spikes and axes, hatchets and wrenches, a dozen types of restraints; coils of thick rope, blood-stiffened, hung from wooden pegs. Great serrated scissors, blades a foot long and beaked like the mandibles of some enormous insect, held their own special place of honor. There was a bucket of water on the floor with leather whips dangling out of it like the tendrils of some wretched black plant. Iron rods with spikes attached and devices made of polished steel hooks sat next to several handmade leather masks with dozens of nails angled inward toward the wearer's face. Small hand-shaped metal boxes filled with clamps and bolts to skewer and split muscle and bone lay carefully lined up across one side. At the bottom, he saw a piece of plywood modified to accommodate rawhide stirrups and a set of retractable brown-toothed clamps with rawhide straps and rusted buckles.

The coals flickered, and Owen felt someone else enter the room.

He turned slowly, took a step backward, and fell into a spot where the floor dropped six inches. The thing lunged into the firelight, and all at once, Owen could make out the shape in front of him, a massive figure, as broad as an ox. It was naked except for a stained leather butcher's apron, his broad shoulders and bare thighs gleaming with sweat. Thick wiry hair matted his flesh and neck like the fur of an ani-mal. Owen's tongue swelled to clog his throat, and he felt himself lapse into a stupor of broad, toxic, logic-devouring terror. Every other detail of the man's face was eclipsed by his reddish yellow eyes, far brighter than the stove, so intense that Owen could've sworn they somehow shone in the long mirror of the man's teeth.

"What the hell . . . ?" he breathed.

One great hand—it felt like many—seized him by the wrist and yanked him off his feet. Tumbling forward, he flew and hit the ground in one of the stalls, facedown on a bed of rotten hay. A sharp object poked him in the leg, and he looked down to see a long, yellowish white object sticking up, a human rib with a rag of fabric still clinging to it. He drew back. The thing was towering over him, its burnished face split open in peals of silent laughter, laughter that somehow mimicked the flickering coals over the walls. The fire was laughing at him. The thing in the apron was laughing at him. It reached under the leather apron and brought out a long, serrated knife whose tip was split open into two different barbed hooks, turning it over and offering it to Owen.

Owen took it.

The thing raised its hand in mocking benediction.

Owen felt himself bringing the blade to his neck, just beneath his chin. He felt no reluctance, only relief to be doing the thing's bidding and bringing an end to his own terror. Through madness, fear, and confusion, he recognized that there was only one thing that the giant wanted from him now.

He jerked the blade toward his throat.

The tips of the blade bit effortlessly into the skin of his neck, the shock hitting him like a slap, breaking the spell. He recoiled, lowering the knife, letting it fall. Blood trickled from the cut, and he touched it, holding pressure there. The gash was long but not deep, although he could feel his blood leaking out between his fingers, pattering onto the floor below.

Throughout it all, the naked giant in the leather apron towered in ragged laughter. Owen knew now what this was: the very face of his family's sickness, the man in black from Grandpa Tommy's song, a being that had destroyed them all throughout the years and had now come, as he'd always known it would, to destroy him.

Then, from outside his immediate realm of consciousness, he saw the towering shape straighten up and turn falteringly to the right.

Owen turned and looked.

At the other end of the room, a shadow hunched against the glow of the stove. What he saw there was a young girl in a tattered blue dress and, standing next to her, holding her hand, his son, Henry. Owen looked again, willing his dying drunkard's brain to focus on the details, no matter how unbelievable.

The girl holding his son's hand was Colette McGuire.

"Father," Colette murmured.

The giant at the bench began to turn slowly around to face her, its grin stretched into rigid angles, arms spread like an invitation to dance. The voice that came out of it was like no human voice or animal sound Owen had ever heard—a cobblestone rasp mixed with a mulish whinny.

Clutching his left hand to his throat, pushing down hard on the place where the blade had found its target, Owen put his right elbow against the stall and levered himself into an upright position. The thing that had stood in front of him was gone. Looking out of the stall, he saw that it had gone back to the workbench, next to the stove, that it was doing something over there with the tools.

"Henry," Owen tried to say, but in the extremity of his pain, he couldn't even whisper it. His throat was an abattoir trough of backed-up blood and leakage. All he could do was raise the knife that the thing had given him—he still held it in his hand—and slam it down hard against the damp, blood-soaked wood of the stall in an attempt to get their attention. It made the softest imaginable sound, not really a sound at all, just a dull ache that traveled up through his forearm to his neural plexus, just enough to snuff out his consciousness in a single stroke. Owen's semiconscious realization, that he should simply have died out there in the woods, should never have wished to see his son again, passed over him with genuine indifference.

He fell down into the stinking hay and let his eyes sink shut.

CHAPTER FIFTY-FOUR

SCOTT TORE THROUGH THE front door of the house without hesitation, down the foyer and through the hallway, the clatter of his own footsteps chasing him back to the dining room. On the floor in front of the air mattress, he saw an old book and read the title: *By Dark Hands*, by H. G. Mast. Glancing it at now, he felt no sense of surprise or revelation. Mast the elder had been passionate about more than murder. He had heard the call of the arts, and Robert Carver's curse had taken the form it had because of his ancestor's passion not just for murder but for the creative act, a shadow that had fallen forward across the decades to envelop the entire family. Scott saw it all now. His run through the woods had been bracing, clearing his mind.

It's pointless. You know it is. You said so yourself. There is no end.

Yes, that was so.

So what possible difference could any of this make?

He didn't have an answer to that. At the moment, he didn't need one. Already he could feel the noxious cloud of energy gathering in the house around him, the ozone in the air growing stronger and more potent until it culminated in an explosion that would blow the roof off the entire world. Something in here smelled of blood. In the corner of the dining room, he ducked into the hole he'd smashed through the wall, wedging his shoulders deeper, crawling into . . . not blackness, not anymore, but a strange, creeping orange light.

He thought of the stove.

Something had lit it.

No, not just something.

It.

Carver.

He walked down the black hallway, the narrow wing stretching out before him in an endless offer of soulless oblivion. He kept moving. He thought of the title of the old book: *By Dark Hands*. And *Helping Hands*. And his own damaged hands. What was a hand but another kind of wing, reaching forward to embrace, to grasp, strangle, and choke? He had been through all of this before, as had his father and grandfather and great-grandfather; there would be a time and place when he would trade it all in and probably get nothing back. It was pointless to worry now about how it all might have been if he'd never found his father's attempt to complete the story—if the things he'd aroused by undertaking the project had been allowed to lie dormant. It made no difference now. The light of his laptop had awakened the Carvers again, and all those hours of energy that he'd thought he'd poured into the story had actually been poured into them, nourishing them with his own lifeblood until they could stand up and take nourishment on their own.

Coming around the corner, he saw what was there and stopped in his tracks.

In front of him, wearing a shabby blue dress like a slave's frock, Colette McGuire crouched over the small, prone body of Henry Mast. Scott's first thought—that she had already killed the boy—was obliterated a moment later when a larger, immeasurably darker form rose towering in front of her. It was garbed in the stained leather apron that Scott had seen hanging by the stove the last time he'd been back here. The thing was unarmed except for the sharp scythe that hung in front of its face, which he realized, with a kind of jolt, was really its grin.

The scythe-faced thing came forward to put its hands on the boy.

"No," Scott said.

Colette's head jerked up—showing the pale face of Rosemary Carver. "Scott?" She shook her head. "You shouldn't have come."

The shape of Robert Carver grew brighter in the stove's light. At the same moment, he unbuckled the leather apron, allowing it to slide from his torso, allowing Scott to see through the gelid skin for what it was—not one body but dozens of smaller ones knit together in a kind of tapestry of corpses. Carver's physical incarnation was made up of all the victims who had died here, tortured women and children who had suffered at the hands of Scott's great-great-grandfather. They clutched at one another, coiled like serpents beneath his skin, their bruised skulls forming Carver's shoulders, multitudes of bony, broken limbs entwined to give shape to the bulbous arms and legs.

As one, the victims of H. G. Mast bent forward and reached for Henry. The boy stared up at the creature in wonder, paralyzed but fully lucid, his expression a crosscut slash of terror.

Scott started forward with the intention of doing anything he could to separate his nephew from the thing, but the moment had come and gone. He'd wasted it on astonishment. Carver swung his arm, and Scott felt the strands of women's greasy, matted hair, tied together to bind the other bodies, acting as a kind of net, a snare that caught and flung him aside. Scott whipped free. Voices shrieked at him through Carver's mouth, bellowed, brayed. With an offhand gesture, the thing batted him sideways, and Scott slammed into Colette, both of them sprawling across the packed dirt floor.

He felt his mind trying to grapple with all that he was witnessing, but there was no room for it. This, then, had been when his father had snapped—bolted from here, headed out to his car and the stretch of road that would ultimately kill him. On the floor beside him, Colette glanced over to read the unspoken question in his face, meeting it with broken hopeless grief. She was only a vessel for Rosemary's father's undying rage, just as Scott was its target—no escape for either of them, now or ever.

The corpses that made up Carver's body were bending forward, and Scott saw them hefting the wooden trapdoor that he had lifted earlier, starting to stuff the boy inside.

The pipe, Scott thought, *the one that runs down underground and out to the pond—*

At last, Henry seemed to shake himself from his terror enough to struggle against what was happening; he snapped and grappled with the thing, but the hands slithered from within its woven pattern to shove him along. Henry screamed, a rising squeak; Carver roared back at the boy with all the force of the avenged dead. The boy burst into tears. Colette ran toward him and Scott followed; Carver swung one great corpse-woven arm—

Something flashed in the orange light, and the arm dropped to the floor.

Scott stared.

It was Owen.

CHAPTER FIFTY- FIVE

SCOTT WATCHED HIS BROTHER come staggering out of one of the stalls, holding a knife in one hand and his throat in the other. He seemed to be wearing a beard of blood, but the wound on his neck wasn't the most galvanizing thing about his appearance. What struck Scott even more powerfully was the expression in Owen's eyes, the riveted-together mask of grim determination to accomplish the task that lay before him.

Without once looking up at Scott or Colette, he dove forward and looped the knife at Carver, burying it in the thing's side and ripping downward. Bodies avalanched where the blade sheared them away, unfolding over the floor—two women in rags, a third on her haunches, clutching a dead infant and hissing like a scalded cat. The uneven, half-carved tower of corpses that remained teetered toward him, reaching, and Owen lashed out again, punching the blade through its face.

Carver tumbled backward and fell. More bodies separated, only to scramble back up into place, while others lay blindly where they'd fallen, glaring from a place Scott couldn't imagine. Carver's face was laughing at him. He knew something, some secret knowledge he'd held for the last century and a half, the outcome of the battle already decided.

Still clutching the knife, Owen made a gurgling sound, blood bubbling through his fingers. He dropped the blade and fell to his knees on the floor next to his son, latching on to the boy and hugging him, Henry flinging his arms around his father. Owen picked up the knife again and cut a swath off his shirt, wrapping it around his throat.

Colette said, "Wait . . ." Extending her arms, she reached for Henry, and Scott saw her face pulsing back and forth between her familiar features and the bleached and twisted hunger of Rosemary Carver. " . . . *my baby*—"

Owen opened his mouth and closed it, gestured at Scott. "Run. Get out of here. Run."

"No." Scott shook his head. "Not again."

Colette screamed, lunging for Henry. Scott moved forward and grabbed her arm. Spinning around, Colette bumped into the open trapdoor, and for a second, Scott held her in open space long enough to see her face become familiar again, realization smoothing her features to a gloss of despair.

Then she fell.

CHAPTER FIFTY-SIX

CARVER'S LAUGHTER RATTLED like a disintegrating cough throughout the wing, echoed in the mouths of the victims as they slunk back into the shadows, the entire house shaking like a huge set of asthmatic lungs. Scott felt blindness rising to smother him like a cloak. The light in the stove was finally waning, but it didn't matter; there was less and less to see. Corpses merged into the walls, their tissue blending with the wood and the dirt, absorbed from whence they'd come. Still their eyes burned on him; he felt them like a bed of nails.

Painstakingly, with monumental effort, Owen had managed to hoist his son up into the crook of his arm. The knife that he'd used to break the bodies apart lay forgotten in the straw. Owen slumped and took a step, then, still holding on to Henry, he glanced back at the trapdoor where Colette had fallen. A sense of realization washed over his face, smoothing it out, making him look both childlike and terribly old.

Scott forced himself into an upright position and looked at his brother. "Coming . . . ?"

Owen didn't answer. From outside, Scott could hear men's voices and barking dogs approaching, getting louder. His brain was a blur of awareness, and then, when he heard the final peal of laughter inside the wing, he felt sudden clarity. He saw that Owen had let go of his son, but he had picked up the knife.

"Owen," Scott said, "come on. Let's *go.*"

"She was trapped like we are." Owen was still staring at the trap-door. "It wasn't her fault."

"I know it wasn't," Scott said, "but—"

"Take Henry. Get out of here."

Before Scott could answer, Owen dove through the trapdoor.

CHAPTER FIFTY-SEVEN

OWEN FELT A SHARP, slanting pain, stabbing him from all sides—no air.

He'd gone spilling and scraping down a rough metal pipe not much bigger than his body, shooting forward on gravity and a glare of ice. It was rough, tearing off scraps of his clothes and skin, and he'd felt little nodules of things clotted to the inside of the pipe as it passed, jagged bones, bits of moldy refuse that hadn't flushed all the way through. Suddenly the pipe was gone. The knife he'd brought with him had disappeared. In suffocating blackness, he rotated slowly and realized that he had been dumped out in gray, airless space.

He was underwater.

The pond.

He turned his face up, already going numb, and water stung his eyes. Overhead, a semitranslucent slab of ice formed the ceiling of his world. In the dull gray light, he saw vague shadows trampling over him, the muted passage of feet, longer shapes, dogs trundling across the surface, voices fading.

A hand took hold of his ankle.

He looked down. Colette stared up at him, hair floating around her face. Owen bent his leg, pulled her upward. She shook her head, expelling bubbles in a rush through her mouth and nose.

There was no more time. Owen took hold of her arm, kicking toward the ice crust, hitting it with his shoulder. It was like ramming a concrete wall. He struck it again. Adrenaline poured through his system, none of it doing any good. Owen curled downward, bent his legs, and kicked at the surface but only succeeded in driving himself deeper into the water. There was nothing to brace against. Colette looked at him and shook her head again, mouth opening and closing, letting out a few more bubbles, weaker this time.

It wasn't her fault.

Owen swam at the ice and rammed it headfirst with all his remaining strength. Something cracked—ice, bone, or both. Then a chunk of the bleak sky slipped free and fell on top of him. Thank God. Everything melted into shades of pale gray, and when his vision refocused, the water around his head was clouding red. Owen realized the only reason he could see it was because daylight was filtering down into the water, but that was all right because—

He groped blindly through the scarlet murk, found Colette's hand. She raised one arm at him, and Owen told himself this might still work out.

All he had to do was lift her up through the hole in the ice.

It should have been easy.

But he suddenly felt very cold, inside and out. He'd been filling his lungs, but not with air. A thick, congested feeling came over him, heavy and indifferent. Up above, in the cloudy light, Colette's legs scissored through the hole, struggling to pull free. As she disappeared to the surface, one foot caught and her shoe slipped off.

Under the ice, Owen watched it fall and realized that he had begun to sink.

Blackness enveloped him. As it did, the congested feeling in his chest went away, and there was no more pain.

It felt like nothing.

All the weight and pain and tiredness, all the fear that he'd worn around like armor throughout the bulk of his adult life was gone, utterly gone, replaced by a feeling of profound peace.

Twenty feet beneath the frozen surface of the pond, Owen Mast died smiling.

CHAPTER FIFTY-EIGHT

THE WOMAN ON THE OTHER side of the glass stared out at the man and the boy. Her face was a question mark, echoed by the sheet of paper she held up in both hands.

Do I know you?

The man gave a nod. "I'm your son." He raised the boy up in his arms. "And this is your grandson, Henry."

The violet eyes sparkled and shone, and she mouthed the last word back to them slowly, as if she were afraid to let it go for fear it wouldn't come back. Tucking her chin, she lifted the crayon and wrote:

Grandson?

"That's right." His voice was gravelly, unsteady. "We came to get you out of here, Mom."

Apprehension in her face now, mixed with realization and a glimmer of familiarity. Her hand moved for the crayon again:

Your name is Scott

"That's right," he said.

I remember another boy. Owen?

"I'm sorry," Scott said. "He's dead."
She blinked, mouth open, then closed again, clamping tight.
"He died saving Henry's mother, Colette McGuire."
A white-hot streak of horror shot across Eleanor Mast's face, as if a dam had broken deep within her. The crayon started jerking across the page again, slashing out words until they crowded the page, an outpouring that Scott couldn't read until she flipped the tablet around and thrust it against the glass.

> *Curse won't end—alive in her—with us always—alive in her—no hope—house in the woods—the black wing—no doors—no windows—lives on in stories—*

"It's okay." Scott put his hand through the narrow slot and touched his mother's hand, holding it gently until she stopped writing and looked at him, tears in her eyes. "I think it's going to be okay." He thought about how the wing had fallen silent that morning, how the sound of inhuman laughter suddenly ceased. How everything had just stopped.

He had looked up at the nearest corner, where the walls and ceiling came together in a crisp, three-cornered edge.

He and Henry had gone back out there, through the woods to the house. The manuscript had still been there on the floor, exactly where he'd left it. Scott gathered it up with his laptop and the painting and the book Owen had found upstairs in the house and an old poster for a play that Grandpa Tom had written. Without a word between them, he and Henry had taken it all outside, dropped it on the ground, doused it in lighter fluid, and burned it, waited until it was nothing more than smoke and ash. He remembered the windless day, how the smoke had gone straight up into the sky, and how they had driven home afterward, neither one of them talking.

"You're leaving here soon," Scott told her. "I want you to come home with me and Henry. You don't have to worry about anything."

Eleanor's hand twitched across the page.

Can't live here anymore. In this town.

"I'm not talking about here," Scott said. "I'm talking about Seattle. That's on the other side of the country. If you want to try."

His mother reached for the crayon and then put it down and gazed at him. Scott put his arm around Henry's shoulders, felt the boy holding himself upright, alert and vigilant, watching his grandmother's mouth turn into a cautious smile. Her voice was rusty, hoarse from lack of practice, but he recognized it instantly.

"Yes," she said.

SONIA WAS WAITING for them in the parking lot, and Scott could see her looking at Henry's expression, trying to decide how to proceed. "How was it?"

"All right."

"Will she be ready to come out when her court order gets reversed?"

"I hope so," Scott said, and held his nephew's hand. He had been on the verge of making up something more upbeat for the boy and realized it wasn't necessary. Henry had already been exposed to the good and the bad, the extremes of human behavior, and diluting the truth now on his account made no sense at all. So he instead just repeated it, as much to himself as Sonia. "I hope so."

THEY DROVE BACK to Milburn, passing the Bijou on the way through town. Scott glanced at Sonia and knew what she was thinking. Colette had barricaded herself inside her house since the day she'd been rescued from the ice, choosing instead to receive visits from the sheriff and various health care providers, psychiatric and otherwise. He had seen her only at funerals since that day, three of them—Owen's, Earl Graham's, and her husband's. Each time she had been escorted by a silent New York attorney and Lonnie Mitchell. Afterward, when Scott asked the sheriff whether Colette was being charged for anything that had happened to Earl, Mitchell had given him a long, hard stare and pointed at the lawyer in the long topcoat. "You know what that means?" Mitchell growled. "That means, *don't ask.*"

So Scott didn't. He had enough on his plate already—court documents that needed to be signed for his mother's release, arrangements for Henry to start school in Seattle. There was something else, another matter whose presence he'd become aware of when Sonia stepped out of the passenger seat in front of Earl Graham's junk emporium and looked back at him with questioning eyes. Although neither of them said anything, Scott knew what he said next would make all the difference.

"Any idea what you're going to do now?"

"Me?" She shrugged, her breath steaming between them like the ghost of words unspoken. "I'm getting out of this town, that's for sure."

"Any particular destination in mind?"

"I've heard it's nice out west."

"We've got some good law schools," he said.

Sonia smiled. "You're going to be busy out there. You're used to being alone, and now you're going to have your mother and Henry, plus your job. . . ."

Scott nodded. "Sounds like I could use some help."

"I wouldn't know where to start."

"I'm not so worried about Henry, but my mom . . . she's going to take a long time to feel safe again. She's going to want some answers. I'll do my best, but it would be nice to have you there."

Sonia seemed to understand. Whether or not she actually did, he wasn't sure, but there would be time to clarify that later, and time for his mother as well, and her questions. Sometime, somewhere, Scott knew someone would tell her the whole story. If the time was right, it might even be him.

In his family, there might never be enough doors or windows, but there would always be stories.

ACKNOWLEDGMENTS

This book occupied an exceptionally long period of my creative life, lingering what felt like indefinitely in that literary neonatal intensive care ward called The Rewrite. Years later, my kids are still drawing on the backs of old manuscript pages.

To that end, I'm profoundly grateful to all of those who sat up with it over late nights, helping it develop its strength, voice, and purpose:

Mark Henry, Matt Ware, Don Laventhall, and my wife, Christina Arndt, all read early drafts and offered valuable insight and support, back when the manuscript was called "The Black Wing." In addition, if you were one of those people who read it early on—including random pages blown down my street on recycling day—feel free to include yourself here.

My agent, Phyllis Westberg, was always there with a kind and encouraging word, even when the draft I was turning in was radically different from the previous one she'd seen. Thanks, Phyllis.

My former editor at Ballantine, Keith Clayton, went through entire hot-eared hours with me on the phone (not to mention massive emails) sorting out what I was trying to say and endeavoring to make it the best it could be.

My spiffy new editor, Mark Tavani, has championed my work at

Ballantine from the beginning, and when the time came, he was ready to step in at a moment's notice.

As always, I'm thankful beyond words to my immediate family, C., J., and V., whose love and understanding have brought light to all the strange and winding rooms of my life.

PHOTO: VEDA RHYS ARNDT-SCHREIBER

JOE SCHREIBER was born in Michigan but spent his formative years in Alaska, Wyoming, and Northern California. His first job out of college was as a house sitter, which gave him ample opportunity to explore some very strange old architecture. He now lives in a decidedly un-haunted house in central Pennsylvania with his wife, two children, and more animals than he can keep track of.

Visit Joe Schreiber online at
www.scaryparent.blogspot.com.